UNCLE FRED
in the
SPRINGTIME

UNCLE FRED in the SPRINGTIME

P. G. WODEHOUSE

W. W. Norton & Company
New York • London

Fist published as a Norton paperback 2012

For information about special discounts for bulk
purchases, please contact W. W. Norton Special Sales
at specialsales@wwnorton.com or 800-233-4830

Manufacturing by Courier Westford
Book design by Judith Abbate
Production manager: Louise Mattarelliano

Library of Congress Cataloging-in-Publication Data

Wodehouse, P. G. (Pelham Grenville), 1881–1975.
Uncle Fred in the springtime / P.G. Wodehouse. —
Norton pbk.
p. cm.
ISBN 978-0-393-34306-9 (pbk.)
1. Blandings Castle (England : Imaginary place)—
Fiction. 2. Shropshire (England)—Fiction.
3. Nobility—Fiction. I. Title.
PR6045.O53U63 2012
823'.912—dc23

2012004357

W. W. Norton & Company, Inc.
500 Fifth Avenue, New York, N.Y. 10110
www.wwnorton.com

W. W. Norton & Company Ltd.
Castle House, 75/76 Wells Street, London W1T 3QT

1 2 3 4 5 6 7 8 9 0

UNCLE FRED
in the
SPRINGTIME

1

THE door of the Drones Club swung open, and a young man in form-fitting tweeds came down the steps and started to walk westwards. An observant passer-by, scanning his face, would have fancied that he discerned on it a keen, tense look, like that of an African hunter stalking a hippopotamus. And he would have been right. Pongo Twistleton—for it was he – was on his way to try to touch Horace Pendlebury-Davenport for two hundred pounds.

To touch Horace Pendlebury-Davenport, if you are coming from the Drones, you go down Hay Hill, through Berkeley Square, along Mount Street and up Park Lane to the new block of luxury flats which they have built where Bloxham House used to be: and it did not take Pongo long to reach journey's end. It was perhaps ten minutes later that Webster, Horace's man, opened the door in answer to his ring.

'What ho, Webster. Mr Davenport in?'

'No, sir. He has stepped out to take a dancing lesson.'

'Well, he won't be long, I suppose, what? I'll come in, shall I?'

'Very good, sir. Perhaps you would not mind waiting in the library. The sitting-room is in some little disorder at the moment.'

'Spring cleaning?'

'No, sir. Mr Davenport has been entertaining his uncle, the Duke of Dunstable, to luncheon, and over the coffee His Grace broke most of the sitting-room furniture with the poker.'

To say that this information surprised Pongo would be correct. To say that he was astounded, however, would be going too far. His Uncle Alaric's eccentricities were a favourite theme of conversation with Horace Davenport, and in Pongo he had always found a sympathetic confidant, for Pongo had an eccentric uncle himself. Though hearing Horace speak of his Uncle Alaric and thinking of his own Uncle Fred, he felt like Noah listening to someone making a fuss about a drizzle.

'What made him do that?'

'I am inclined to think, sir, that something may have occurred to annoy His Grace.'

This seemed plausible, and in the absence of further data Pongo left it at that. He made his way to the small apartment dignified by the name of library, and wandering to the window stood looking out on Park Lane.

It was a cheerless prospect that met his eyes. Like all English springs, the one which had just come to London seemed totally unable to make up its fat-headed mind whether it was supposed to be that ethereal mildness of which the poet sings or something suitable for ski-ers left over from the winter. A few moments before, the sun had been shining with extraordinary brilliance, but now a sort of young blizzard was raging, and the spectacle had the effect of plunging Pongo into despondency.

Horace was engaged to marry his sister Valerie, but was it conceivable, he asked himself, that any man, even to oblige a future brother-in-law, would cough up the colossal sum of two hundred potatoes? The answer, he felt, was in the negative, and with a mournful sigh he turned away and began to pace the room.

If you pace the library of Number 52 Bloxham Mansions, starting at the window and going straight across country, your outward journey takes you past the writing-table. And as Pongo reached this writing-table, something there attracted his eye. From beneath the blotter the end of a paper was protruding, and on it were written the intriguing words:

Signed

CLAUDE POTT

(*Private Investigator*)

They brought him up with as round a turn as if he had seen a baronet lying on the floor with an Oriental paper-knife of antique design in his back. An overwhelming desire came upon him to see what all this was about. He was not in the habit of reading other people's letters, but here was one which a man of the nicest scruples could scarcely be expected to pass up.

The thing was cast in narrative form, being, he found on examination, a sort of saga in which the leading character—a star part, if ever there was one—was somebody referred to as The Subject. From the activities of this individual Claude Pott seemed unable to tear himself away.

The Subject, who appeared to be abroad somewhere, for there was frequent mention of a Casino, was evidently one of those people who live for pleasure alone. You didn't catch The Subject doing good to the poor or making a thoughtful study of local political conditions. When he—or she—was not entering Casino in comp. of friends (two male, one female) at 11.17 p.m., he—or she, for there was no clue as to whether this was a story with a hero or a heroine—was playing tenn., riding h's, out on the golf links, lunching with three f's, driving to Montreuil with one m., or dancing with party consisting of four m's, ditto f's, and in this latter case keeping it up into the small hours. Pongo was familiar with the expression 'living the life of Riley,' and that it was a life of this nature that The Subject had been leading was manifest in the document's every sentence.

But what the idea behind the narrative could be he found himself unable to divine. Claude Pott had a nice, crisp style, but his work was marred by the same obscurity which has caused complaint in the case of the poet Browning.

He had begun to read it for the third time, hoping for enlightenment, when the click of a latchkey came to his ears, and as he hastily restored the paper to its place the door opened and there entered a young man of great height but lacking the width of shoulder and ruggedness of limb which make height impressive. Nature, stretching Horace Davenport out, ha2d forgotten to stretch him sideways, and one could have pictured Euclid, had they met, nudging a friend and saying, 'Don't look now, but this chap coming along illustrates exactly what I was telling you about a straight line having length without breadth.'

Farthest north of this great expanse there appeared a tortoise-shell-rimmed-spectacled face of so much amiability of expression that Pongo, sighting it, found himself once again hoping for the best.

'What ho, Horace,' he said, almost exuberantly.

'Hullo, Pongo. You here? Has Webster told you about my uncle's latest?'

'He did just touch on it. His theory is that the old boy was annoyed about something. Does that seem to fit the facts?'

'Absolutely. He was annoyed about quite a number of things. In the first place, he was going off to the country to-day and he had been counting on that fellow Baxter, his secretary, to go with him. He always likes to have someone with him on a railway journey.'

'To dance before him, no doubt, and generally entertain him?'

'And at the last moment Baxter said he would have to stay on in London to do some work at the British Museum in connection with that Family History Uncle Alaric has been messing about with for years. This made him shirty, for a start. He seemed to think it came under the head of being thwarted.'

'A touch of thwarting about it, perhaps.'

'And before coming to me he had been to see my cousin Ricky, and Ricky had managed to put his back up about something. So he was in dangerous mood when he got here. And we had scarcely sat down to lunch, when up popped a soufflé looking like a diseased custard. This did not help to ease the strain. And when we had had our coffee, and the time came for him to catch his train and he told me to go to the station with him and I said I couldn't, that seemed to touch him off. He reached for the poker and started in.'

'Why wouldn't you go to the station with him?'

'I couldn't. I was late for my dancing lesson.'

'I was going to ask you about that. What's this idea of your suddenly taking dancing lessons?'

'Valerie insisted on it. She said I danced like a dromedary with the staggers.'

Pongo did not blame his sister. Indeed, in comparing her loved one to a dromedary with the staggers she had been, he thought, rather complimentary.

'How are you coming along?'

'I think I'm making progress. Polly assures me so. Polly says I shall be able to go to the Ball to-morrow night. The Bohemian Ball at the Albert Hall. I'm going as a Boy Scout. I want to take Valerie to it and surprise her. Polly thinks I can get by all right.'

'But isn't Val at Le Touquet?'

'She's flying back to-day.'

'Oh, I see. Tell me, who is this Polly who has crept into your conversation?'

'She's the girl who's teaching me. I met her through Ricky. She's a friend of his. Polly Pott. A nice, sympathetic sort of girl I'd always found her, so when this business of staggering dromedaries came up, I asked her if she would give me a few lessons.'

A pang of pity for this heroine shot through Pongo. He himself was reading for the Bar and had sometimes felt like cracking under the strain of it all, but he saw that compared with Polly Pott he was on velvet. Between trying to extract some meaning from the rambling writings of the Messrs. Coke and Littleton and teaching dancing to Horace Davenport there was a substantial difference, and it was the person on whom life had thrust the latter task who must be considered to have drawn the short straw. The trouble was, he reflected, that Horace was so tall. A chap of that length didn't really get on to what his feet were doing till some minutes after it had happened. What you wanted, of course, was to slice him in half and have two Horaces.

'Polly Pott, eh? Any relation to Claude Pott, private investigator?'

'His daughter. What do you know about Claude Pott, private investigator?'

Pongo stirred uneasily. Too late, he saw that he had rather invited the question.

'Well, the fact is, old man, happening to pass the writing-table just now, and chancing inadvertently to catch sight of that document—'

'I wish you wouldn't read my letters.'

'Oh, I wouldn't. But I could see that this wasn't a letter. Just a document. So I ran my eye over it. I thought it might possibly be something with reference to which you were going to seek my advice, knowing me to be a bit of a nib in legal matters, and I felt that a lot of time would be saved if I had the *res* at my fingers' ends.'

'And now I suppose you'll go racing off to Valerie to tell her I had her watched by detectives while she was at Le Touquet.'

A blinding light flashed upon Pongo.

'Great Scott! Was that what the thing was about?'

He pursed his lips—not too tightly, for he was still hoping to float that loan, but tightly enough to indicate that the Twistletons had their pride and resented their sisters being tailed up by detectives. Horace read his thoughts correctly.

'Yes, I know, but you don't realize the position, Pongo. It was the Drones Club week-end at Le Touquet. The thought of the girl I loved surrounded by about eighty-seven members of the Drones in the lax atmosphere of a foreign pleasure resort while I was far away was like a knife in my heart. Polly happened to mention that her father was a private investigator, never happier than when putting on a false nose and shadowing people, and the temptation was more than I could resist. Pongo, for Heaven's sake don't breathe a word about this to Valerie. If she has a fault, it is that she's touchy. The sweetest of her sex, but a bit apt to go in off the deep end, when stirred. I can trust you?'

Pongo unpursed his lips. He understood all and pardoned all.

'Of course, old man. She shall never learn from me. You don't suppose I would wreck the happiness of my best friend . . . my oldest friend . . . my dearest friend . . . Horace, old top,' said Pongo, for it was a Twistleton trait to recognize when the iron was hot, 'I wonder if . . . I wonder whether . . . I wonder if you could possibly . . .'

'Mr Claude Pott,' announced Webster at the door.

To Pongo Twistleton, whose idea of a private investigator was a hawk-faced man with keen, piercing eyes and the general deportment of a leopard, Claude Pott came as a complete surprise. Hawks have no chins. Claude Pott had two. Leopards pad. Pott waddled. And his eyes, so far from being keen and piercing, were dull and expressionless, seeming, as is so often the case with those who go through life endeavouring to conceal their thoughts from the world, to be covered with a sort of film or glaze.

He was a stout, round, bald, pursy little man of about fifty, who might have been taken for a Silver Ring bookie or a minor Shakespearian actor—and, oddly enough, in the course of a life in which he had played many parts, he had actually been both.

'Good afternoon, Mr D.,' said this gargoyle.

'Hullo, Mr Pott. When did you get back?'

'Last night, sir. And thinking it over in bed this morning it occurred to me that it might be best if I were to deliver the concluding portion of my report verbally, thus saving time.'

'Oh, there's some more?'

'Yes, sir. I will apprise you of the facts,' said Claude Pott, giving Pongo a rather hard stare, 'when you are at liberty.'

'Oh, that's all right. You may speak freely before Mr Twistleton. He knows all. This is Mr Twistleton, The Subject's brother.'

'Pongo to pals,' murmured that young man weakly. He was finding the hard stare trying.

The austerity of the investigator's manner relaxed.

'Mr Pongo Twistleton? Then you must be the nephew of the Earl of Ickenham that he used to talk about.'

'Yes, he's my uncle.'

'A splendid gentleman. One of the real old school. A sportsman to his fingertips.'

Pongo, though fond of his uncle, could not quite bring himself to share this wholehearted enthusiasm.

'Yes, Uncle Fred's all right, I suppose,' he said. 'Apart from being loopy to the tonsils. You know him, do you?'

'I do indeed, sir. It was he who most kindly advanced me the money to start in business as a private investigator. So The Subject is Lord I's niece, is she? How odd! That his lordship should have financed me in my venture, I mean, and before I know where I am, I'm following his niece and taking notes of her movements. Strange!' said Mr Pott. 'Queer!'

'Curious,' assented Pongo.

'Unusual,' said Claude Pott.

'Bizarre,' suggested Pongo.

'Most. Shows what a small world it is.'

'Dashed small.'

Horace, who had been listening to these philosophical exchanges with some impatience, intervened.

'You were going to make your report, Mr Pott.'

'Coo!' said Claude Pott, called to order. 'That's right, isn't it? Well then, Mr D., to put the thing in a nutshell, I regret to have to inform you that there's been what you might call a bit of an unfortunate occurrence. On the nineteenth Ap., which was yesterday, The Subject, having lunched at Hotel Picardy with party consisting of two females, three males, proceeded to the golf club, where she took out her hockey-knockers and started playing round with one associate, the junior professional, self following at a cautious distance. For some time nothing noteworthy transpired, but at the fourteenth hole . . . I don't know if you happen to be familiar with the golf links at Le Touquet, sir?'

'Oh, rather.'

'Then you will be aware that as you pass from the fourteenth tee along the fairway you come opposite a house with a hedge in front of it. And just as The Subject came opposite this house, there appeared behind the hedge two males, one with cocktail shaker. They started yodelling to The Subject, evidently inviting her to step along and have one, and The Subject, dismissing her associate, went through the gate in the hedge and by the time I came up was lost to sight in the house.'

A soft groan broke from Horace Davenport. He had the air of a man who was contemplating burying his face in his hands.

'Acting in your interests, I, too, passed through the gate and crept to the window from behind which I could hear chat and revelry in progress. And I was just stooping down to investigate further, when a hand fell on my shoulder and, turning, I perceived one male. And at the same moment The Subject, poking her head out of the window, observed "Nice work, Barmy. That's the blighter that's been following me about all the week. You be knocking his head off, while Catsmeat phones for the police. We'll have him sent to the guillotine for ingrowing molestation." And I saw that there was only one course for me to pursue.'

'I wouldn't have thought even that,' said Pongo, who had been following the narrative with close attention.

'Yes, sir—one. I could clear myself by issuing a full statement.'

A sharp, agonized cry escaped Horace Davenport.

'Yes, sir. I'm sorry, but there was no alternative. I had no desire to get embroiled with French rozzers. I issued my statement. While the male, Barmy, was calling me a trailing arbutus and the male, Catsmeat, was saying did anyone know the French for "police" and The Subject was talking about horsewhips, I explained the situation fully. It took me some time to get the facts into their heads, but I managed it finally and was permitted to depart, The Subject saying that if she ever set eyes on me again—'

'Miss Twistleton,' announced Webster.

'Well, good-bye, all,' said Claude Pott.

A critic who had been disappointed by the absence of the leopard note in Mr Pott's demeanour would have found nothing to complain of in that of Pongo's sister Valerie. She was a tall, handsome girl, who seemed to be running a temperature, and her whole aspect, as she came into the room, was that of some jungle creature advancing on its prey.

'Worm!' she said, opening the conversation.

'Valerie, darling, let me explain!'

'Let *me* explain,' said Pongo.

His sister directed at him a stare of a hardness far exceeding that of Mr Pott.

'Could you possibly keep your fat head out of this?'

'No, I couldn't keep my fat head out of it,' said Pongo. 'You don't think I'm going to stand supinely by and see a good man wronged, do you? Why should you barge in here, gnashing your bally teeth, just because Horace sicked Claude Pott, private investigator, on to you? If you had any sense, you would see that it was a compliment, really. Shows how much he loves you.'

'Oh, does it? Well—'

'Valerie, darling!'

The girl turned to Pongo.

'Would you,' she said formally, 'be good enough to ask your friend not to address me as "Valerie, darling." My name is Miss Twistleton.'

'Your name,' said Pongo, with brotherly sternness, 'will be mud if you pass up an excellent bet like good old Horace Davenport— the whitest man I know—simply because his great love made him want to keep an eye on you during Drones Club week-end.'

'I did not—'

'And as events have proved he was thoroughly justified in the course he took. You appear to have been cutting up like a glamour girl at a Hollywood party. What about those two males, one with cocktail shaker?'

'I did not—'

'And the m. you drove to Montreuil with?'

'Yes,' said Horace, for the first time perking up and showing a little of the Pendlebury-Davenport fire. 'What about the m. you drove to Montreuil with?'

Valerie Twistleton's face was cold and hard.

'If you will allow me to speak for a moment and not keep interrupting every time I open my mouth, I was about to say that I did not come here to argue. I merely came to inform you that our engagement is at an end, and that a notice to that effect will appear in *The Times* to-morrow morning. The only explanation I can think of that offers a particle of excuse for your conduct is that you have finally gone off your rocker. I've been expecting it for months. Look at your Uncle Alaric. Barmy to the back teeth.'

Horace Davenport was in the depths, but he could not let this pass.

'That's all right about my Uncle Alaric. What price your Uncle Fred?'

'What about him?'

'Loopy to the tonsils.'

'My Uncle Fred is not loopy to the tonsils.'

'Yes, he is. Pongo says so.'

'Pongo's an ass.'

Pongo raised his eyebrows.

'Cannot we,' he suggested coldly, 'preserve the decencies of debate?'

'This isn't a debate. As I told you before, I came here simply to inform Mr Davenport that our engagement is jolly well terminated.'

There was a set look on Horace's face. He took off his spectacles, and polished them with an ominous calm.

'So you're handing me the mitten?'

'Yes, I am.'

'You'll be sorry.'

'No, I shan't.'

'I shall go straight to the devil.'

'All right, trot along.'

'I shall plunge into a riot of reckless living.'

'Go ahead.'

'And my first step, I may mention, will be to take Polly Pott to that Bohemian Ball at the Albert Hall.'

'Poor soul! I hope you will do the square thing by her.'

'I fail to understand you.'

'Well, she'll need a pair of crutches next day. In common fairness you ought to pay for them.'

There was a silence. Only the sound of tense breathing could be heard—the breathing of a man with whom a woman has gone just too far.

'If you will be kind enough to buzz off,' said Horace icily, 'I will be ringing her up now.'

The door slammed. He went to the telephone.

Pongo cleared his throat. It was not precisely the moment he would have chosen for putting his fortune to the test, had he been free to choose, but his needs were immediate, the day was already well advanced and no business done, and he had gathered that Horace's time in the near future was likely to be rather fully occupied. So now he cleared his throat and, shooting his cuffs, called upon the splendid Twistleton courage to nerve him for his task.

'Horace, old man.'

'Hullo?'

'Horace, old chap.'

'Hullo? Polly?'

'Horace, old egg.'

'Half a minute. There's somebody talking. Well?'

'Horace, old top, you remember what we were starting to chat about when the recent Pott blew in. What I was going to say, when we were interrupted, was that owing to circumstances over which I had no—or very little—control. . . .'

'Buck up. Don't take all day over it.'

Pongo saw that preambles would have to be dispensed with.

'Can you lend me two hundred quid?'

'No.'

'Oh? Right ho. Well, in that case,' said Pongo stiffly, 'tinkerty-tonk.'

He left the room and walked round to the garage where he kept his Buffy-Porson two-seater, and instructed the proprietor to have it in readiness for him on the morrow.

'Going far, sir?'

'To Ickenham, in Hampshire,' said Pongo.

He spoke moodily. He had not planned to reveal his financial difficulties to his Uncle Fred, but he could think of no other source of revenue.

2

HAVING put the finishing touches to his nephew's sitting-room and removed himself from Bloxham Mansions in a cab, the Duke of Dunstable, feeling much better after his little bit of exercise, had driven to Paddington Station and caught the 2.45 train to Market Blandings in the county of Shropshire. For he had invited himself— he was a man of too impatient spirit to hang about waiting for other people to invite him—to spend an indefinite period as the guest of Clarence, ninth Earl of Emsworth, and his sister, Lady Constance Keeble, at that haunt of ancient peace, Blandings Castle.

The postcard which he had dispatched some days previously announcing his impending arrival and ordering an airy ground-floor bedroom with a southern exposure and a quiet sitting-room in which he could work with his secretary, Rupert Baxter, on his history of the family had had a mixed reception at the Blandings breakfast-table.

Lord Emsworth, frankly appalled, had received the bad news with a sharp 'Eh, what? Oh, I say, dash it!' He had disliked the Duke in a dreamy way for forty-seven years, and as for Rupert Baxter he had hoped never to be obliged to meet him again either in this world or the next. Until fairly recently that efficient young man had been his own secretary, and his attitude towards him was a little like that of some miraculously cured convalescent towards the hideous disease which has come within an ace of laying him low. It was true, of course, that this time the frightful fellow would be infesting the castle in the capacity of somebody else's employee, but he drew small comfort from that. The mere thought of being under the same roof with Rupert Baxter was revolting to him.

Lady Constance, on the other hand, was pleased. She was a devoted admirer of the efficient Baxter, and there had been a time, when the world was young, when she and the Duke of Dunstable had whispered together in dim conservatories and been the last couple to straggle home from picnics. And though nothing had come of it—it was long before he succeeded to the title, and they shipped him abroad at about that time to allow an England which he had made too hot for him to cool off a little—the memory lingered.

Lord Emsworth lodged a protest, though realizing as he did so that it was purely formal. He was, and always had been, a cipher in the home.

'It's only about a week since he was here last.'

'It is nearly seven months.'

'Can't you tell him we're full up?'

'Of course I can't.'

'The last time he was here,' said Lord Emsworth broodingly, 'he poked the Empress in the ribs with an umbrella.'

'Well, I am certainly not going to offend one of my oldest friends just because he poked your pig with an umbrella,' said Lady Constance. 'I shall write to Alaric and tell him that we shall be delighted to have him for as long as he cares to stay. I see that he says he must be on the ground floor, because he is nervous of fire. He had better have the Garden Suite.'

And so it was in that luxurious set of apartments that the Duke awoke on the morning following his luncheon-party at Bloxham Mansions. For some time he lay gazing at the sunlight that filtered through the curtains which covered the French windows opening on the lawn: then, ringing the bell, he instructed the footman to bring him toast, marmalade, a pot of China tea, two lightly boiled eggs and *The Times*. And it was perhaps twenty minutes later that

Lady Constance, sunning herself on the terrace, was informed by Beach, her butler, that His Grace would be glad if she would step to his room for a moment.

Her immediate sensation, on receiving this summons, was one of apprehension and alarm. The story which the Duke had told at dinner on the previous night, at great length and with a ghoulish relish, of the lesson which he had taught his nephew Horace had made a deep impression on her, and she fully expected on reaching the Blue Room to find it—possibly owing to some lapse from the required standard in His Grace's breakfast—a devastated area. It was with profound relief that she saw that all was well. The ducal poker remained a potential threat in the background, but it had not been brought into operation as yet, and she looked at the mauve-pajamaed occupant of the bed with that quiet affection which hostesses feel towards guests who have not smashed their furniture—blended with the tenderness which a woman never quite loses for the man who has once breathed words of love down the back of her neck.

'Good morning, Alaric.'

''Morning, Connie. I say, who the devil's that whistling feller?'

'What do you mean?'

'I mean a whistling feller. A feller who whistles. There's been a blighter outside my window ever since I woke up, whistling the "Bonny Bonny Banks of Loch Lomond."'

'One of the gardeners, I expect.'

'Ah!' said the Duke quietly.

Pongo Twistleton had been surprised that a private investigator could look like Claude Pott, and he would have been equally surprised if he had been introduced to the Duke of Dunstable and informed that this was the notorious sitting-room-wrecker of whom he had heard so much. The Duke did not look a killer. Except for the Dunstable nose, always a little startling at first sight, there was nothing obviously formidable and intimidating about Horace's

Uncle Alaric. A bald head . . . A cascade of white moustache . . . Prominent blue eyes . . . A rather nice old bird, you would have said.

'Was that what you wanted to see me about?'

'No. Have the car ready to take me to the station directly after lunch. I've got to go to London.'

'But you only came last night.'

'It doesn't matter what happened last night. It's what has happened this morning. I glance through my *Times*, and what do I see? My nephew Horace has gone and got his engagement broken off.'

'What!'

'You heard.'

'But why?'

'How the dickens should I know why? It's just because I don't know why that I've got to go and find out. When an engagement has been broken off *The Times* doesn't print long reports from its special correspondent. It simply says "The marriage arranged between George Tiddlypush and Amelia Stick-in-the-mud will not take place."'

'The girl was Lord Ickenham's niece, wasn't she?'

'Still is.'

'I know Lady Ickenham, but I have never met Lord Ickenham.'

'Nor have I. But she's his niece, just the same.'

'They say he is very eccentric.'

'He's potty. Everybody's potty nowadays, except a few people like myself. It's the spirit of the age. Look at Clarence. Ought to have been certified years ago.'

'Don't you think that it's simply that he is dreamy and absent-minded?'

'Absent-minded be blowed. He's potty. So's Horace. So's my other nephew, Ricky. You take my advice, Connie. Never have nephews.'

Lady Constance's sigh seemed to say that he spoke too late.

'I've got dozens, Alaric.'

'Potty?'

'I sometimes think so. They seem to do the most extraordinary things.'

'I'll bet they don't do such extraordinary things as mine.'

'My nephew Ronald married a chorus girl.'

'My nephew Ricky writes poetry.'

'My nephew Bosham once bought a gold brick from a man in the street.'

'And now he wants to sell soup.'

'Bosham?'

'Ricky. He wants to sell soup.'

'Sell soup?'

'Good God, Connie, don't repeat everything I say, as if you were an echo in the Swiss mountains. I tell you he wants to sell soup. I go and see him yesterday, and he has the impertinence, if you please, to ask me to give him five hundred pounds to buy an onion soup bar. I refused to give him a penny, of course. He was as sick as mud. Not so sick as Horace will be, though, when he's finished with me. I shall start by disembowelling him. Go and order that car.'

'Well, it does seem a shame that you should have to go to London on a lovely day like this.'

'You don't think I want to go, do you? I've got to go.'

'Couldn't you tell Mr Baxter to go and see Horace? He is still in London, isn't he?'

'Yes, he is, the shirking, skrimshanking, four-eyed young son of a what-not, and I'm quite convinced that he stayed there because he was planning to go on a toot the moment my back was turned. If I can bring it home to him, by George, I'll sack him as soon as he shows his ugly face here. No, I couldn't tell Baxter to go and see Horace. I'm not going to have my nephew, halfwitted though he is, subjected to the inquisition of a dashed underling.'

There were several points in this speech, which, if it had not been for the thought of that poker which hung over Blandings Castle like a sword of Damocles, Lady Constance would have liked to criticize. She resented the suggestion that Rupert Baxter was a man capable of going on toots. She did not consider his face ugly. And it pained her to hear him described as a dashed underling. But there are times when the tongue must be curbed. She maintained a discreet silence, from which she emerged a few moments later with a suggestion.

'I know! Bosham is going to London this morning. Why couldn't Horace drive him back in his car? Then you could have your talk with him without any trouble or inconvenience.'

'The first sensible word you've spoken since you came into this room,' said the Duke approvingly. 'Yes, tell Bosham to rout him out and bring him back alive or dead. Well, I can't stay here talking to you all day, Connie. Got to get up, got to get up. Where's Clarence?'

'Down at the pig-sty, I suppose.'

'Don't tell me he's still mooning over that pig of his.'

'He's quite absurd about it.'

'Quite crazy, you mean. If you want to know what I think, Connie, it's that pig that's at the root of his whole trouble. It's a very bad influence in his life, and if something isn't done soon to remove it you'll find him suddenly sticking straws in his hair and saying he's a poached egg. Talking of eggs, send me up a dozen.'

'Eggs? But haven't you had your breakfast?'

'Of course I've had my breakfast.'

'I see. But you want some more,' said Lady Constance pacifically. 'How would you like them done?'

'I don't want them done at all. I don't want eating eggs. I want throwing eggs. I intend to give that whistling feller a sharp lesson. Hark! There he is again. Singing now.'

'Alaric,' said Lady Constance, a pleading note in her voice, 'must you throw eggs at the gardeners?'

'Yes.'

'Very well,' said Lady Constance resignedly, and went off to avert the threatened horror by removing the vocalist from the danger zone.

Her thoughts, as she went, were long, long thoughts.

Lord Emsworth, meanwhile, unaware of the solicitude which he was causing, was down in the meadow by the kitchen garden, drooping over the comfortable sty which housed his pre-eminent sow, Empress of Blandings, twice in successive years silver medallist in the Fat Pigs' class at the Shropshire Agricultural Show. The noble animal, under his adoring eyes, was finishing a late breakfast.

The ninth Earl of Emsworth was a resilient man. It had not taken him long to get over the first sharp agony of the discovery that Rupert Baxter was about to re-enter his life. This morning, Baxter was forgotten, and he was experiencing that perfect happiness which comes from a clear conscience, absence of loved ones, congenial society and fine weather. For once in a way there was nothing which he was trying to conceal from his sister Constance, no disrupting influences had come to mar his communion with the Empress, and the weather, as almost always in this favoured spot, was wonderful. We have seen spring being whimsical and capricious in London, but it knew enough not to try anything of that sort on Blandings Castle.

The only concern Lord Emsworth had was a fear that this golden solitude could not last, and the apprehension was well founded. A raucous cry shattered the drowsy stillness and, turning, he perceived, as Claude Pott would have said, one male. His guest, the Duke, was crossing the meadow towards him.

"Morning, Clarence.'

'Good morning, Alaric.'

Lord Emsworth forced a welcoming smile to his lips. His breeding—and about fifteen thousand words from Lady Constance from time to time—had taught him that a host must wear the mask. He tried his hardest not to feel like a stag at bay.

'Seen Bosham anywhere?'

'No. No, I have not.'

'I want a word with him before he leaves. I'll wait here and intercept him on his way out. He's going to London to-day, to bring Horace here. His engagement has been broken off.'

This puzzled Lord Emsworth. His son and heir, Lord Bosham, who was visiting the castle for the Bridgeford races, had been, he felt pretty sure, for some years a married man. He mentioned this.

'Not Bosham's engagement. Horace's.'

Again Lord Emsworth was at a loss.

'Who is Horace?'

'My nephew.'

'And he is engaged?'

'He was. Ickenham's niece.'

'Who is?'

'The girl he was engaged to.'

'Who is Ickenham?'

'Her uncle.'

'Oh,' said Lord Emsworth, brightening. The name had struck a chord in his memory. 'Oh, Ickenham? Of course. Ickenham, to be sure. I know Ickenham. He is a friend of my brother Galahad. I think they used to be thrown out of night clubs together. I am glad Ickenham is coming here.'

'He isn't.'

'You said he was.'

'I didn't say he was. I said Horace was.'

The name was new to Lord Emsworth.

'Who,' he asked, 'is Horace?'

'I told you two seconds ago,' said the Duke, with the asperity which never left him for long, 'that he was my nephew. I have no reason to believe that conditions have altered since.'

'Oh?' said Lord Emsworth. 'Ah? Yes. Yes, to be sure. Your nephew. Well, we must try to make his stay pleasant. Perhaps he is interested in pigs. Are you interested in pigs, Alaric? You know my sow, Empress of Blandings, I think. I believe you met when you were here in the summer.'

He moved aside to allow his guest an uninterrupted view of the superb animal. The Duke advanced to the rail, and there followed a brief silence—on Lord Emsworth's side reverent, on that of the Duke austere. He had produced a large pair of spectacles from his breast pocket and through them was scrutinizing the silver medallist in a spirit only too plainly captious and disrespectful.

'Disgusting!' he said at length.

Lord Emsworth started violently. He could scarcely believe that he had heard aright.

'What!'

'That pig is too fat.'

'Too fat?'

'Much too fat. Look at her. Bulging.'

'But my dear Alaric, she is supposed to be fat.'

'Not as fat as that.'

'Yes, I assure you. She has already been given two medals for being fat.'

'Don't be silly, Clarence. What would a pig do with medals? It's no good trying to shirk the issue. There is only one word for that pig—gross. She reminds me of my Aunt Horatia, who died of apoplexy during Christmas dinner. Keeled over half-way through her second helping of plum pudding and never spoke again. This animal might be her double. And what do you expect? You stuff her and stuff her and stuff her, and I don't suppose she gets a lick of exercise from one week's end to another. What she wants is a crackling good gallop every morning, and no starchy foods. That would get her into shape.'

Lord Emsworth had recovered the pince-nez which emotion had caused, as it always did, to leap from his nose. He replaced them insecurely.

'Are you under the impression,' he said, for when deeply moved he could be terribly sarcastic, 'that I want to enter my pig for the Derby?'

The Duke had been musing. He had not liked that nonsense about pigs being given medals and he was thinking how sad all this was for poor Connie. But at these words he looked up sharply. An involuntary shudder shook him, and his manner took on a sort of bedside tenderness.

'I wouldn't, Clarence.'

'Wouldn't what?'

'Enter this pig for the Derby. She might not win, and then you would have had all your trouble for nothing. What you want is to get her out of your life. And I'll tell you what I'll do. Listen, my dear Clarence,' said the Duke, patting his host's shoulder, 'I'll take this pig over—lock, stock, and barrel. Yes, I mean it. Have her sent to my place—I'll wire them to expect her—and in a few weeks' time she will be a different creature. Keen, alert, eyes sparkling. And you'll be different, too. Brighter. Less potty. Improved out of all knowledge . . . Ah, there's Bosham. Hi, Bosham! Half a minute, Bosham, I want a word with you.'

For some moments after his companion had left him, Lord Emsworth remained leaning limply against the rail of the sty. The sun was bright. The sky was blue. A gentle breeze caressed the Empress's tail, as it wiggled over the trough. But to him the heavens seemed darkened by a murky mist, and there appeared to be an east wind blowing through the world. It was not for some time that he became aware that a voice was speaking his name, but he heard it at last and pulling together with a powerful effort, saw his sister Constance.

She was asking him if he was getting deaf. He said No, he was not getting deaf.

'Well, I've been shouting at you for ever so long. I wish you would listen to me sometimes. Clarence, I have come to have a talk about Alaric. I am very worried about him. He seems to have got so odd.'

'Odd? I should say he was odd. Do you know what, Connie? He came to me just now—'

'He was asking me to give him eggs to throw at the gardeners.'

At a less tense moment, her words would have shocked Lord

Emsworth. An English landed proprietor of the better type comes to regard himself as *in loco parentis* to those in his employment, and if visitors start throwing eggs at them he resents it. But now he did not even lose his pince-nez.

'And do you know what he said to me?'

'He can't be sane, if he wants to throw eggs at gardeners.'

'He can't be sane, if he wants me to give him the Empress.'

'Does he?'

'Yes.'

'Then, of course,' said Lady Constance, 'you will have to.'

This time Lord Emsworth did lose his pince-nez, and lose them thoroughly. They flew at the end of their string like leaves in a storm. He stared incredulously.

'What!'

'You *are* getting deaf.'

'I am not getting deaf. When I said "What!" I didn't mean "What?" I meant "What!!"'

'What on earth are you talking about?'

'I'm talking about this extraordinary remark of yours. I tell you this frightful Duke wants me to give him the Empress, and instead of being appalled and horrified and—er—appalled you say "Of course you will have to!" Without turning an eyelash! God bless my soul, do you imagine for an instant—'

'And do you imagine for an instant that I am going to run the risk of having Alaric career through the castle with a poker? If he destroyed all the furniture in his nephew Horace's sitting-room just because Horace wouldn't go to the station and see him off, what do you think he would do in a case like this? I do not intend to have my home wrecked for the sake of a pig. Personally, I think it's a blessing that we are going to get rid of the miserable animal.'

'Did you say "miserable animal"?'

'Yes, I did say "miserable animal." Alaric was telling me that he thought it a very bad influence in your life.'

'Dash his impertinence!'

'And I quite agree with him. In any case, there is no use arguing about it. If he wants the pig, he must have it.'

'Oh, very well, very well, very well, very well,' said Lord Emsworth. 'I suppose the next thing he'll want will be the castle, and you'll give him that. Be sure to tell him not to be afraid to ask for it, if he takes a fancy to it. I think I will go and read a little in the library, before Alaric decides to have all my books packed up and shipped off.'

It was a good exit speech—mordant—bitter, satirical—but it brought no glow of satisfaction to Lord Emsworth as he uttered it. His heart was bowed down with weight of woe. The experience gained from a hundred battles had taught him that his sister Constance always got her way. One might bluster and one might struggle, one might raise hands to heaven and clench fists and shake them, but in the end the result was always the same—Connie got what she wanted.

As he sat some ten minutes later in the cloistered coolness of the library, vainly trying to concentrate his attention on *Whiffle On The Care Of The Pig*, a feeling of being alone and helpless in a hostile world came upon Lord Emsworth. What he needed above all else in this crisis which had come to blast his life was a friend . . . an ally . . . a sympathetic adviser. But who was there to whom he could turn? Bosham was useless. Beach, his butler, was sympathetic, but not a constructive thinker. And his brother Galahad, the only male member of the family capable of coping with that family's females, was away. . . .

Lord Emsworth started. A thought had struck him. Musing on Galahad, he had suddenly remembered that friend of his, that redoubtable Lord Ickenham of whom the Duke had been talking just now.

The Hon. Galahad Threepwood was a man of high standards. He weighed people before stamping them with the seal of his approval, and picked his words before he spoke. If Galahad Threepwood said a man was hot stuff, he used the phrase not carelessly but in its deepest sense. And not once but many times had Lord Emsworth heard him bestow this accolade on Frederick, Earl of Ickenham.

His eyes gleamed behind their pince-nez with a new light. He was planning and scheming. *Debrett's Peerage*, standing over there on its shelf, would inform him of this wonder-man's address, and what more simple than to ring him up on the telephone and arrange a meeting and then pop up to London and place the facts before him and seek his advice. A man like that would have a hundred ideas for the saving of the Empress. . . .

The gleam died away. In classing the act of popping up to London as simple, he saw that he had erred. While this ghastly Duke remained on the premises, there was not the slightest hope of Connie allowing him to get away, even for a night. Boys who stood on burning decks had a better chance of leaving their post than the master of Blandings Castle when there were visitors.

He was just reaching feebly for his *Whiffle*, which he had dropped in his anguish, hoping that its magic pages would act as an opiate, when Lady Constance burst into the room.

'Clarence!'

'Eh?'

'Clarence, did you tell Alaric you wanted to enter your pig for the Derby?'

'No, I told him I didn't.'

'Then he misunderstood you. He said you did. And he wants me to get a brain specialist down to observe you.'

'I like his dashed cheek!'

'So you must go to London immediately.'

Once more *Whiffle* fell from Lord Emsworth's limp hand.

'Go to London?'

'Now, please, Clarence, don't be difficult. There is no need for you to tell me how you dislike going to London. But this is vitally important. Ever since Alaric arrived, I have been feeling that he ought to be under the observation of some good brain specialist, but

I couldn't think how it was to be managed without offending him. This has solved everything. Do you know Sir Roderick Glossop?'

'Never heard of him.'

'He is supposed to be quite the best man in that line. Lady Gimblett told me he had done wonders for her sister's problem child. I want you to go to London this afternoon and bring him back with you. Give him lunch at your club to-morrow and explain the whole situation to him. Assure him that expense is no object, and that he must come back with you. He will tell us what is the best thing to be done about poor Alaric. I am hopeful that some quite simple form of treatment may be all that is required. You must catch the two o'clock train.'

'Very well, Connie. If you say so.'

There was a strange look on Lord Emsworth's face as the door closed. It was the look of a man who has just found himself on the receiving end of a miracle. His knees were trembling a little as he rose and walked to the book-case, where the red and gold of *Debrett's Peerage* gleamed like the ray of a lighthouse guiding a storm-tossed mariner.

Beach, the butler, hearing the bell, presented himself at the library.

'M'lord?'

'Oh, Beach, I want you to put in a trunk telephone call for me. I don't know the number, but the address is Ickenham Hall, Ickenham, Hampshire. I want a personal call to Lord Ickenham.'

'Very good, m'lord.'

'And when you get it,' said Lord Emsworth, glancing nervously over his shoulder, 'have it put through to my bed-room.'

3

IF your Buffy-Porson is running well, the journey from London to Hampshire does not take long. Pongo Twistleton, making good time, arrived at Ickenham Hall a few minutes before noon—at about the moment, in fact, when Lord Emsworth in far-off Shropshire was sitting down in the library of Blandings Castle to his *Whiffle On The Care Of The Pig*.

Half-way up the drive, where the rhododendrons masked a sharp turning, he nearly collided with the Hall Rolls, proceeding in the opposite direction, and a glimpse of luggage on its grid caused him to fear that he might just have missed his uncle. But all was well. Reaching the house, he found him standing on the front steps.

Frederick Altamont Cornwallis Twistleton, fifth Earl of Ickenham, was a tall, slim, distinguished-looking man with a jaunty moustache and an alert and enterprising eye. In actual count of time, he was no longer in his first youth. The spring now enlivening England with its alternate sunshine and blizzards was one of many that had passed over his head, leaving it a becoming iron-grey. But just as the years had failed to deprive him of his slender figure, so had they been impotent to quench his indomitable spirit. Together with a juvenile waist-line, he still retained the bright enthusiasms and the fresh, unspoiled outlook of a slightly inebriated under-graduate—though to catch him at his best, as he would have been the first to admit, you had to catch him in London.

It was for this reason that Jane, Countess of Ickenham, had prudently decided that the evening of her husband's life should be spent exclusively at his rural seat, going so far as to inform him that if he ever tried to sneak up to London she would skin him with a blunt knife. And if, as he now stood on the steps, his agreeable face seemed to be alight with some inner glow, this was due to the reflection that she had just left for a distant spot where she proposed to remain for some considerable time. He was devoted to his helpmeet, never wavering in the opinion that she was the sweetest thing that had ever replied 'Yes' to a clergyman's 'Wilt thou?' but there was no gainsaying the fact that her absence would render it easier for him to get that breath of London air which keeps a man from growing rusty and puts him in touch with the latest developments of modern thought.

At the sight of his nephew, his cheerfulness increased. He was very fond of Pongo, in whose society many of his happiest and most instructive hours had been passed. A day which they had spent together at the Dog Races some months before still haunted the young man's dreams.

'Why, hullo, my boy,' he cried. 'Delighted to see you. Park the scooter and come in. What a morning! Warm, fragrant, balmy, yet with just that nip in the air that puts a fellow on his toes. I saw one of those Western pictures at our local cinema last night, in which a character described himself as being all spooked up with zip and vinegar. That is precisely how I feel. The yeast of spring is fermenting in my veins, and I am ready for anything. You've just missed the boss.'

'Was that Aunt Jane I saw going off in the car?'

'That was the Big White Chief.'

The information relieved Pongo. He respected and admired his aunt, but from boyhood days she had always inspired him with a certain fear, and he was glad that he had not got to meet her while he was passing through his present financial crisis. Like so many aunts, she was gifted with a sort of second sight and one glance at his face would almost certainly have told her that he was two hundred in the red. From that to the confession that his difficulties were due to unsuccessful speculations on the turf would have been the shortest of steps. He did not like to think what would happen if she discovered his recent activities.

'She's motoring to Dover to catch the afternoon boat. She is off to the South of France to nurse her mother, who is having one of her spells.'

'Then you're all alone?'

'Except for your sister Valerie.'

'Oh, my gosh. Is she here?'

'She arrived last night, breathing flame through her nostrils. You've heard about her broken engagement? Perhaps you have come here with the idea of comforting her in her distress?'

'Well, not absolutely. In fact, between you and me, I'm not any too keen on meeting her at the moment. I rather took Horace's side in the recent brawl, and our relations are distant.'

Lord Ickenham nodded.

'Yes, now that you mention it, I recollect her saying something about your being some offensive breed of insect. An emotional girl.'

'Yes.'

'But I can't understand her making such heavy weather over the thing. Everybody knows a broken engagement doesn't amount to anything. Your aunt, I remember, broke ours six times in all before making me the happiest man in the world. Bless her! The sweetest, truest wife man ever had. I hope her mother responds to treatment and that she will be back with me soon. But not too soon. You know, Pongo, it's an odd thing that the detective Horace commissioned to chase Valerie across the ice with blood-hounds should have been old Pott. Mustard Pott, we used to call him. I've known him for years.'

'Yes, he was telling me. You started him as a sleuth.'

'That's right. A versatile chap, Mustard. There aren't many

things he hasn't done in his time. He was on the stage once, I believe. Then he took to Silver Ring bookeying. Then he ran a club. And I rather suspect him of being a defrocked butler. Though what Nature really intended him to be, I have always felt, was a confidence-trick man. Which, by the way, is a thing I've wanted to have a shot at all my life, but never seemed able to get round to somehow.'

'What rot.'

'It isn't rot. You shouldn't mock at an old man's daydreams. Every time I read one of those bits in the paper about Another Victim Of The Confidence Trick, I yearn to try it for myself, because I simply cannot bring myself to believe that there are people in the world mugs enough to fall for it. Well, young Pongo, how much?'

'Eh?'

'I can see in your eye that you've come to make a touch. What's the figure?'

Such ready intelligence on the part of an uncle should have pleased a nephew, but Pongo remained sombre. Now that the moment had come, his natural pessimism had asserted itself again.

'Well, it's rather a lot.'

'A fiver?'

'A bit more than that.'

'Ten?'

'Two hundred.'

'Two—*what*? How in the world did you manage to get in the hole for a sum like that?'

'I came a bit of a mucker at Lincoln, being led astray by my advisers, and when I tried to get it back at Hurst Park things came unstuck again, and the outcome and upshot is that I owe a bookie named George Budd two hundred quid. Do you know George Budd?'

'Since my time. When I was a prominent figure on the turf, George Budd was probably in his cradle, sucking his pink toes.'

'Well, he isn't sucking any pink toes now. He's a tough egg.

Bingo Little had a bit on the slate with him last winter, and when he started trying to break it gently to him that he might not be able to pay up, this Budd said he did hope he would—'

'So the modern bookie feels like that, does he? The ones in my time always used to.'

'—because he said he knew it was silly to be superstitious but he had noticed that every time anyone did him down for money some nasty accident happened to them. He said it was like some sort of fate. And he summoned a great beefy brute called Erb and dangled him before Bingo's eyes. Erb called on me yesterday.'

'What did he say?'

'He didn't say anything. He seemed to be one of those strong, silent men. He just looked at me and nodded. So if you could possibly see your way, Uncle Fred, to advancing—'

Lord Ickenham shook his head regretfully.

'Alas, my boy, the ear which you are trying to bite, though not unresponsive, is helpless to assist. There has been a shake-up in the Treasury department here. Some little time ago, your aunt unfortunately decided to take over the family finances and administer them herself, leaving me with just that bit of spending money which a man requires for tobacco, self-respect, golf-balls and what not. My limit is a tenner.'

'Oh, my gosh! And Erb's going to call again on Wednesday.'

There was a wealth of sympathy and understanding in Lord Ickenham's eye, as he patted his nephew's shoulder. He was gazing back across the years and seeing himself, an ardent lad in the twenties, thoughtfully glueing a large black moustache above his lips, his motive being to deceive and frustrate a bygone turf commissioner doing business under the name of Jimmy Timms, the Safe Man.

'I know just how you must be feeling, my boy. We have all gone through it, from the Archbishop of Canterbury, I imagine, downwards. Thirty-six years ago, almost to this very day, I was climbing out of a window and shinning down a waterspout to avoid a muscular individual named Syd, employed by a bookie who was my creditor at the moment in very much the same executive capacity as this Erb of yours. I got away all right, I remember, though what I have always thought must have been an ormolu clock missed me by inches. There is only one thing to be done. You must touch Horace Davenport.'

A bitter smile wreathed Pongo's lips.

'Ha!' he said briefly.

'You mean you have already tried? And failed? Too bad. Still, I wouldn't despair. No doubt you went the wrong way to work. I fancy that we shall find that when tactfully approached by a man of my presence and dignity he will prove far more plastic. Leave it to me. I will get into his ribs for you. There are no limits, literally none, to what I can accomplish in the springtime.'

'But you can't come to London.'

'Can't come to London? I don't understand you.'

'Didn't Aunt Jane say she would skin you if you did?'

'In her whimsical way she did say something to that effect, true. But you appear to have forgotten that she is on her way to the South of France.'

'Yes—leaving Valerie here to keep an eye on you.'

'I see what you mean. Yes, now that you mention it, there may possibly have been some idea in her mind that Valerie would maintain an affectionate watch over my movements during her absence. But be of good cheer. Valerie is not making a long stay. She will be returning to London with you in your car.'

'What?'

'Yes. She does not know it yet—in fact, I understood her to say that she was proposing to remain some weeks—but I think you will find her at your side.'

'What do you mean? You can't chuck her out.'

'My dear boy!' said Lord Ickenham, shocked. 'Of course not. But one has one's methods. Ah, there she is,' he went on, as a girlish figure came round the corner of the house. 'Valerie, my dear, here's Pongo.'

Valerie Twistleton had paused to stare at a passing snail—coldly and forbiddingly, as if it had been Horace Davenport. Looking up, she transferred this cold stare to her brother.

'So I see,' she said distantly. 'What's he doing here?'

'He has come to take you back to London.'

'I have no intention whatsoever—'

'Nothing,' proceeded Lord Ickenham, 'could be more delightful than to have you with me to cheer my loneliness, but Pongo feels—and I must say I agree with him—that you are making a great mistake in running away like this.'

'Doing *what?*'

'I'm afraid that is the construction people will place on the fact of your leaving London after what has happened. You know what people are. They sneer. They jibe. They laugh behind the back. It will be different, of course, with your real friends. They will merely feel a tender pity. They will look on you as the wounded animal crawling to its lair, and will understand and sympathize. But I repeat that in my opinion you are making a mistake. We Twistletons have always rather prided ourselves on keeping the stiff upper lip in times of trouble, and I confess that if I were in your place my impulse would be to show myself in my usual haunts—gay, smiling, debonair . . . Yes, Coggs?'

The butler had appeared from the hall.

'A trunk call for you, m'lord.'

'I will come at once. Be thinking it over, my dear.'

For some moments there had been proceeding from Valerie Twistleton a soft noise like the escape of steam. It now ceased, and her teeth came together with a sharp, unpleasant click.

'Can you wait ten minutes while I pack, Pongo?' she said. 'I will try not to keep you longer.'

She passed into the house, and Pongo lit a reverent cigarette. He did not approve of his Uncle Fred, but he could not but admire his work.

Lord Ickenham returned, looking about him.

'Where's Valerie?'

'Upstairs, packing.'

'Ah, she decided to leave, then? I think she was wise. That was old Emsworth on the 'phone. I don't think you've met him, have you? Lives at Blandings Castle in Shropshire. I hardly know him myself, but he is the brother of a very old pal of mine. He wants me to lunch with him at his club to-morrow. It will fit in quite nicely. We'll get this business of Horace over with in the morning. I'll meet you at the Drones at about twelve. And now come in and have a quick one. Bless my soul, it's wonderful to think that to-morrow I shall be in London. I feel like a child about to be taken to the circus.'

Pongo's feelings, as he followed his uncle to the smoking-room, were more mixed. It was stimulating, of course, to think that by his arts the other might succeed in inducing Horace Davenport to join the Share-The-Wealth movement, but the picture of him loose in London was one that tended definitely to knit the brow. As always when Lord Ickenham proposed to share with him the bracing atmosphere of the metropolis, he found himself regarding with apprehension the shape of things to come.

A thoughtful member of the Drones had once put the thing in a nutshell.

'The trouble with Pongo's Uncle Fred,' he had said, and the Drones is about the only place nowadays where you hear sound, penetrating stuff like this, 'is that, though sixty if a day, he becomes on arriving in London as young as he feels—which is, apparently, a youngish twenty-two. He has a nasty way of lugging Pongo out into the open and there, right in the public eye, proceeding to step high, wide and plentiful. I don't know if you happen to know what the word "excesses" means, but those are what Pongo's Uncle Fred, when in London, invariably commits.'

The young man's face, as he sipped his cocktail, was a little drawn and anxious.

4

His Uncle Fred's theory that Horace Davenport, scientifically worked, would develop pay gold had impressed Pongo Twistleton a good deal both when he heard it and during the remainder of the day. Throughout the drive back to London it kept him in optimistic mood. But when he woke on the following morning the idea struck him as unsound and impractical.

It was hopeless, he felt, to expect to mace any one given person for a sum like two hundred pounds. The only possible solution of his financial worries was to open a subscription list and let the general public in on the thing. He decided to look in at the Drones immediately and test the sentiment of the investors. And having arrived there, he was gratified to note that all the indications seemed to point to a successful flotation.

The atmosphere in the smoking-room of the Drones Club on the return of its members from their annual week-end at Le Touquet was not always one of cheerfulness and gaiety—there had been years when you might have mistaken the place for the Wailing Wall of Jerusalem—but to-day a delightful spirit of happiness prevailed. The dingy gods who preside over the *chemin-de-fer* tables at Continental Casinos had, it appeared, been extraordinarily kind to many of the Eggs, Beans and Crumpets revelling at the bar. And Pongo, drinking in the tales of their exploits, had just decided to raise the assessment of several of those present another ten pounds, when through the haze of cigarette smoke he caught sigh of a familiar face. On a chair at the far end of the room sat Claude Pott.

It was not merely curiosity as to what Mr Pott was doing there or a fear lest he might be feeling lonely in these unaccustomed surroundings that caused Pongo to go and engage him in conversation. At the sight of the private investigator, there had floated into his mind like drifting thistledown the thought that it might be possible to start the ball rolling by obtaining a small donation from him. He crossed the room with outstretched hand.

'Why, hullo, Mr Pott. What brings you here?'

'Good morning, sir. I came with Mr Davenport. He is at the moment in the telephone booth, telephoning.'

'I didn't know old Horace ever got up as early as this.'

'He has not retired to bed yet. He went to a dance last night.'

'Of course, yes. The Bohemian Ball at the Albert Hall. I remember. Well, it's nice seeing you again, Mr Pott. You left a bit hurriedly that time we met.'

'Yes,' said Claude Pott meditatively. 'How did you come out with The Subject?'

'Not too well. She threw her weight about a bit.'

'I had an idea she would.'

'You were better away.'

'That's what I thought.'

'Still,' said Pongo heartily, 'I was very sorry you had to go, very. I could see that we were a couple of chaps who were going to get along together. Will you have a drink or something?'

'No, thank you, Mr T.'

'A cigarette or something?'

'No, thank you.'

'A chair or something? Oh, you've got one. I say, Mr Pott,' said Pongo, 'I was wondering—'

The babble at the bar had risen to a sudden crescendo. Oofy Prosser, the club's tame millionaire, was repeating for the benefit of some new arrivals the story of how he had run his bank seven times, and there had come into Mr Pott's eyes a dull glow, like the phosphorescent gleam on the stomach of a dead fish.

'Coo!' he said, directing at Oofy the sort of look a thoughtful vulture in the Sahara casts at a dying camel. 'Seems to be a lot of money in here this morning.'

'Yes. And talking of money—'

'Now would be just the time to run the old Hat Stakes.'

'Hat Stakes?'

'Haven't you ever heard of the Hat Stakes? It sometimes seems to me they don't teach you boys nothing at your public schools. Here's the way it works. You take somebody, as it might be me, and he opens a book on the Hat Race, the finish to be wherever you like—call it that door over there. See what I mean? The punters would bet on what sort of hat the first bloke coming in through that door would be wearing. You, for instance, might feel like having a tenner—'

Pongo flicked a speck of dust from his companion's sleeve.

'Ah, but I haven't got a tenner,' he said. 'And that's precisely why I was saying that I wondered—'

'—on Top Hat. Then if a feller wearing a top hat was the first to come in, you'd cop.'

'Yes, I see the idea. Amusing. Ingenious.'

'But you can't play the Hat Stakes nowadays, with everybody wearing these Homburgs. There wouldn't be enough starters. Cor!'

'Cor!' agreed Pongo sympathetically. 'You'd have to make it clothes or something, what? But you were speaking of tenners, and while on that subject . . . Stop me if you've heard this before . . .'

Claude Pott, who had seemed about to sink into a brooding reverie, came out of his meditations with a start.

'What's that you said?'

'I was saying that while on the subject of tenners—'

'Clothes!' Mr Pott rose from his chair with a spasmodic leap, as if he had seen The Subject entering the room. 'Well, strike me pink!'

He shot for the door at a speed quite remarkable in a man of his build. A few moments later, he shot back again, and suddenly the Eggs, Beans and Crumpets assembled at the bar were shocked to discover that some bounder, contrary to all club etiquette, was making a speech.

'Gentlemen!'

The babble died away, to be succeeded by a stunned silence, through which there came the voice of Claude Pott, speaking with all the fervour and *brio* of his Silver Ring days.

'Gentlemen and sportsmen, if I may claim your kind indulgence for one instant! Gentlemen and sportsmen, I know gentlemen and sportsmen when I see them, and what I have been privileged to overhear of your conversation since entering this room has shown me that you are all gentlemen and sportsmen who are ready at all times to take part in a little sporting flutter.'

The words 'sporting flutter' were words which never failed to touch a chord in the members of the Drones Club. Something resembling warmth and sympathy began to creep into the atmosphere of cold disapproval. How this little blister had managed to worm his way into their smoking-room they were still at a loss to understand, but the initial impulse of those present to bung him out on his ear had softened into a more friendly desire to hear what he had to say.

'Pott is my name, gentlemen—a name at one time, I venture to assert, not unfamiliar to patrons of the sport of kings, and though I have retired from active business as a turf commission agent I am still willing to make a little book from time to time to entertain sportsmen and gentlemen, and there's no time like the present. Here we all are—you with the money, me with the book—so I say again, gentlemen, let's have a little flutter. Gentlemen all, the Clothes Stakes are about to be run.'

Few members of the Drones are at their brightest and alertest in the morning. There was a puzzled murmur. A Bean said, 'What did he say?' and a Crumpet whispered, 'The what Stakes?'

'I was explaining the how-you-do-it of the Hat Stakes to my friend Mr Twistleton over there, and the Clothes Stakes are run on precisely the same principle. There is at the present moment a gentleman in the telephone booth along the corridor, and I have just taken the precaution to instruct a page-boy to shove a wedge under the door, thus ensuring that he will remain there and so accord you all ample leisure in which to place your wagers. Coo!' said Claude Pott, struck by an unpleasant idea. 'Nobody's going to come along and let him out, are they?'

'Of course not!' cried his audience indignantly. The thought of anybody wantonly releasing a fellow member who had got stuck in the telephone booth, a thing that only happened once in a blue moon, was revolting to them.

'Then that's all right. Now then, gentlemen, the simple question you have to ask yourselves is—What is the gentleman in the telephone booth wearing? Or putting it another way—What's he got on? Hence the term Clothes Stakes. It might be one thing, or it might be another. He might be in his Sunday-go-to-meetings, or he might have been taking a dip in the Serpentine and be in his little bathing suit. Or he may have joined the Salvation Army. To give you a lead, I am offering nine to four against Blue Serge, four to one Pin-Striped Grey Tweed, ten to one Golf Coat and Plus Fours, a hundred to six Gymnasium Vest and Running Shorts, twenty to one Court Dress as worn at Buckingham Palace, nine to four the field. And perhaps you, sir,' said Mr Pott, addressing an adjacent Egg, 'would be good enough to officiate as my clerk.'

'That doesn't mean I can't have a bit on?'

'By no means, sir. Follow the dictates of your heart and fear nothing.'

'What are you giving Herringbone Cheviot Lounge?'

'Six to one Herringbone Cheviot Lounge, sir.'

'I'll have ten bob.'

'Right, sir. Six halves Herringbone Cheviot Lounge. Ready money, if you please, sir. It's not that I don't trust you, but I'm not

allowed by law. Thank you, sir. Walk up, walk up, my noble sportsmen. Nine to four the field.'

The lead thus given them removed the last inhibitions of the
company. Business became brisk, and it was not long before Mr
Pott had vanished completely behind a mass of eager punters.

Among the first to invest had been Pongo Twistleton. Hastening to the hall porter's desk, he had written a cheque for his last ten
pounds in the world, and he was now leaning against the bar, filled
with the quiet satisfaction of the man who has spotted the winner
and got his money down in good time.

For from the very inception of these proceedings it had been
clear to Pongo that Fortune, hitherto capricious, had at last decided
that it was no use trying to keep a good man down and had handed
him something on a plate. To be a successful punter, what you
need is information, and this he possessed in abundant measure.
Alone of those present, he was aware of the identity of the gentleman in the telephone booth, and he had the additional advantage
of knowing the inside facts about the latter's wardrobe.

You take a chap like—say—Catsmeat Potter-Pirbright, that
modern Brummel, and you might guess for hours without hitting
on the precise suit he would be wearing on any given morning.
But with Horace Pendlebury-Davenport it was different. Horace
had never been a vivacious dresser. He liked to stick to the old and
tried till they came apart on him, and it was this idiosyncrasy of
his which had caused his recent *fiancée*, just before her departure
for Le Touquet, to take a drastic step.

Swooping down on Horace's flat, at a moment when Pongo was
there chatting with its proprietor, and ignoring her loved one's protesting cries, Valerie Twistleton had scooped up virtually his entire
outfit and borne it away in a cab, to be given to the deserving poor.
She could not actually leave the unhappy man in the nude, so she
had allowed him to retain the shabby grey flannel suit he stood up
in and also the morning clothes which he was reserving for the
wedding day. But she had got away with all the rest, and as no tai-

lor could have delivered a fresh supply at this early date, Pongo had felt justified in plunging to the uttermost. The bulk of his fortune on Grey Flannel at ten to one and a small covering bet on Morning Suit, and there he was, sitting pretty.

And he was just sipping his cocktail and reflecting that while his winnings must necessarily fall far short of the stupendous sum which he owed to George Budd, they would at least constitute something on account and remove the dark shadow of Erb at any rate temporarily from his life, when like a blow on the base of the skull there came to him the realization that he had overlooked a vital point.

The opening words of his conversation with Claude Pott came back to him, and he remembered that Mr Pott, in addition to informing him that Horace was in the telephone booth, had stated that the latter had attended the Bohemian Ball at the Albert Hall and had not been to bed yet. And like the knell of a tolling bell there rang in his ears Horace's words: 'I am going as a Boy Scout.'

The smoking-room reeled before Pongo's eyes. He saw now why Claude Pott had leaped so enthusiastically at the idea of starting these Clothes Stakes. The man had known it would be a skinner for the book. The shrewdest and most imaginative Drone would never think of Boy Scouts in telephone booths at this hour of the morning.

He uttered a stricken cry. At the eleventh hour the road to wealth had been indicated to him, and owing to that ready-money clause he was not in a position to take advantage of the fact. And then he caught sight of Oofy Prosser at the other end of the bar, and saw how by swift, decisive action he might save his fortunes from the wreck.

The attitude of Oofy Prosser towards the Clothes Stake had been from the first contemptuous and supercilious, like that of a Wolf of Wall Street watching small boys scrambling for pennies. This Silver Ring stuff did not interest Oofy. He held himself aloof from it, and as the latter slid down the bar and accosted him he tried to hold himself aloof from Pongo. It was only by clutching his coat sleeve and holding on to it with a fevered grip that Pongo was able to keep him rooted to the spot.

'I say, Oofy—'

'No,' replied Oofy Prosser curtly. 'Not a penny!'

Pongo danced a few frantic dance steps. Already there was a lull over by the table where Mr Pott was conducting his business, and the closing of the book seemed imminent.

'But I want to put you on to a good thing!'

'Oh?'

'A cert.'

'Ah?'

'An absolute dashed cast-iron cert.'

Oofy Prosser sneered visibly.

'I'm not betting. What's the use of winning a couple of quid? Why, last Sunday at the big table at Le Touquet—'

Pongo sped towards Claude Pott, scattering Eggs, Beans and Crumpets from his path.

'Mr Pott!'

'Sir?'

'Any limit?'

'No, sir.'

'I've a friend here who wants to put on something big.'

'Ready money only, Mr T., may I remind you? It's the law.'

'Nonsense. This is Mr Prosser. You can take his cheque. You must have heard of Mr Prosser.'

'Oh, Mr Prosser? Yes, that's different. I don't mind breaking the law to oblige Mr Prosser.'

Pongo, bounding back to the bar, found there an Oofy no longer aloof and supercilious.

'Do you really know something, Pongo?'

'You bet I know something. Will you cut me in for fifty?'

'All right.'

'Then put your shirt on Boy Scout,' hissed Pongo. 'I have first-

hand stable information that the bloke in the telephone booth is
Horace Davenport, and I happen to know that he went to a fancy-
dress dance last night as a Boy Scout and hasn't been home to
change yet.'

'What! Is that right?'

'Absolutely official.'

'Then it's money for jam!'

'Money for pickles,' asserted Pongo enthusiastically. 'Follow me
and fear nothing. And don't forget I'm in for the sum I mentioned.'

With a kindling eye he watched his financial backer force his
way into the local Tattersall's, and it was at this tense moment that
a page-boy came up and informed him that Lord Ickenham was
waiting for him in the hall. He went floating out to meet him, his
feet scarcely touching the carpet.

Lord Ickenham watched his approach with interest.

'Aha!' he said.

'Aha!' said Pongo, but absently, as one who has no time for formal greetings. 'Listen, Uncle Fred, slip me every bally cent you've
got on you. I may just be able to get it down before the book closes.
Your pal, Claude Pott, came here with Horace Davenport—'

'I wonder what Horace was doing, bringing Mustard to the
Drones. Capital chap, of course, but quite the wrong person to let
loose in a gathering of impressionable young men.'

Pongo's manner betrayed impatience.

'We haven't time to go into the ethics of the thing. Suffice it
that Horace did bring him, and he shut Horace up in the telephone
booth and started a book on what sort of clothes he had on. How
much can you raise?'

'To wager against Mustard Pott?' Lord Ickenham smiled gently. 'Nothing, my dear boy, nothing. One of the hard lessons Life
will teach you, as you grow to know him better, is that you can't
make money out of Mustard. Hundreds have tried it, and hundreds have failed.'

Pongo shrugged his shoulders. He had done his best.

'Well, you're missing the chance of a lifetime. I happen to know that Horace went to a dance last night as a Boy Scout, and I have it from Pott's own lips that he hasn't been home to change. Oofy Prosser is carrying me for fifty.'

It was evident from his expression that Lord Ickenham was genuinely shocked.

'Horace Davenport went to a dance as a Boy Scout? What a ghastly sight he must have looked. I can't believe this. I must verify it. Bates,' said Lord Ickenham, walking over to the hall-porter's desk, 'were you here when Mr Davenport came in?'

'Yes, m'lord.'

'How did he look?'

'Terrible, m'lord.'

It seemed to Pongo that his uncle had wandered from the point.

'I concede,' he said, 'that a chap of Horace's height and skinniness ought to have been shrewder than to flaunt himself at a public dance in the costume of a Boy Scout. Involving as it does, knickerbockers and bare knees—'

'But he didn't, sir.'

'What!'

The hall porter was polite, but firm.

'Mr Davenport didn't go to no dance as no Boy ruddy Scout, if you'll pardon me contradicting you, sir. More like some sort of negroid character, it seemed to me. His face was all blacked up, and he had a spear with him. Gave me a nasty turn when he come through.'

Pongo clutched the desk. The hall-porter's seventeen stone seemed to be swaying before his eyes.

'Blacked up?'

A movement along the passage attracted their attention. Claude Pott, accompanied by a small committee, was proceeding to the telephone booth. He removed the wedge from beneath the door, and as he opened it there emerged a figure.

Nature hath framed strange fellows in her time, but few stranger than the one that now whizzed out of the telephone booth, whizzed down the corridor, whizzed past the little group at the desk and, bursting through the door of the club, whizzed down the steps and into a passing cab.

The face of this individual, as the hall porter had foreshadowed, was a rich black in colour. Its long body was draped in tights of the same sombre hue, surmounted by a leopard's skin. Towering above his head was a head-dress of ostrich feathers, and in its right hand it grasped an assegai. It was wearing tortoise-shell-rimmed spectacles.

Pongo, sliding back against the desk, found his arm gripped by a kindly hand.

'Shift ho, my boy, I think, eh?' said Lord Ickenham.

'There would appear to be nothing to keep you here, and a meeting with Oofy Prosser at this moment might be fraught with pain and embarrassment. Let us follow Horace—he seemed to be homing—and hold an enquiry into this in-and-out running of his. Tell me, how much did you say Oofy Prosser was carrying you for? Fifty pounds?'

Pongo nodded bleakly.

'Then let us assemble the facts. Your assets are nil. You owe George Budd two hundred. You now owe Oofy fifty. If you don't pay Oofy, he will presumably report you to the committee and have you thrown into the street, where you will doubtless find Erb waiting for you with a knuckleduster. Well,' said Lord Ickenham, impressed, 'nobody can say you don't lead a full life. To a yokel like myself all this is very stimulating. One has the sense of being right at the pulsing heart of things.'

They came to Bloxham Mansions, and were informed by Webster that Mr Davenport was in his bath.

5

THE Horace who entered the library some ten minutes later in pajamas and a dressing-gown was a far more prepossessing spectacle than the ghastly figure which had popped out of the Drones Club telephone booth, but he was still patently a man who had suffered. His face, scrubbed with butter and rinsed with soap and water, shone rosily, but it was a haggard face, and the eyes were dark with anguish.

Into these eyes, as he beheld the senior of his two visitors, there crept a look of alarm. Horace Davenport was not unfamiliar with stories in which the male relatives of injured girls called on young men with horsewhips.

Lord Ickenham's manner, however, was reassuring. Though considering him weak in the head, he had always liked Horace, and he was touched by the forlornness of his aspect.

'How are you, my dear fellow? I looked in earlier in the day, but you were out.'

'Yes, Webster told me.'

'And when I saw you at the Drones just now, you seemed pressed for time and not in the mood for conversation. I wanted to have a talk with you about this unfortunate rift between yourself and Valerie. She has given me a fairly comprehensive eyewitness's report of the facts.'

Horace seemed to swallow something jagged.

'Oh, has she?'

'Yes. I was chatting with her last night, and your name happened to come up.'

'Oh, did it?'

'Yes. In fact, she rather dwelt on you. Valerie—we must face it—is piqued.'

'Yes.'

'But don't let that worry you,' said Lord Ickenham cheerily. 'She'll come round. I'm convinced of it. When you reach my age, you will know that it is an excellent sign when a girl speaks of a man as a goggle-eyed nit-wit and says that her dearest wish is to dip him in boiling oil and watch him wriggle.'

'Did she say that?'

'Yes, she was most definite about it—showing, I feel, that love still lingers. My advice is—give her a day or two to cool off, and then start sending her flowers. She will tear them to shreds. Send some more. She will rend them to ribbons. Shoot in a further supply. And very soon, if you persevere, you will find that the little daily dose is having its effect. I anticipate a complete reconciliation somewhere about the first week in May.'

'I see,' said Horace moodily. 'Well, that's fine.'

Lord Ickenham felt a trifle ruffled.

'You don't seem pleased.'

'Oh, I am. Oh yes, rather.'

'Then why do you continue to look like a dead fish on a slab?'

'Well, the fact is, there's something else worrying me a bit at the moment.'

Pongo broke a silence which had lasted for some twenty minutes. Since entering the apartment he had been sitting with folded arms, as if hewn from the living rock.

'Oh, is there?' he cried. 'And there's something that's jolly well worrying me at the moment. Did you or did you not, you blighted Pendlebury-Davenport, definitely and specifically state to me that

you were going to that Ball as a Boy Scout? Come on now. Did you
or didn't you?'

'Yes, I did. I remember. But I changed my mind.'

'Changed your mind! Coo!' said Pongo, speaking through
tightly clenched teeth and borrowing from the powerful vocabu-
lary of Claude Pott to give emphasis to his words. 'He changed his
mind! He changed his bally mind! Ha! Coo! Cor!'

'Why, what's up?'

'Oh, nothing. You have merely utterly and completely ruined
me, that's all.'

'Yes, my dear Horace,' said Lord Ickenham, 'I'm afraid you
have let Pongo down rather badly. When Pongo joins the Foreign
Legion, the responsibility will be yours. You give him your solemn
assurance that you are going to the Ball in one costume and actually attend it in another. Not very British.'

'But why does it matter?'

'There was some betting in the club smoking-room on what you
were wearing, and Pongo, unhappy lad, plunging in the light of what
he thought was inside knowledge on Boy Scout, took the knock.'

'Oh, I say! I'm frightfully sorry.'

'Too late to be sorry now.'

'The thing was, you see, that Polly thought it would be fun if I
went as a Zulu warrior.'

'Evidently a girl of exotic and rather unwholesome tastes. The
word "morbid" is one that springs to the lips. Who is this Polly?'

'Pott's daughter. She went to the Ball with me.'

Lord Ickenham uttered an exclamation.

'Not little Polly Pott? Good heavens, how time flies. Fancy Polly
being old enough to go to dances. I knew her when she was a kid.
She used to come and spend her holidays at Ickenham. A very jolly
child she was, too, beloved by all. Quite grown up now, eh? Well,
well, we're none of us getting younger. I was a boy in the early fif-
ties when I saw her last. So you took Polly to the Ball, did you?'

'Yes. You see, the original idea was that Valerie was to have gone. But when she gave me the bird, I told her I would take Polly instead.'

'Your view being, of course, that that would learn her? A fine, defiant gesture. Did Pott go along?'

'No, he wasn't there.'

'Then what was he doing at the Drones with you?'

'Well, you see, he had come to Marlborough Street to pay my fine, and we sort of drifted on there afterwards. I suppose I had some idea of buying him a drink or something.'

A faint stir of interest ruffled the stone of Pongo's face.

'What do you mean, your fine? Were you pinched last night?'

'Yes. There was a bit of unpleasantness at the Ball, and they scooped me in. It was Ricky's fault.'

'Who,' asked Lord Ickenham, 'is Ricky?'

'My cousin. Alaric Gilpin.'

'Poet. Beefy chap with red hair. It was he who introduced this girl Polly to Horace,' interpolated Pongo, supplying additional footnotes. 'She was giving him dancing lessons.'

'And how did he come to mix you up in unpleasantness?'

'Well, it was like this. Ricky, though I didn't know it, is engaged to Polly. And another thing I didn't know was that he hadn't much liked the idea of her giving me dancing lessons and, when she told him I was taking her to the Ball, expressly forbade her to go. So when he found us together there . . . I say, he wasn't hanging about outside when you arrived, was he?'

'I saw no lurking figure.'

'He said he was going to look in to-day and break my neck.'

'I didn't know poets broke people's necks.'

'Ricky does. He once took on three simultaneous costermongers in Covent Garden and cleaned them up in five minutes. He had gone there to get inspiration for a pastoral, and they started chi-iking him, and he sailed in and knocked them base over apex into a pile of Brussels sprouts.'

'How different from the home life of the late Lord Tennyson. But you were telling us about this trouble at the Ball.'

Horace mused for a moment, his thoughts in the stormy past.

'Well, it was after the proceedings had been in progress for about a couple of hours that it started. Polly was off somewhere, hobnobbing with pals, and I was having a smoke and resting the ankles, when Ricky appeared and came up and joined me. He said a friend of his had given him a ticket at the last moment and he thought he might as well look in for a bit, so he hired a Little Lord Fauntleroy suit and came along. He was perfectly all right then—in fact, exceptionally affable. He sat down and tried to borrow five hundred pounds from me to buy an onion soup bar.'

Lord Ickenham shook his head.

'You are taking me out of my depth. We rustics who don't get up to London much are not in touch with the latest developments of modern civilization. What is an onion soup bar?'

'Place where you sell onion soup,' explained Pongo. 'There are lots of them round Piccadilly Circus way these days. You stay open all night and sell onion soup to the multitude as they reel out of the bottle-party places. Pots of money in it, I believe.'

'So Ricky said. A pal of his, an American, started one a couple of years ago in Coventry Street and, according to him, worked the profits up to about two thousand quid a year. But apparently he has got homesick and wants to sell out and go back to New York, and he's willing to let Ricky have the thing for five hundred. And Ricky wanted me to lend it to him. And he was just getting rather eloquent and convincing, when he suddenly broke off and I saw that he was glaring at something over my shoulder.'

'Don't tell me,' said Lord Ickenham. 'Let me guess. Polly?'

'In person. And then the whole aspect of affairs changed. He had just been stroking my arm and saying what pals we had always been and asking me if I remembered the days when we used to go ratting together at my father's place, and he cheesed it like a flash.

He turned vermilion, and the next moment he had started kicking up a frightful row . . . cursing me . . . cursing Polly . . . showing quite a different side to his nature, I mean to say. Well, you know how it is when you do that sort of thing at a place like the Albert Hall. People began to cluster round, asking questions. And what with one thing and another, I got a bit rattled, and I suppose it was because I was rattled that I did it. It was a mistake, of course. I see that now.'

'Did what?'

'Jabbed him with my assegai. Mind you,' said Horace, 'I didn't mean to. It wasn't as if I had had any settled plans. I was just trying to hold him off. But I misjudged the distance, and the next thing I knew he was rubbing his stomach and coming for me with a nasty glint in his eyes. So I jabbed him again, and then things hotted up still further. And what really led to my getting arrested was that he managed to edge past the assegai and land me a juicy one on the jaw.'

Lord Ickenham found himself unable to reconcile cause and effect.

'But surely no policeman, however flat-footed, would take a man into custody for being landed a juicy one on the jaw. You have probably got your facts twisted. I expect we shall find, when we look into it, that it was Ricky who was taken to Marlborough Street.'

'No, you see what happened was this juicy one on the jaw made me a bit dizzy, and I didn't quite know what I was doing. Everything was a sort of blur, and I just jabbed wildly in the general direction of what I thought was the seat of the trouble. And after a while I discovered that I was jabbing a female dressed as Marie Antoinette. It came as a great surprise to me. As a matter of fact, I had been rather puzzled for some moments. You see, I could feel the assegai going into some yielding substance, and I was surprised that Ricky was so squashy and had such a high voice. And then, as I say, I found it wasn't Ricky, but this woman.'

'Embarrassing.'

'It was a bit. The man who was with the woman summoned the cops. And what made it still more awkward was that by that time Ricky was nowhere near. Almost at the start of the proceedings, it appeared, people had gripped him and bustled him off. So that when the policeman arrived and found me running amuck with an assegai apparently without provocation, it was rather difficult to convince him that I wasn't tight. In fact, I didn't convince him. The magistrate was a bit terse about it all this morning. I say, are you sure Ricky wasn't hanging about outside?'

'We saw no signs of him.'

'Then I'll get dressed and go round and see Polly.'

'With what motive?'

'Well, dash it, I want to tell her to go and explain to Ricky that my behaviour towards her throughout was scrupulously correct. At present, he's got the idea that I'm a kind of . . . Who was the chap who was such a devil with the other sex? . . . Donald something.'

'Donald Duck?'

'Don Juan. That's the fellow I mean. Unless I can convince Ricky immediately that I'm not a Don Juan and was not up to any funny business with Polly, the worst will happen. You've no notion what he was like last night. Absolutely frothing at the mouth. I must go and see her at once.'

'And if he comes in while you are there?'

Horace, half-way to the door, halted.

'I never thought of that.'

'No.'

'You think it would be better to telephone her?'

'I don't think anything of the sort. You can't conduct a delicate negotiation like this over the telephone. You need the language of the eye . . . those little appealing gestures of the hand . . . Obviously you must entrust the thing to an ambassador. And what better ambassador could you have than Pongo here?'

'Pongo?'

'A silver-tongued orator, if ever there was one. Oh, I know

what you are thinking,' said Lord Ickenham. 'You feel that there may be a coolness on his side, due to the fact that you recently refused to lend him a bit of money. My dear boy, Pongo is too big and fine to be unwilling to help you out because of that. Besides, in return for his services you will of course naturally slip him the trifle he requires.'

'But he said he wanted two hundred pounds.'

'Two hundred and fifty. He doesn't always speak distinctly.'

'But that's a frightful lot.'

'To a man of your wealth as the price of your safety? You show a cheeseparing spirit which I do not like to see. Fight against it.'

'But, dash it, why does everybody come trying to touch *me*?'

'Because you've got the stuff, my boy. It is the penalty you pay for having an ancestress who couldn't say No to Charles the Second.'

Horace chewed a dubious lip.

'I don't see how I can manage—'

'Well, please yourself, of course. Tell me about this fellow Ricky, Pongo. A rather formidable chap, is he? Robust? Well-developed? Muscular? His strength is as the strength of ten?'

'Definitely, Uncle Fred.'

'And in addition to that he appears to be both jealous and quick-tempered. An unpleasant combination. One of those then, I imagine, who if he inflicted some serious injury on anyone, would be the first to regret it after he had calmed down, but would calm down about ten minutes too late. I've met the type. There was a chap named Bricky Bostock in my young days who laid a fellow out for weeks over some misunderstanding about a girl, and it was pitiful to see his remorse when he realized what he had done. Used to hang about outside the hospital all the time the man was in danger, trembling like a leaf. But, as I said to him, "What's the use of trembling like a leaf now? The time to have trembled like a leaf was when you had your hands on his throat and were starting to squeeze the juice out of him."'

'It'll be all right about that two-fifty, Pongo,' said Horace.

'Thanks, old man.'

'When can you go and see Polly?'

'The instant I've had a bit of lunch.'

'I'll give you her address. You will find her a most intelligent girl, quick to understand. But pitch it strong.'

'Leave it to me.'

'And impress upon her particularly that there is no time to waste. Full explanations should be made to Ricky by this evening at the latest. And now,' said Horace, 'I suppose I'd better go and dress.'

The door closed. Lord Ickenham glanced at his watch.

'Hullo,' he said. 'I must be off. I have to go to the Senior Conservative Club to meet old Emsworth. So good-bye, my dear boy, for the present. I am delighted that everything has come out so smoothly. We shall probably meet at Pott's. I am going to slip round there after lunch and see Polly. Give her my love, and don't let Mustard lure you into any card game. A dear, good chap, one of the best, but rather apt to try to get people to play something he calls Persian Monarchs. When he was running that club of his, I've known him to go through the place like a devouring flame, leaving ruin and desolation behind him on every side.'

6

THE method of Lord Emsworth, when telling a story, being to repeat all the unimportant parts several times and to diverge from the main stream of narrative at intervals in order to supply lengthy character studies of the various persons involved in it, luncheon was almost over before he was able to place his guest in full possession of the facts relating to the Empress of Blandings. When eventually he had succeeded in doing so, he adjusted his pince-nez and looked hopefully across the table.

'What do you advise, my dear Ickenham?'

Lord Ickenham ate a thoughtful cheese straw.

'Well, it is obvious that immediate steps must be taken through the proper channels, but the question that presents itself is "What steps?"'

'Exactly.'

'We have here,' said Lord Ickenham, illustrating by means of a knife, a radish and a piece of bread, 'one pig, one sister, one Duke.'

'Yes.'

'The Duke wants the pig.'

'Quite.'

'The sister says he's got to have it.'

'Precisely.'

'The pig, no doubt, would prefer to be dissociated from the affair altogether. Very well, then. To what conclusion do we come?'

'I don't know,' said Lord Emsworth.

'We come to the conclusion that the whole situation pivots on the pig. Eliminate the pig, and we see daylight. "What, no pig?" says the Duke, and after a little natural disappointment turns his thoughts to other things—I don't know what, but whatever things Dukes do turn their thoughts to. There must be dozens. This leaves us with the simple problem—How is the existing state of what I might call "plus pig" to be converted into a state of "minus pig"? There can be only one answer, my dear Emsworth. The pig must be smuggled away to a place of safety and kept under cover till the Duke has blown over.'

Lord Emsworth, as always when confronted with a problem, had allowed his lower jaw to sag restfully.

'How?' he asked.

Lord Ickenham regarded him with approval.

'I was expecting you to say that. I knew your razor-like brain would cut cleanly to the heart of the thing. Well, it ought not to be difficult. You creep out by night with an accomplice and—one shoving and one pulling—you load the animal into some vehicle and ship her off to my family seat, where she will be looked after like a favourite child till you are ready to receive her again. It is a long journey from Shropshire to Hampshire, of course, but she can stop off from time to time for a strengthening bran-mash or a quick acorn. The only point to be decided is who draws the job of accomplice. Who is there at Blandings that you can trust?'

'Nobody,' said Lord Emsworth promptly.

'Ah? That seems to constitute an obstacle.'

'I suppose you would not care to come down yourself?'

'I should love it, and it is what I would have suggested. But unfortunately I am under strict orders from my wife to remain at Ickenham. My wife, I should mention, is a woman who believes in a strong centralized government.'

'But you aren't at Ickenham.'

'No. The Boss being away, I am playing hookey at the moment. But I have often heard her mention her friend Lady Constance Keeble, and were I to come to Blandings Lady Constance would inevitably reveal the fact to her sooner or later. Some casual remark in a letter, perhaps, saying how delightful it had been to meet her old bit of trouble at last and how my visit had brightened up the place. You see what I mean?'

'Oh, quite. Yes, quite, dash it.'

'My prestige in the home is already low, and a substantiated charge of being A. W. O. L. would put a further crimp in it, from which it might never recover.'

'I see.'

'But I think,' said Lord Ickenham, helping himself to the radish which had been doing duty as Lady Constance, 'that I have got the solution. There is always a way. We must place the thing in the hands of Mustard Pott.'

'Who is Mustard Pott?'

'A very dear and valued friend of mine. I feel pretty sure that, if we stress the fact that there is a bit in it for him, he would be delighted to smuggle pigs. Mustard is always ready and anxious to add to his bank balance. I was intending to call upon him after lunch, to renew our old acquaintance. Would you care to come along and sound him?'

'It is a most admirable idea. Does he live far from here?'

'No, quite close. Down in the Sloane Square neighbourhood.'

'I ask because I have an appointment with Sir Roderick Glossop at three o'clock. Connie told me to ask him to lunch, but I was dashed if I was going to do that. Do you know Sir Roderick Glossop, the brain specialist?'

'Only to the extent of having sat next to him at a public dinner not long ago.'

'A talented man, I believe.'

'So he told me. He spoke very highly of himself.'

'Connie wants me to bring him to Blandings, to observe the Duke, and he made an appointment with me for three o'clock. But I am all anxiety to see this man Pott. Would there be time?'

'Oh, certainly. And I think we have found the right way out of the impasse. If it had been a question of introducing Mustard into the home, I might have hesitated. But in this case he will put up at the local inn and confine himself entirely to outside work. You won't even have to ask him to dinner. The only danger I can see is that he may get this pig of yours into a friendly game and take her last bit of potato peel off her. Still, that is a risk that must be faced.'

'Of course.'

'Nothing venture, nothing have, eh?'

'Precisely.'

'Then suppose we dispense with coffee and go round and see him. We shall probably find my nephew Pongo there. A nice boy. You will like him.'

Pongo Twistleton had arrived at Claude Pott's residence at about the time when Lord Emsworth and his guest were leaving the Senior Conservative Club, and had almost immediately tried to borrow ten pounds from him. For even though Horace Davenport had guaranteed in the event of his soothing Ricky Gilpin to underwrite his gambling losses, he could not forget that he was still fiscally crippled, and he felt that he owed it to himself to omit no word or act which might lead to the acquisition of a bit of the needful.

In the sleuth hound of 6, Wilbraham Place, Sloane Square, however, he speedily discovered that he had come up against one of the Untouchables, a man to whom even Oofy Prosser, that outstanding non-partner, would have felt compelled to raise his hat. Beginning by quoting from Polonius' speech to Laertes, which a surprising number of people whom you would not have suspected of familiarity with the writings of Shakespeare seem to know, Mr Pott had gone on to say that lending money always made him feel as if he were rubbing velvet the wrong way, and that in any case he would not lend it to Pongo, because he valued his friendship too highly. The surest method of creating a rift between two pals, explained Mr Pott, was for one pal to place the other pal under a financial obligation.

It was, in consequence, into an atmosphere of some slight strain that the Lords Emsworth and Ickenham entered a few moments later. And though the mutual courtesies of the latter and Claude Pott, getting together again after long separation, lightened the gloom temporarily, the clouds gathered once more when Mr Pott, having listened to Lord Emsworth's proposal, regretfully declined to have anything to do with removing the Empress from her sty and wafting her away to Ickenham Hall.

'I couldn't do it, Lord E.'

'Eh? Why not?'

'It wouldn't be in accordance with the dignity of the profession.'

Lord Ickenham resented this superior attitude.

'Don't stick on such beastly side, Mustard. You and your bally dignity! I never heard such swank.'

'One has one's self-respect.'

'What's self-respect got to do with it? There's nothing *infra dig* about snitching pigs. If I were differently situated, I'd do it like a shot. And I'm one of the haughtiest men in Hampshire.'

'Well, between you and me, Lord I,' said Claude Pott, discarding loftiness and coming clean, 'there's another reason. I was once bitten by a pig.'

'Not really?'

'Yes, sir. And ever since then I've had a horror of the animals.'

Lord Emsworth hastened to point out that the present was a special case.

'You can't be bitten by the Empress.'

'Oh, no? Who made that rule?'

'She's as gentle as a lamb.'

'I was once bitten by a lamb.'

Lord Ickenham was surprised.

'What an extraordinary past you seem to have had, Mustard. One whirl of excitement. One of these days you must look me up and tell me some of the things you haven't been bitten by. Well, if you won't take the job on, you won't, of course. But I'm disappointed in you.'

Mr Pott sighed slightly, but it was plain that he did not intend to recede from his attitude of civil disobedience.

'I suppose I shall now have to approach the matter from another angle. If you're seeing Glossop at three, Emsworth, you'd better be starting.'

'Eh? Oh, ah, yes. True.'

'You leaving us, Lord E?' said Mr Pott. 'Which way are you going?'

'I have an appointment in Harley Street.'

'I'll come with you,' said Mr Pott, who had marked down the dreamy peer as almost an ideal person with whom to play Persian Monarchs and wished to cement their acquaintanceship. 'I've got to see a man up in that direction. We could share a cab.'

He escorted Lord Emsworth lovingly to the door, and Lord Ickenham stood brooding.

'A set-back,' he said. 'An unquestionable set-back. I had been relying on Mustard. Still, if a fellow's been bitten by pigs I suppose his views on associating with them do get coloured. But how the devil does a man *get* bitten by a pig? I wouldn't have thought they would ever meet on that footing. Ah, well, there it is. And now what about Polly? There seems to be no signs of her. Is she out?'

Pongo roused himself from a brown study.

'She's in her room, Pott told me. Dressing or something, I take it.'

Lord Ickenham went to the door.

'Ahoy!' he shouted. 'Polly!'

There came in reply from somewhere in the distance a voice which even in his gloom Pongo was able to recognize as silvery.

'Hullo?'

'Come here. I want to see you.'

'Who's there?'

'Frederick Altamont Cornwallis Twistleton, fifth Earl of good old Ickenham. Have you forgotten your honorary uncle Fred?'

'Oo!' cried the silvery voice. There was a patter of feet in the passage, and a kimono-clad figure burst into the room.

'Uncle Fur-RED! Well, it is nice seeing you again!'

'Dashed mutual, I assure you, my dear. I say, you've grown.'

'Well, it's six years.'

'So it is, by Jove.'

'You're just as handsome as ever.'

'Handsomer, I should have said. And you're prettier than ever. But what's become of your legs?'

'They're still there.'

'Yes, but when I saw you last they were about eight feet long, like a colt's.'

'I was at the awkward age.'

'You aren't now, by George. How old are you, Polly?'

'Twenty-one.'

'Gol durn yuh, l'il gal, as my spooked-up-with-vinegar friend would say, you're a peach!'

Lord Ickenham patted her hand, put his arm about her waist and kissed her tenderly. Pongo wished he had thought of that himself. He reflected moodily that this was always the way. In the course of their previous adventures together, if there had ever been any kissing or hand-patting or waist-encircling to be done, it had always been his nimbler uncle who had nipped in ahead of him and attended to it. He coughed austerely.

'Oh, hullo! I'd forgotten you were there,' said Lord Ickenham, apologetically. 'Miss Polly Pott . . . My nephew—such as he is— Pongo Twistleton.'

'How do you do?'

'How do you do?' said Pongo.

He spoke a little huskily, for he had once more fallen in love at first sight. The heart of Pongo Twistleton had always been an open door with 'Welcome' clearly inscribed on the mat, and you never knew what would walk in next. At brief intervals during the past few years he had fallen in love at first sight with a mixed gaggle or assortment of females to the number of about twenty, but as he gazed at this girl like an ostrich goggling at a brass door-knob it seemed to him that here was the best yet. There was something about her that differentiated her from the other lodgers.

It was not the fact that she was small, though the troupe hitherto had tended to be on the tall and willowy side. It was not that her eyes were grey and soft, while his tastes previously had rather lain in the direction of the dark and bold and flashing. It was something about her personality—a matiness, a simplicity, an absence of that lipsticky sophistication to which the others had been so addicted. This was a cosy girl. A girl you could tell your troubles to. You could lay your head in her lap and ask her to stroke it.

Not that he did, of course. He merely lit a cigarette.

'Won't you . . . sit down?' he said.

'What I'd really like to do,' said Polly Pott, 'is to lie down—and go to sleep. I'm a wreck, Uncle Fred. I was up nearly all last night at a dance.'

'We know all about your last night's goings-on, my child,' said Lord Ickenham. 'That is why we are here. We have come on behalf of Horace Davenport, who is in a state of alarm and despondency on account of the unfriendly attitude of your young man.'

The girl laughed—the gay, wholehearted laugh of youth. Pongo remembered that he had laughed like that in the days before he had begun to see so much of his Uncle Fred.

'Ricky was marvellous last night. You ought to have seen him jumping about, trying to dodge Horace's spear.'

'He speaks of breaking Horace's neck.'

'Yes, I remember he said something about that. Ricky's got rather a way of wanting to break people's necks.'

'And we would like you to get in touch with him immediately and assure him that this will not be necessary, because Horace's behaviour towards you has always been gentlemanly, respectfull— in short, *preux* to the last drop. I don't know if this public menace you're engaged to has ever heard of Sir Galahad but, if so, convey the idea that the heart of that stainless knight might have been even purer if he had taken a tip or two from Horace.'

'Oh, but everything is quite all right now. I've calmed Ricky down, and he had forgiven Horace. Has Horace been worrying?'

'That is not overstating it. Horace *has* been worrying.'

'I'll ring him up and tell him there's no need to, shall I?'

'On no account,' said Lord Ickenham. 'Pongo will handle the whole affair, acting as your agent. It would be tedious to go into the reasons for this, but you can take it from me that it is essential. You had better be toddling off, Pongo, and bringing the roses back to Horace's cheeks.'

'I will.'

'The sooner you get that cheque, the better. Run along. I will remain and pick up the threads with Polly. I feel that she owes me an explanation. The moment my back is turned, she appears to have gone and got engaged to a young plug-ugly who seems to possess all the less engaging qualities of a Borneo head-hunter. Tell me about this lad of yours, Polly,' said Lord Ickenham, as the door closed. 'You seem to like them tough. Where did you find him? On Devil's Island?'

'He brought Father home one night.'

'You mean Father brought him home.'

'No, I don't. Father couldn't walk very well, and Ricky was practically carrying him. Apparently Father had been set upon in the street by some men who had a grudge against him—I don't know why.'

Lord Ickenham thought he could guess. He was well aware that, given a pack of cards, Claude Pott could offend the mildest lamb. Indeed, it was a tenable theory that this might have been the cause of his once having been bitten by one.

'And Ricky happened to be passing, and he jumped in and res-cued him.'

'How many men were there?'

'Thousands, I believe.'

'But he wouldn't mind that?'

'Oh, no.'

'He just broke their necks.'

'I expect so. He had a black eye. I put steak on it.'

'Romantic. Did you fall in love at first sight?'

'Oh, yes.'

'My nephew Pongo always does. Perhaps it's the best way. Saves time. Did he fall in love with you at first sight?'

'Oh, yes.'

'I begin to think better of this Borstal exhibit. He will probably wind up in Broadmoor, but he has taste.'

'You would never have thought so, though; he just sat and glared at me with his good eye, and growled when I spoke to him.'

'Uncouth young wart-hog.'

'He's nothing of the kind. He was shy. Later on, he got better.'

'And when he was better, was he good?'

'Yes.'

'I wish I could have heard him propose. The sort of chap who would be likely to think up something new.'

'He did, rather. He grabbed me by the wrist and nearly broke it and told me to marry him. I said I would.'

'Well, you know your own business best, of course. What does your father think of it?'

'He doesn't approve. He says Ricky isn't worthy of me.'

'What a judge!'

'And he's got an extraordinary idea into his head that if I'm encouraged I may marry Horace. He was encouraging me all this morning. It's just because Ricky hasn't any money, of course. But I don't care. He's sweet.'

'Would you call that the *mot juste*?'

'Yes, I would. Most of the time he's an absolute darling. He can't help being jealous.'

'Well, all right. I suppose I shall have to give my consent. Bless you, my children. And here is a piece of advice which you will find useful in your married life. Don't watch his eyes. Watch his knees. They will tell you when he is setting himself for a swing. And when he swings, roll with the punch.'

'But when am I going to get any married life? He makes practically nothing with his poetry.'

'Still, he may have a flair for selling onion soup.'

'But how are we going to find the money to buy the bar? And his friend won't hold the offer open for ever.'

'I see what you mean, and I wish I could help you, my dear. But I can't raise anything like the sum you need. Hasn't he any money at all?'

'There's a little bit his mother left him, but he can't get at the capital. He tried to borrow some from his uncle. Do you know the Duke of Dunstable?'

'Only from hearing Horace speak of him.'

'He seems an awful old man. When Ricky told him he wanted five hundred pounds to buy an onion soup bar, he was furious.'

'Did he say he wanted to get married?'

'No. He thought it would be better not to.'

'I don't agree with him. He should have told Dunstable all about it and shown him your photograph.'

'He didn't dare risk it.'

'Well, I think he missed a trick. The ideal thing, of course, would be if you could meet Dunstable without him knowing who you are and play upon him like a stringed instrument. Because you could, you know. You've no notion what a pretty, charming girl you are, Polly. You'd be surprised. When you came in just now, I was stunned. I would have given you anything you asked, even unto half my kingdom. And I see no reason why Dunstable's reactions should not be the same. Dukes are not above the softer emotions. If some-how we could work it so that you slid imperceptibly into his life. . . .'

He looked up, annoyed. The door-bell had rung.

'Callers? Just when we need to be alone in order to concentrate. I'll tell them to go to blazes.'

He went down the passage. His nephew Pongo was standing on the mat.

7

Pongo's manner was marked by the extreme of agitation. His eyes were bulging, and he began to pour out his troubles almost before the door was open. There was nothing in his bearing of a young man who has just concluded a satisfactory financial deal.

'I say, Uncle Fred, he's not there! Horace, I mean. At his flat, I mean. He's gone, I mean.'

'Gone?'

'Webster told me he had just left in his car with a gentleman.'

Lord Ickenham, while appreciating his nephew's natural chagrin, was disposed to make light of the matter.

'A little after-luncheon spin through the park with a crony, no doubt. He will return.'

'But he won't, dash it!' cried Pongo, performing the opening steps of a sort of tarantella. 'That's the whole point. He took a lot of luggage with him. He may be away for weeks. And George Budd planning to unleash Erb on me if I don't pay up by Wednesday!'

Lord Ickenham perceived that the situation was more serious than he had supposed.

'Did Webster say where he was off to?'

'No. He didn't know.'

'Tell me the whole story in your own words, my boy, omitting no detail, however slight.'

Pongo marshalled his facts.

'Well, apparently the first thing that happened was that Horace, having lunched frugally off some tinned stuff, sent Webster out to take a look round and see if Ricky was hanging about, telling him—if he wasn't—to go round to the garage and get his car, as he thought he would take a drive in order to correct a slight headache. He said it caught him just above the eyebrows,' added Pongo, mindful of the injunction not to omit details.

'I see. And then?'

'Webster came back and reported that the car was outside but Ricky wasn't, and Horace said "Thanks". And Horace went to the front door and opened it, as a preliminary to making his get-away, and there on the mat, his hand just raised to press the bell, was this bloke.'

'What sort of bloke?'

'Webster describes him as a pink chap.'

'Park Lane seems to have been very much congested with pink chaps to-day. I had a chat there with one this morning. Some convention up in town, perhaps. What was his name?'

'No names were exchanged. Horace said "Oh, hullo!" and the chap said "Hullo!" and Horace said "Did you come to see me?" and the chap said "Yes", and Horace said "Step this way," or words to that effect, and they went into the library. Webster states that they were closeted there for some ten minutes, and then Horace rang for Webster and told him to pack his things and put them in the car. And Webster packed his things and put them in the car and came back to Horace and said "I have packed your things and put them in the car, sir," and Horace said "Right ho" and shot out, followed by the pink chap. Webster describes him as pale and anxious-looking, as if he were going to meet some doom.'

Lord Ickenham pondered. The story, admirably clear in its construction and delivery, left no room for doubt concerning the probability of an extended absence on the part of the young seigneur of 52, Bloxham Mansions.

'H'm!' he said. 'Well, it's a little awkward that this should have arisen just now, my boy, because I am not really at liberty to weigh the thing and decide what is to be done for the best. Just at the moment my brain is bespoke. I am immersed in a discussion of ways and means with Polly. She is in trouble, poor child.'

All that was fine and chivalrous in Pongo Twistleton rose to the surface. He had been expecting to reel for some time beneath the stunning blow of Horace's disappearance, but now he forgot self.

'Trouble?'

He was deeply concerned. As a rule, when he fell in love at first sight, his primary impulse was a desire to reach out for the adored object and start handling her like a sack of coals, but the love with which this girl inspired him was a tender, chivalrous love. Her appeal was to his finer side, not to the caveman who lurked in all the Twistletons. He wanted to shield her from a harsh world. He wanted to perform knightly services for her. She was the sort of girl he could see himself kissing gently on the forehead and then going out into the sunset. And the thought of her being in trouble gashed him like a knife.

'Trouble? Oh, I say! Why, what's the matter?'

'The old, old story. Like so many of us, she is in sore need of the ready, and does not see where she is going to get it. Her young man has this glittering opportunity of buying a lucrative onion-soupery, which would enable them to get married, but he seeks in vain for someone to come across with the purchase price. Owing to that unfortunate affair at the Ball, he failed to enlist Horace's sympathy. The Duke of Dunstable, whom he also approached, proved equally unresponsive. I was starting to tell Polly, when you arrived, that the only solution is for her to meet Dunstable and fascinate him, and we were wondering how this was to be con-trived. Step along and join us. Your fresh young intelligence may be just what we require. Here is Pongo, Polly,' he said, rejoining the girl. 'It is possible that he may have an idea. He nearly had one about three years ago. At any rate, he wishes to espouse your cause. Eh, Pongo?'

'Oh, rather.'

'Well, then, as I was saying, Polly, the solution is for you to meet the Duke, but it must not be as Ricky's *fiancée*—'

'Why not?' asked Pongo, starting to display the fresh young intelligence.

'Because he wouldn't think me good enough,' said Polly.

'My dear,' Lord Ickenham assured her, patting her hand, 'if you are good enough for me, you are good enough for a blasted, pop-eyed Duke. But the trouble is that he is the one who has to be conciliated, and it would be fatal to make a bad start. You must meet him as a stranger. You must glide imperceptibly into his life and fascinate him before he knows who you are. We want to get him saying to himself "A charming girl, egad! Just the sort I could wish my nephew Ricky to marry." And then along comes the anthropoid ape to whom you have given your heart and says he thinks so, too. All that is quite straight. But how the dickens are you to glide imperceptibly into his life? How do you establish contact?'

Pongo bent himself frowningly to the problem. He was aware of a keen agony at the reflection that the cream of his brain was being given to thinking up ways of getting this girl married to another man, but together with the agony there was a comfortable glow, as he felt that the opportunity of helping her had been accorded him. He reminded himself of Cyrano de Bergerac.

'Difficult,' he said. 'For one thing, the Duke's away somewhere. I remember Horace telling me that it was because he wouldn't go to the station and see him off that he broke up the sitting-room with the poker. Of course, he may just have been going home. He has a lair in Wiltshire, I believe.'

'No, I know where he's gone. He is at Blandings Castle.'

'Isn't that your pal Emsworth's place?'

'It is.'

'Well, then, there you are,' said Pongo, feeling how lucky it was that there was a trained legal mind present to solve all perplexities. 'You get Emsworth to invite Miss Pott down there.'

Lord Ickenham shook his head.

'It is not quite so simple as that, I fear. You have a rather inaccurate idea of Emsworth's position at Blandings. He was telling me about it at lunch and, broadly, what it amounts to is this. There may be men who are able to invite unattached and unexplained girls of great personal charm to their homes, but Emsworth is not one of them. He has a sister, Lady Constance Keeble, who holds revisionary powers over his visiting list.'

Pongo caught his drift. He remembered having heard his friend Ronnie Fish speak of Lady Constance Keeble in a critical spirit, and Ronnie's views had been endorsed by others of his circle who had encountered the lady.

'If Emsworth invited Polly to stay, Lady Constance would have her out of the place within five minutes of her arrival.'

'Yes, I understand she's more or less of a fiend in human shape,' assented Pongo. 'Never met her myself, but I have it from three separate sources—Ronnie Fish, Hugo Carmody and Monty Bodkin—that strong men run like rabbits to avoid meeting her.'

'Precisely. And so . . . Oh, my Lord, that bell again!'

'I'll go,' said Polly, and vanished in the direction of the front door.

Lord Ickenham took advantage of her absence to point out the fundamental difficulty of the position.

'You see, Pongo, the real trouble is old Mustard. If Polly had a presentable father, everything would be simple. Emsworth may not be able to issue invitations to unattached girls, but even he, I imagine, would be allowed to bring a friend and his daughter to stay. But with a father like hers this is not practicable. I wouldn't for the world say a word against Mustard—one of Nature's gentlemen—but his greatest admirer couldn't call him a social asset to a girl. Mustard—there is no getting away from it—looks just what he is—a retired Silver Ring bookie who for years has been doing himself too well on the starchy foods. And even if he were an Adonis, I would still be disinclined to let him loose in a refined English home. I say this is no derogatory sense, of course. One of my oldest pals. Still, there it is.'

Pongo felt that the moment had come to clear up a mystery. Voices could be heard in the passage, but there was just time to put the question which had been perplexing him ever since Polly Pott had glided imperceptibly into his life.

'I say, how does a chap like that come to be her father?'

'He married her mother. You understand the facts of life, don't you?'

'You mean she's his stepdaughter?'

'I was too elliptical. What I should have said was that he married the woman who subsequently became her mother. A delightful creature she was, too.'

'But why did a delightful creature marry Pott?'

'Why does anyone marry anybody? Why does Polly want to marry a modern poet of apparently homicidal tendencies? Why have you wanted to marry the last forty-six frightful girls you've met? . . . But hist!'

'Eh?'

'I said "Hist!"'

'Oh, hist?' said Pongo, once more catching his drift. The door had opened, and Polly was with them again.

She was accompanied by Lord Emsworth, not looking his best.

The ninth Earl of Emsworth was a man who in times of stress always tended to resemble the Aged Parent in an old-fashioned melodrama when informed that the villain intended to foreclose the mortgage. He wore now a disintegrated air, as if somebody had removed most of his interior organs. You see the same sort of thing in stuffed parrots when the sawdust has leaked out of them. His pince-nez were askew, and his collar had come off its stud.

'Could I have a glass of water?' he asked feebly, like a hart heated in the chase.

Polly hurried off solicitously, and Lord Ickenham regarded his brother Peer with growing interest.

'Something the matter?'

'My dear Ickenham, a disastrous thing has happened.'

'Tell me all.'

'What I am to say to Connie, I really do not know.'

'What about?'

'She will be furious.'

'Why?'

'And she is a woman who can make things so confoundedly uncomfortable about the place when she is annoyed. Ah, thank you, my dear.'

Lord Emsworth drained the contents of the glass gratefully, and became more lucid.

'You remember, my dear Ickenham, that I left you to keep an appointment with Sir Roderick Glossop, the brain specialist. My sister Constance, I think I told you, had given me the strictest instructions to bring him back to Blandings, to observe Dunstable. Dunstable's behaviour has been worrying her. He breaks furniture with pokers and throws eggs at gardeners. So Connie sent me to bring Glossop.'

'And—?'

'My dear fellow, he won't come!'

'But why should that upset you so much? Lady Constance surely can't blame you for not producing brain specialists, if they're too busy to leave London.'

Lord Emsworth moaned softly.

'He is not too busy to leave London. He refuses to come because he says I insulted him.'

'Did you?'

'Yes.'

'How?'

'Well, it started with my calling him "Pimples." He didn't like it.'

'I don't quite follow you.'

'Who do you think this Sir Roderick Glossop turned out to be, Ickenham? A boy whom I had known at school. A most unpleasant boy with a nasty, superior manner and an extraordinary number of spots on his face. I was shown in, and he said: "Well, it's a long time since we met, eh?" And I said: "Eh?" And he said: "You don't remember me, eh?" And I said: "Eh?" And then I took a good look at him, and I said "God bless my soul! Why, it's Pimples!"'

'An affecting reunion.'

'I recall now that he seemed to flush, and his manner lost its cordiality. It took on that supercilious superiority which I had always so much resented, and he asked me brusquely to state my business. I told him all about Dunstable wanting the Empress, and he became most offensive. He said something about being a busy man and having no time to waste, and he sneered openly at what he called "this absurd fuss" that was being made about what he described as "a mere pig."'

Lord Emsworth's face darkened. It was plain that the wound still throbbed.

'Well, I wasn't going to stand that sort of thing from young Pimples. I told him not to be a conceited ass. And he, I think, called me a doddering old fool. Something of that general nature, at any rate. And one word led to another, and in the end I confess that I did become perhaps a little more outspoken than was prudent. I remembered that there had been a scandal connected with his name—something to do with overeating himself and being sick at the house supper—and rather injudiciously I brought this up. And shortly afterwards he was ringing the bell for me to be shown out and telling me that nothing would induce him to come to Blandings after what had occurred. And now I am wondering how I am to explain to Constance.'

Lord Ickenham nodded brightly. There had come into his eyes a gleam which Pongo had no difficulty in recognizing. He had observed it on several previous occasions, notably during that visit to the Dog Races just before his uncle's behaviour had attracted

the attention of the police. He could read its message. It meant
that some pleasing inspiration had floated into Lord Ickenham's
mind, and it caused a strong shudder to pass through his frame,
together with a wish that he were far away. When pleasing inspira-
tions floated into Lord Ickenham's mind, the prudent man made
for the nearest bomb-proof shelter.

'This is all most interesting.'

'It is a terrible state of affairs.'

'On the contrary, nothing more fortunate could have happened.
I now see daylight.'

'Eh?'

'You were not here when we were holding our conference just
now, my dear Emsworth, or your lightning mind would long ere
this have leaped at my meaning. Briefly, the position is as follows.
It is essential that young Polly . . . By the way, you don't know each
other, do you? Miss Polly Pott, only daughter of Claude ("Mustard") Pott—Lord Emsworth.'

'How do you do?'

'It is essential, I was saying, that Polly goes to Blandings and
there meets and fascinates Dunstable.'

'Why?'

'She desires his approval of her projected union with his nephew,
a young thug named Ricky Gilpin.'

'Ah?'

'And the snag against which we had come up, when you arrived,
was the problem of how to get her to Blandings. You, we felt, were
scarcely in a position to invite her by herself and there are various
reasons, into which I need not go, why old Mustard should not trail
along. Everything is now simple. You are in urgent need of a Sir
Roderick Glossop. She is in urgent need of an impressive father.
I am prepared to play both roles. To-morrow, by a suitable train,
Sir Roderick Glossop will set out with you for Blandings Castle,
accompanied by his daughter and secretary—'

'Hey!' said Pongo, speaking abruptly.

Lord Ickenham surveyed him with mild surprise.

'You are surely not proposing to remain in London, my dear boy? Didn't you·tell me that you were expecting a visit from Erb on Wednesday?'

'Oh!'

'Exactly. You must obviously get away and lie low somewhere. And what better haven could you find than Blandings Castle? But perhaps you were thinking that you would rather go there as my valet?'

'No, I'm dashed if I was.'

'Very well, then. Secretary it shall be. You follow what I am driving at, Emsworth?'

'No,' said Lord Emsworth, who seldom followed what people were driving at.

'I will run through the agenda again.'

He did so, and this time a faint light of intelligence seemed to brighten Lord Emsworth's eye.

'Oh, ah, yes. Yes, I think I see what you mean. But can you—'

'Get away with it? My dear fellow! Pongo here will tell you that on one occasion last year, in the course of a single afternoon in the suburb of Valley Fields, I impersonated with complete success not only an official from the bird shop, come to clip the claws of the parrot at The Cedars, Mafeking Road, but Mr Roddis, owner of The Cedars, and a Mr J. G. Bulstrode, a resident of the same neighbourhood. And I have no doubt that, if called upon to do so, I could have done them a very good parrot, too. The present task will be a childishly simple one to a man of my gifts. When were you thinking of returning to Blandings?'

'I should like to catch the five o'clock train this afternoon.'

'That will fit in admirably with our plans. You will go down today on the five o'clock train and announce that Sir Roderick Glossop will be arriving to-morrow with his secretary, and that you have invited him to bring his charming daughter. What good trains have you? The two-forty-five? Excellent. We will catch that, and there we shall be. I don't think that even you, Pongo, can pick any holes in that scenario.'

'I can tell you this, if you care to hear it, that you're definitely cuckoo and that everything is jolly well bound to go wrong and land us in the soup.'

'Nothing of the kind. I hope he isn't frightening you, Polly.'

'He is.'

'Don't let him. When you get to know Pongo better,' said Lord Ickenham, 'you will realize that he is always like this—moody, sombre, full of doubts and misgivings. Shakespeare drew Hamlet from him. You will feel better, my boy, when you have had a drink. Let us nip round to my club and get a swift one.'

8

THE two-forty-five express—Paddington to Market Blandings, first stop Oxford—stood at its platform with that air of well-bred reserve which is characteristic of Paddington trains, and Pongo Twistleton and Lord Ickenham stood beside it, waiting for Polly Pott. The clock over the bookstall pointed to thirty-eight minutes after the hour.

Anyone ignorant of the difference between a pessimist and an optimist would have been able to pick up a useful pointer or two by scanning the faces of this nephew and this uncle. The passage of time had done nothing to relieve Pongo's apprehensions regarding the expedition on which he was about to embark, and his mobile features indicated clearly the concern with which he was viewing the future. As always when fate had linked his movements with those of the head of the family, he was feeling like a man floating over Niagara Falls in a barrel.

Lord Ickenham, on the other hand, was all that was jovial and debonair. Tilting his hat at a jaunty angle, he gazed about him with approval at the decorous station which has for so many years echoed to the tread of county families.

'To one like myself,' he said, 'who, living in Hampshire, gets out of the metropolis, when he is fortunate enough to get into it, *via* Waterloo, there is something very soothing in the note of refined calm which Paddington strikes. At Waterloo, all is hustle and bus-

tle, and the society tends to be mixed. Here a leisured peace pre-
vails, and you get only the best people—cultured men accustomed
to mingling with basset hounds and women in tailored suits who
look like horses. Note the chap next door. No doubt some son of
the ruling classes, returning after a quiet jaunt in London to his
huntin', shootin', and fishin'.'

The individual to whom he alluded was a swarthy young man
who was leaning out of the window of the adjoining compartment,
surveying the Paddington scene through a pair of steel-rimmed
spectacles. Pongo, who thought he looked a bit of a blister, said
so, and the rancour of his tone caused Lord Ickenham to shoot a
quick, reproachful glance at him. Feeling himself like a school-
boy going home for Christmas, he wanted happy, smiling faces
about him.

'I don't believe you're enjoying this, Pongo. I wish you would try
to get the holiday spirit. That day down at Valley Fields you were
the life and soul of the party. Don't you like spreading sweetness
and light?'

'If by spreading sweetness and light, you mean gatecrashing a
strange house and—'

'Not so loud,' said Lord Ickenham warningly, 'stations have ears.'

He led his nephew away down the platform, apologizing with
a charming affability to the various travellers with whom the latter collided from time to time in his preoccupation. One of these,
a portly man of imposing aspect, paused for an instant on seeing
Lord Ickenham, as if wavering on the verge of recognition. Lord
Ickenham passed on with a genial nod.

'Who was that?' asked Pongo dully.

'I haven't an idea,' said Lord Ickenham. 'I seem to have a vague
recollection of having met him somewhere, but I can't place
him and do not propose to institute enquiries. He would probably turn out to be someone who was at school with me, though
some years my junior. When you reach my age, you learn to avoid
these reunions. The last man I met who was at school with me,

though some years my junior, had a long white beard and no teeth. It blurred the picture I had formed of myself as a sprightly young fellow on the threshold of life. Ah, here's Polly.'

He moved forward with elastic step and folded the girl in a warm embrace. It seemed to Pongo, not for the first time, that this man went out of his way to kiss girls. On the present occasion, a fatherly nod would amply have met the case.

'Well, my dear, so here you are. Did you have any trouble getting away?'

'Trouble?'

'I should have supposed that your father would have been curious as to where you were off to. But no doubt you told him some frank, straightforward story about visiting a school friend.'

'I told him I was going to stay with you for a few days. Of course, he may have thought I meant that I was going to Ickenham.'

'True. He may. But it wouldn't have done to have revealed the actual facts to him. He might have disapproved. There is an odd, Puritan streak in old Mustard. Well, everything seems to be working out capitally. You're looking wonderful, Polly. If this Duke has a spark of human feeling in him, he cannot fail to fall for you like a ton of bricks. You remind me of some radiant spirit of the Spring. Pongo, on the other hand, does not. There is something worrying Pongo, and I can't make out what it is.'

'Ha!'

'Don't say "Ha!" my boy. You ought to be jumping with joy at the thought of going to a delightful place like Blandings Castle.'

'I ought, ought I? How about Lady Constance?'

'What about her?'

'She's waiting for us at the other end, isn't she? And what a pill! Ronnie Fish says she has to be seen to be believed. Hugo Carmody paled beneath his tan as he spoke of her. Monty Bodkin strongly suspects that she conducts human sacrifices at the time of the full moon.'

'Nonsense. These boys exaggerate so. Probably a gentle, sweet-faced lady of the old school, with mittens. You must fight against this tendency of yours to take the sombre view. Where you get your streak of pessimism from, I can't imagine. Not from my side of the family. Nothing will go wrong. I feel it in my bones. I am convinced that this is going to be one of my major triumphs.'

'Like that day at the Dog Races.'

'I wish you would not keep harping on that day at the Dog Races. I have always maintained that the constable acted far too precipitately on that occasion. They are letting a rather neurotic type of man into the Force nowadays. Well, if we are going to Blandings Castle for a restful little holiday, I suppose we ought to be taking our seats. I notice an official down the platform fidgeting with a green flag.'

They entered their compartment. The young man in spectacles was still leaning out of the window. As they passed him, he eyed them keenly—so keenly, indeed, that one might have supposed that he had found in these three fellow-travellers something to view with suspicion. This, however, was not the case. Rupert Baxter, formerly secretary to Lord Emsworth and now secretary to the Duke of Dunstable, always eyed people keenly. It was pure routine.

All that he was actually feeling at the moment was that the elder of the two men looked a pleasant old buffer, that the younger seemed to have something on his mind, and that the girl was a pretty girl. He also had a nebulous idea that he had seen her before somewhere. But he did not follow up this train of thought. Substituting a travelling-cap for the rather forbidding black hat which he was wearing, he took his seat and leaned back with closed eyes. And presently Rupert Baxter slept.

In the next compartment, Lord Ickenham was attending to some minor details.

'A thing we have got to get settled before our arrival,' he said, 'is the question of names. Nothing is more difficult than to think of a good name on the spur of the moment. That day at the Dog Races, I remember, we were well on our way to the police station before

I was able to select "George Robinson" for myself and to lean over to Pongo and whisper that he was Edwin Smith. And I felt all the while that, as names, they were poor stuff. They did not satisfy the artist in me. This time we must do much better. I, of course, automatically become Sir Roderick Glossop. You, Polly, had better be Gwendoline. "Polly" seems to me not quite dignified enough for one in your position. But what of Pongo?'

Pongo bared his teeth in a bitter smile.

'I wouldn't worry about me. What I am going to be called is "this man." "Ptarmigan," Lady Constance will say, addressing the butler—'

'Ptarmigan isn't a bad name.'

'"Ptarmigan, send for Charles and Herbert and throw this man out. And see that he lands on something sharp."'

'That pessimistic streak again! Think of some movie stars, Polly.'

'Fred Astaire?'

'No.'

'Warner Baxter?'

'Baxter would be excellent, but we can't use it. It is the name of the Duke's secretary. Emsworth was telling me about him. It would be confusing to have two Baxters about the place. Why, of course. I've got it. Glossop. Sir Roderick Glossop, as I see it, was one of two brothers and, as so often happens, the younger brother did not equal the elder's success in life. He became a curate, dreaming away the years in a country parish, and when he died, leaving only a copy of Hymns Ancient and Modern and a son called Basil, Sir Roderick found himself stuck with the latter. So with the idea of saving something out of the wreck he made him his secretary. That's what I call a nice, well-rounded story. Telling it will give you something to talk about to Lady Constance over the pipes and whisky in her boudoir. If you get to her boudoir, that is to say. I am not quite clear as to the social standing of secretaries. Do they mingle with the nobs or squash in with the domestic staff?'

A flicker of animation lit up Pongo's sombre eyes.

'I'll be dashed if I squash in with any domestic staff.'

'Well, we'll try you on the nobs,' said Lord Ickenham doubt-fully. 'But don't blame me if it turns out that that's the wrong thing and Lady Constance takes her lorgnette to you. God bless my soul, though, you can't compare the lorgnettes of to-day with the ones I used to know as a boy. I remember walking one day in Grosvenor Square with my aunt Brenda and her pug dog Jabber-wocky, and a policeman came up and said that the latter ought to be wearing a muzzle. My aunt made no verbal reply. She merely whipped her lorgnette from its holster and looked at the man, who gave one choking gasp and fell back against the railings, without a mark on him but with an awful look of horror in his staring eyes, as if he had seen some dreadful sight. A doctor was sent for, and they managed to bring him round, but he was never the same again. He had to leave the Force, and eventually drifted into the grocery business. And that is how Sir Thomas Lipton got his start.'

He broke off. During his remarks, a face had been peering in through the glass door of the compartment, and now entered a portly man of imposing aspect with a large, round head like the dome of St. Paul's. He stood framed in the doorway, his manner majestic but benevolent.

'Ah,' he said. 'So it was you, Ickenham. I thought I recognized you on the platform just now. You remember me?'

Now that he was seeing him without his hat, Lord Ickenham did, and seemed delighted at the happy chance that had brought them together again.

'Of course.'

'May I come in, or am I interrupting a private conversation?'

'Of course come in, my dear fellow. We were only talking about lorgnettes. I was saying that in the deepest and fullest sense of the word there are none nowadays. Where are you off to?'

'My immediate objective is an obscure station in Shropshire of the name of Market Blandings. One alights there, I understand, for Blandings Castle.'

'Blandings Castle?'

'The residence of Lord Emsworth. That is my ultimate destination. You know the place?'

'I have heard of it. By the way, you have not met my daughter and nephew. My daughter Gwendoline and my nephew Basil—Sir Roderick Glossop.'

Sir Roderick Glossop seated himself, shooting a keen glance at Polly and Pongo as he did so. Their demeanour had aroused his professional interest. From the young man, as Lord Ickenham performed the ceremony of introduction, there had proceeded a bubbling grunt like that of some strong swimmer in his agony, while the girl's eyes had become like saucers. She was now breathing in an odd, gasping sort of way. It was not Sir Roderick's place to drum up trade by suggesting it, but he found himself strongly of the opinion that these young folks would do well to place themselves in the care of a good nerve specialist.

Lord Ickenham, apparently oblivious to the seismic upheaval which had left this nephew a mere pile of ruins, had begun to prattle genially.

'Well, Glossop, it's extraordinarily nice, seeing you again. We haven't met since that dinner of the Loyal Sons of Hampshire, where you got so tight. How are all the loonies? It must be amazingly interesting work, sitting on people's heads and yelling to somebody to hurry up with the strait waistcoat.'

Sir Roderick Glossop, who had stiffened, relaxed. The monstrous suggestion that he had been intemperate at the annual banquet of the Loyal Sons of Hampshire had offended him deeply, nor had he liked that reference to sitting on people's heads. But he was a man who pined without conversation, and in order to carry on this particular conversation it appeared to be necessary to accept his companion's peculiar way of expressing himself.

'Yes,' he said, 'the work, though sometimes distressing, is as you say, full of interest.'

'And you're always at it, I suppose? You are going to Blandings Castle now, no doubt, to inspect some well-connected screwball?'

Sir Roderick pursed his lips.

'You are asking me to betray confidences, I fear, my dear Ickenham. However, I may perhaps gratify your curiosity to the extent of saying that my visit is a professional one. A friend of the family has been giving evidence of an overexcited nervous condition.'

'There is no need to be coy with me, Glossop. You are going to Blandings to put ice on the head of the chap with the egg-throwing urge.'

Sir Roderick started.

'You appear singularly well-informed.'

'I had that one straight from the stable. Emsworth told me.'

'Oh, you know Emsworth?'

'Intimately. I was lunching with him yesterday, and he went off to see you. But when I ran into him later in the day, he rather hinted that things had not gone too well between you, with the result that you had refused to interest yourself in this unbalanced egg-jerker.'

Sir Roderick flushed.

'You are perfectly correct. Emsworth's manner left me no alternative but to decline the commission. But this morning I received a letter from his sister, Lady Constance Keeble, so charming in its tone that I was constrained to change my mind. You know Lady Constance?'

'What, dear old Connie? I should say so! A lifelong friend. My nephew Basil there looks on her as a second mother.'

'Indeed? I have not yet met her myself.'

'You haven't? Capital!'

'I beg your pardon?'

'You still have that treat in store,' explained Lord Ickenham.

'Lady Constance expressed so strong a desire that I should go to Blandings that I decided to overlook Emsworth's discourtesy. The summons comes at a singularly inopportune time, unfortunately, for I have an important conference in London to-morrow afternoon. However, I have been looking up the trains, and I see that there is one that leaves Market Blandings at eight-twenty in the morning, arriving at Paddington shortly before noon, so I shall be able to make my examination and return in time.'

'Surely a single examination won't work the trick?'

'Oh, I think so.'

'I wish I had a brain like yours,' said Lord Ickenham. 'What an amazing thing. I suppose you could walk down a line of people, giving each of them a quick glance, and separate the sheep from the goats like shelling peas. . . . "Loony . . . not loony. . . . This one wants watching. . . . This one's all right. . . . Keep an eye on this chap. Don't let him get near the breadknife. . . ." Extraordinary. What do you do exactly? Ask questions? Start topics and observe reactions?'

'Yes, I suppose you might say—broadly—that that is the method I employ.'

'I see. You bring the conversation round to the subject of birds, for instance, and if the fellow says he's a canary and hops on to the mantelpiece and starts singing, you sense that there is something wrong. Yes, I understand. Well, it seems to me that, if it's as simple as that, you could save yourself a lot of trouble by making your examination now.'

'I do not understand you.'

'You're in luck, Glossop. The man Emsworth wants you to run the rule over is on the train. You'll find him in the compartment next door. A dark chap with spectacles. Emsworth asked me to keep an eye on him during the journey, but if you want my opinion—there's nothing wrong with the fellow at all. Connie was always such a nervous little soul, bless her. I suppose some chance remark of his about eggs gave her the idea that he had said he wanted to throw them, and she went all of a twitter. Why don't you go in and engage him in conversation and note the results? If there's anything wrong with him, that sixth sense of yours will enable you to spot it in a second. If he's all right, on the other hand, you could leave the train at Oxford and return to London in comfort.'

'It is a most admirable idea.'

'Don't mention my name, of course.'

'My dear Ickenham, you may trust me to exercise perfect discretion. The whole thing will be perfectly casual. I shall embark on our little talk quite simply and naturally by asking him if he can oblige me with a match.'

'Genius!' said Lord Ickenham.

The silence which followed Sir Roderick's departure was broken by a groan from Pongo.

'I knew something like this would happen,' he said.

'But my dear boy,' protested Lord Ickenham, 'what has happened, except that I have been refreshed by an intelligent chat with a fine mind, and have picked up some hints on deportment for brain specialists which should prove invaluable? The old Gawd-help-us will alight at Oxford—'

'So will I jolly well alight at Oxford!'

'And return to your flat? I wonder if you will find Erb waiting for you on the doorstep?'

'Oh, gosh!'

'Yes, I thought you had overlooked that point. Pull yourself together, my dear Pongo. Stiffen the sinews, summon up the blood. Everything is going to be all right. You seem thoughtful, Polly.'

'I was only wondering why Lord Emsworth called him Pimples.'

'You mean he hasn't any now? No, I noticed that,' said Lord Ickenham. 'It is so often the way. We start out in life with more pimples than we know what to do with, and in the careless arrogance of youth think they are going to last for ever. But comes a day when we suddenly find that we are down to our last half-dozen. And then those go. There is a lesson in this for all of us. Ah, Glossop, what news from the front?'

Sir Roderick Glossop radiated satisfaction.

'You were perfectly correct, my dear Ickenham. Absolutely nothing wrong. No indication whatsoever of any egg-fixation. There was no basis at all for Lady Constance's alarm. I should describe the man as exceptionally intelligent. But I was surprised to find him so young.'

'We all were once.'

'True. But I had imagined from Lady Constance's letter that he was far older. Whether she said so or not, I cannot recall, but the impression I gathered was that he was a contemporary of Emsworth's.'

'Probably looks younger than he is. The country air. Or as a child he may have been fed on Bevo.'

'Ah,' said Sir Roderick non-committally. 'Well, if I am to leave the train at Oxford, I must be getting back to my compartment and collecting my things. It has been a great pleasure meeting you again, Ickenham, and I am exceedingly obliged for that very thoughtful suggestion of yours. I confess that I was not looking forward to an early morning journey. Good-bye.'

'Good-bye.'

'Good-bye,' said Polly.

'Good-bye,' said Pongo, speaking last and speaking with difficulty. He had been sitting for some moments in a deep silence, broken only by an occasional sharp, whistling intake of breath. Sir Roderick carried away with him an impression of a sombre and introspective young man. He mentioned him later in a lecture to the Mothers of West Kensington as an example of the tendency of post-war youth towards a brooding melancholia.

Lord Ickenham, too, seemed to feel that he needed cheering up, and for the remainder of the journey spared no effort to amuse and entertain. All through the afternoon he maintained a high level of sprightliness and gaiety, and it was only when they had alighted at Market Blandings station that he found himself compelled to strike a jarring note.

Market Blandings station, never a congested area, was this evening more than usually somnolent and deserted. Its only occupants were a porter and a cat. The swarthy young man got out and walked to the end of the train, where the porter was extracting luggage from the van. Polly wandered off to fraternize with the cat. And Lord Ickenham, having bought Pongo a penny-worth of butterscotch from the slot machine, was just commenting on the remissness of his host and hostess in not sending anyone down to meet so distinguished a guest, when there came on to the platform a solid man in the middle thirties. The afterglow of the sunset lit up his face, and it was at this point that Lord Ickenham struck the jarring note.

'I wonder if you remember, Pongo,' he said, 'that when you looked in on me at Ickenham the day before yesterday I mentioned that it had always been the ambition of my life to play the confidence trick on someone? Owing to all the rush and bustle of this Emsworth business, I quite forgot to tell you that yesterday morning the opportunity arose.'

'What!'

'Yes. Before coming to the Drones, I went to call on Horace Davenport, and finding him not at home, waited for a while in the street outside his flat. And while I was doing so a pink chap came along, and it seemed to me that if ever I was going to make the experiment, now was the time. There was something about this fellow that told me that I could never hope for a better subject. And so it proved. He handed me over his wallet, and I walked off with it. The whole affair was a triumph of mind over matter, and I am modestly proud of it.'

It had always been an axiom with Pongo Twistleton that his Uncle Fred was one of those people who ought not to be allowed at large, but he had never suspected that the reasons for not allowing him at large were so solidly based as this. He clutched his brow.

As had happened that day at the Dog Races, this man seemed to have taken him into a strange nightmare world.

'I sent the wallet back, of course. My interest in the experiment was purely scientific. I had no thought of vulgar gain. The chap's card was inside, and I shipped it off by registered post. And the reason why I mention it now . . . Do you see the fellow coming along the platform?'

Pongo turned an ashen face.

'You don't mean—?'

'Yes,' said Lord Ickenham, with a breezy insouciance which cut his nephew like a knife, 'that's the chap.'

9

'HIS name,' said Lord Ickenham, 'is Bosham. It was on the card I found in his wallet. But I distinctly remember that the address on the card was some place down in Hampshire, not far from my own little dosshouse, so it seems extremely odd that he should be here. It looks to me like one of those strained coincidences which are so inartistic. Unless he's a ghost.'

Pongo, who might have been taken for one himself by a short-sighted man, found speech. For some moments he had been squeaking and gibbering like the sheeted dead in the Roman streets a little ere the mightiest Julius fell.

'Bosham is Lord Emsworth's son,' he said hollowly.

'Is he, indeed? I am not very well up in the Peerage. I seldom read it except to get a laugh out of the names. Then that explains it,' said Lord Ickenham heartily. 'He must have been on a visit to Blandings, and when he ran up to London for the day to get his hair cut the Duke told him on no account to fail, while there, to go and slap his nephew Horace on the back and give him his best. It was perfectly natural that his pilgrimage to Bloxham Mansions should chance to synchronize with mine. How simple these apparently extraordinary things are, when you go into them.'

'He's coming this way.'

'He would be. I presume he is here to escort us to the castle.'

'But, dash it, what are you going to do?'

'Do? Why, nothing.'

'Well, I'll bet he will. Do you mean to tell me that if a chap has the confidence trick played on him by a chap, and meets the chap again, he isn't going to set about the chap?'

'My dear boy, for a young man who has enjoyed the advantage of having a refined uncle constantly at his elbow, you seem singularly ignorant of the manners and customs of good society. We bloods do not make scenes in public places.'

'You think he will wait till later before having you pinched?'

Lord Ickenham clicked his tongue.

'My dear Pongo, you have a gift for taking the dark view that amounts almost to genius. I should imagine that the prophet Isaiah as a young man must have been very like you. Tell me—I don't want to turn till I can see the whites of his eyes—where is our friend? Does he approach?'

'He's sort of backing and filling at the moment.'

'I quite understand. It is the decent diffidence of the English upper classes. All his life he has been brought up in the creed that there is nothing that is more beastly bad form than accosting a stranger, and he is wondering if I am indeed the Sir Roderick Glossop of whom he has heard so much. He shrinks from taking a chance. I think it must be your presence that is bothering him. No doubt Emsworth completely forgot to mention that I should be accompanied by my secretary, and this has made him confused. "It may be Glossop," he is saying to himself. "I wouldn't be prepared to bet it isn't Glossop. But if it is Glossop, who's the chap with him? There was nothing in my instructions about chaps-with-Glossop." And so he backs and fills. Well, this gives us time to go further into the matter we were discussing. What on earth leads you to suppose that this Bosham will denounce me for having played the confidence trick on him? The moment I say that I am Sir Roderick Glossop, the eagerly awaited guest, he will naturally assume that he was deceived by a chance resemblance. Where is he now?'

'Just abaft the try-your-weight machine.'

'Then watch me turn and nonplus him,' said Lord Ickenham, and pivoted gracefully. 'Excuse me, sir,' he said. 'I wonder if you could inform me if there is any possibility of my obtaining a vehicle of some sort here, to take me to Blandings Castle?'

He had not overestimated the effect of his manoeuvre. Lord Bosham halted as if he had walked into a lamp-post, and stood gaping.

The heir to the Earldom of Emsworth was a slow thinker, but he was not incapable of inductive reasoning. He had been told to meet an elderly gentleman who would arrive on the two-forty-five train en route for Blandings Castle. The only elderly gentleman who had arrived on the two-forty-five train en route for Blandings Castle was the elderly gentleman before him. This elderly gentleman, therefore, must be that elderly gentleman. In which case, he was Sir Roderick Glossop, the eminent brain-specialist, and so could not be, as in that first instant of seeing his face he had been prepared to swear he was, the pleasant stranger who had relieved him of his wallet in Park Lane.

For Lord Bosham, though he lived a secluded life in a remote corner of Hampshire, was sufficiently in touch with things to know that eminent brain-specialists do not go about playing the confidence trick on people. Every young man starting out in the world, he was aware, has his choice. He can become an eminent brain-specialist, or he can become a confidence trickster. But not both.

'Are you Sir Roderick Glossop?' he asked, his round eyes drinking in those features that had seemed so familiar.

'That is my name.'

'Oh? Ah? Mine's Bosham. We—er—we haven't met before, by any chance?'

'Unfortunately, no. The loss,' said Lord Ickenham, courteously but inaccurately, 'was mine. But I have heard of you. When I saw him yesterday, Lord Emsworth spoke with a fatherly warmth of your many gifts.'

'Ah? Well, I tooled down in the car to meet you.'

'Vastly civil of you, my dear Bosham.'

'You've got some luggage in the van, I take it, what? I'll slide along and see to it.'

'Thank you, thank you.'

'Then we can tool up to the castle.'

'Precisely what I would have suggested myself. Is there a large party there?'

'Eh? Oh, no. Only my father and my aunt and the Duke and Horace Davenport.'

'Horace Davenport?'

'The Duke's nephew. Well, I'll be sliding along and seeing about that luggage.'

He slid, and Pongo resumed his imitation of the sheeted dead.

'Well?' he said, at length becoming coherent. 'Now what? On arrival at this ghastly castle, we shall immediately find ourselves cheek by jowl with a chap who knows you, knows Miss Pott and has been a close pal of mine for years. "Hullo, Pongo!" he will say, bounding up, as we stand chatting with Lady Constance. "Hullo, Lord Ickenham! Golly, Polly, isn't this jolly, here we all are, what?" If you have nothing else to do at the moment, you might be trying that one over on your bazooka.'

Lord Ickenham did not reply. He was looking down the platform. At the far end, a reunion seemed to be taking place between Lord Bosham and the swarthy young man who had occupied the adjoining compartment on the train. They had just shaken hands, and were now engaged in conversation.

'You were saying, my boy?' he asked, coming out of his thoughts.

Pongo repeated the substance of his remarks.

'Yes, I see what you mean,' agreed Lord Ickenham. 'You must always remember, however, that there is nothing either good or bad, but thinking makes it so. Still, in feeling that a problem has arisen I am not saying that you are not right. I confess that I had not anticipated Horace. Fate seems to have arranged that this shall be Old Home Week at Blandings Castle. We only need Mustard Pott and my dear wife to have what you might call a full hand.'

'Could we get hold of him before he spills the beans, and explain things to him and ask him to sit in?'

Lord Ickenham shook his head.

'I think not. Horace is a nice boy, but he would be a total loss as a conspirator.'

'Then what are we going to do?'

'Keep cool.'

'A fat lot of help keeping cool will be.'

'This is the pessimist in you speaking again. What I was about to say was that we must keep cool and level heads and deny our identity.'

'And you think he will swallow that? Ha!'

'I wish you wouldn't say "Ha!" Why shouldn't he swallow it? Who can say what limits, if any, there are to what Horace Davenport will swallow? With an uncle like his, if he is anything of a student of heredity, he must frequently have speculated on the possibility of his little grey cells suddenly turning blue on him. I imagine that he will think that it is this disaster that has happened. Still, I feel that we would do well to separate, so that we steal upon him little by little, as it were, instead of confronting him in a solid bunch. If the distance is not too great, I shall walk to the castle, allowing you and Polly to go on ahead in the car and pave the way.'

'Or we might all walk back to London.'

'My dear boy, do try to rid yourself of this horrible defeatist attitude. You have seen for yourself how stout denial of identity affected our friend Bosham. All you have to do, when you meet Horace, is to give him a cold stare and say that your name is Basil. That in itself should carry conviction, for who would say his name was Basil if he did not know that it could be proved against him? As for Polly, I have no misgivings. She will hold her end up. She is Mustard's daughter and must have been taught to tell the tale as soon as her infant lips could lisp. And if you don't think it's difficult to say "lips could lisp," try it yourself. You might step over and explain the situation to her. And now,' said Lord Ickenham, with relish, 'we come to another small difficulty.'

A sound like the dying gurgle of a siphon of soda water proceeded from Pongo.

'Oh, golly! Don't tell me there's something else?'

A happy smile was playing over Lord Ickenham's handsome face.

'Things are certainly being made somewhat intricate for us on this little expedition of ours,' he said contentedly. 'I had anticipated strolling in over the red carpet and being accepted without demur at my face value, but apparently this is not to be.'

'What the dickens has happened?'

'It is not so much what has happened as what is going to happen. If you glance along the platform, you will note that Bosham is returning, accompanied not only by a porter in a uniform much too tight for him but by our dark friend in the spectacles. Does it not occur to you that when Bosham introduces me to him, he may feel that Sir Roderick Glossop has changed a bit since he saw him last?'

'Oh, my aunt!'

'Yes, stimulating, isn't it?'

'Perhaps Glossop didn't tell him he was Glossop.'

'If you suppose that Glossop could be alone with anyone for two minutes without telling him he was Glossop, you are a very indifferent reader of character.'

'We must clear out of here at once!'

Lord Ickenham was shocked.

'Clear out? That is no way for a member of a proud family to talk. Did Twistletons clear out at Agincourt and Crecy? At Malplaquet and Blenheim? When the Old Guard made their last desperate charge up the blood-soaked slopes of Waterloo, do you suppose that Wellington, glancing over his shoulder, saw a Twistleton sneaking off with ill-assumed carelessness in the direction of Brussels? We Twistletons do not clear out, my boy. We stick around, generally long after we have outstayed our welcome. I feel sure that I shall be able to find some way of dealing with the matter. All it needs is a little thought, and my brain is at its brightest this evening. Run along and explain things to Polly, and I will have everything comfortably adjusted by the time you return. . . . Ah, Bosham, my dear fellow, I see that you have collected our impedimenta. Very good of you to have bothered.'

'Eh? Oh no, not a bit.'

'Tell me, Bosham, is it far to the castle?'

'About a couple of miles.'

'Then I think, if you don't mind, that I will walk. It would be pleasant to stretch my legs.'

Lord Bosham seemed relieved.

'Well, that's fine, if you'd like to. Might have been a bit of a squash in the car. I didn't know Baxter was turning up. This is Mr Baxter the Duke's secretary—Sir Roderick Glossop.'

'How do you do? I am very glad you did turn up, Mr Baxter,' said Lord Ickenham, beaming upon the dark young man, who was eyeing him with silent intentness. 'It gives me the opportunity of discussing that poor fellow on the train. I saw him go into your compartment, but I hesitated to intrude upon you and ask you what you made of him. One of my patients,' explained Lord Ickenham. 'He suffers from delusions—or did. I am hopeful that my treatment may have been effective. Certainly he seemed normal enough while he was talking to me. But in these cases a relapse often comes like a flash, and I know the presence of strangers excites him. Did he by any chance tell you he was Mussolini?'

'He did not.'

'Or Shirley Temple?'

'He told me that he was Sir Roderick Glossop.'

'Then I am in distinguished company. Not that it is anything to joke about, of course. The whole thing is terribly sad and disheartening. Evidently all my work has gone for nothing. It almost makes one lose confidence in oneself.'

'I should not have thought that you were a man who easily lost his self-confidence.'

'Kind of you to say so, my dear fellow. No, as a rule, I do not. But absolute failure like this. . . . Ah, well, one must keep one's flag flying, must one not? You humoured him, I hope? It is always the best and safest plan. Well, here are my daughter and my nephew Basil, who acts as my secretary. This is Lord Bosham, my dear, Lord Emsworth's son. And Mr Baxter. I was telling them that I thought I would walk to the castle. I am feeling a little cramped after the journey. We shall meet at Philippi.'

To reach Blandings Castle from Market Blandings, you leave the latter, if you can bear to tear yourself away from one of the most picturesque little towns in England, by way of the High Street. This, ending in a flurry of old-world cottages, takes you to a broad highway, running between leafy hedges that border pasture land and barley fields, and you come eventually to the great stone gates by the main lodge and through these to a drive which winds uphill for some three quarters of a mile. A testing bit, this last, for the indifferent pedestrian. Beach, the butler, who sometimes walked to Market Blandings and back to discipline his figure, always felt a sinking feeling as he approached it.

Lord Ickenham took it in his stride. The recent happenings on the station platform had left him pleasantly exhilarated, and he was all eagerness to get to his destination and see what further entertainment awaited him in the shape of obstacles and problems. Breasting the slope with a song on his lips, he had reached the last of the bends in the drive and was pausing to admire the grey bulk of the castle as it stood out against the saffron sky, when he observed coming towards him a man of his own age but much fatter and not half so beautiful.

'Hoy!' cried this person.

'Hoy!' responded Lord Ickenham civilly.

The fact that he had heard Horace Davenport speak of his uncle Alaric as a baldheaded old coot with a walrus moustache had enabled him to identify the newcomer without difficulty. Few coots could have had less hair than this man, and any walrus would have been proud to possess the moustache at which he was puffing.

'You the brain chap?'

Rightly concluding that this was a crisper and neater way of saying 'psychiatrist,' Lord Ickenham replied that he was.

'The others are in the hall, having drinks and things. When I heard you were walking up, I thought I'd come along and meet you. Dunstable's my name. The Duke of Dunstable.'

They fell into step together. The Duke produced a bandanna handkerchief and mopped his forehead with it. The evening was warm, and he was not in the best of condition.

'I wanted a quiet talk—' he began.

'Speaking of Dukes,' said Lord Ickenham, 'did you ever hear the one about the Duke and the lady snake-charmer?'

It was a jocund little tale, slightly blue in spots, and he told it well. But though his companion was plainly amused, his chief emotion appeared to be perplexity.

'Are you really Sir Roderick Glossop?'

'Why do you ask?'

'Man at the club told me he was a pompous old ass. But you're not a pompous old ass.'

'Your friend probably met me in my professional capacity. You know how it is. One puts on a bit of dog in office hours, to impress the customers. I dare say you have done the same thing yourself in the House of Lords.'

'That's true.'

'But you were saying something about wanting a quiet talk.'

'Exactly. Before Connie could get hold of you and stuff you up with a lot of nonsense. Emsworth's sister, Lady Constance Keeble. She's like all women—won't face facts. The first thing she's going to do when she meets you is to try to pull the wool over your eyes and persuade you that he's as sane as I am. Quite understandable, no doubt. Her brother, and all that.'

'You are speaking of Lord Emsworth?'

'Yes. What did you make of him?'

'He seemed clean and sober.'

Again the Duke appeared a little puzzled.

'Why shouldn't he be sober?'

'Don't think I am complaining,' Lord Ickenham hastened to assure him. 'I was pleased.'

'Oh? Well, as I was saying, Connie will try to make you think that the whole thing has been much exaggerated and that he's simply dreamy and absent-minded. Don't let her fool you. The man's potty.'

'Indeed?'

'No question about it. The whole family's potty. You saw Bosham at the station. There's a loony for you. Goes up to London and lets a chap play the confidence trick on him. "Give me your wallet to show you trust me," says the chap. "Right ho," says Bosham. Just like that. Ever meet the other boy—Freddie Threepwood? Worse than Bosham. Sells dog-biscuits. So you can get a rough idea what Emsworth must be like. Man can't have two sons like that and be sane himself, I mean to say. You've got to start with that idea well in your head, or you'll never get anywhere. Shall I tell you about Emsworth?'

'Do.'

'Here are the facts. He's got a pig, and he's crazy about it.'

'The good man loves his pig.'

'Yes, but he doesn't want to run it in the Derby.'

'Does Emsworth?'

'Told me so himself.'

Lord Ickenham looked dubious.

'I doubt if the Stewards would accept a pig. You might starch its ears and enter it as a greyhound for the Waterloo Cup, but not the Derby.'

'Exactly. Well, that shows you.'

'It does, indeed.'

The Duke puffed at his moustache approvingly, so that it flew before him like a banner. It pleased him to find this expert in such complete agreement with his views. The man, he could see, knew his business, and he decided to abandon reserve and lay bare the skeleton in his own cupboard. He had not intended to draw attention to the dark shadow which had fallen on the house of Dunstable, but he saw now that it would be best to tell all. In the hall which he had just left, strange and disconcerting things had been happening, and he wanted a skilled opinion on them.

'A nice little place Emsworth has here,' said Lord Ickenham, as they reached the broad gravel sweep that flanked the terrace.

'Not so bad. Makes it all the sadder that he'll probably end his days in Colney Hatch. Unless you can cure him.'

'I seldom fail.'

'Then I wish,' said the Duke, coming out with it, 'that while you're here you would take a look at my nephew Horace.'

'Is he giving you cause for anxiety?'

'Acute anxiety.'

The Duke, about to unveil the Dunstable skeleton, checked himself abruptly and blew furiously at his moustache. From some spot hidden from them by thick shrubberies there had come the sound of a pleasant tenor voice. It was rendering the 'Bonny Bonny Banks of Loch Lomond', and putting a good deal of feeling into it.

'Gah! That whistling feller again!'

'I beg your pardon?'

'Chap who comes whistling and singing outside my window,' said the Duke, like the heroine of an old-fashioned novelette speaking of her lover. 'I've been trying to get to grips with him ever since I arrived, but he eludes me. Well I can wait. I've got a dozen best new-laid eggs in my room, and sooner or later . . . But I was telling you about Horace.'

'Yes, I want to hear all about Horace. Your nephew, you say?'

'One of them. My late brother's son. He's potty. The other's my late sister's son. He's potty, too. My late brother was potty. So was my late sister.'

'And where would you rank Horace in this galaxy of goofiness? Is he, in your opinion, above or below the family average?'

The Duke considered.

'Above. Decidedly above. After what happened in the hall just now, most emphatically above. Do you know what happened in the hall just now?'

'I'm sorry, no. I'm a stranger in these parts myself.'

'It shocked me profoundly.'

'What happened in the hall?'

'And always the "Bonny Bonny Banks of Loch Lomond",' said the Duke peevishly. 'A song I've hated all my life. Who wrote the beastly thing?'

'Burns, I believe. But you were going to tell me what happened in the hall.'

'Yes. So I was. It showed me that I had wronged that chap Baxter. I expect you met Baxter at the station. My secretary. He was on your train. He should have come down with me, but he insisted on remaining in London on the plea that he had work to do in connection with a history of my family that I'm writing. I didn't believe him. It seemed to me that he had a furtive look in his eye. My feeling all along was that he was planning to go on some toot. And when Horace told me this morning that he had seen him at some dance or other a couple of nights ago, leaping about all over the place in the costume of a Corsican brigand, I was all ready for him. The moment his foot crossed the threshold, I sacked him. And then this thing happened in the hall.'

'You were going to tell me about that, weren't you?'

'I am telling you about it. It was when we were in the hall. Connie had taken your daughter out to show her the portraits in the gallery, though why any girl should be supposed to be anxious to look at that collection of gargoyles is more than I can imagine. I should be vastly surprised to learn that there was an uglier lot of devils in the whole of England than Emsworth's ancestors. However, be that as it may, Connie had taken your daughter to see them, leaving Bosham and your nephew and myself in the hall. And in comes Horace. And no sooner had I directed his attention to your nephew than he gives a jump and says "Pongo!" See? "Pongo!" Like that. Your nephew looked taken aback, and said in a low voice that his name was Basil.'

'Brave lad!'

'What?'

'I said "Brave lad!"'

'Why?'

'Why not?' argued Lord Ickenham.

The Duke turned this over for a moment, and seemed to see justice in it.

'What had happened, you see, was that Horace had mistaken him for a friend of his. Well, all right. Nothing so very remarkable about that, you are saying. Sort of thing that might happen to anyone. Quite. But mark the sequel. If Burns thought "Loch Lomond" rhymes with "before ye,"' said the Duke, with a return of his peevishness, 'he must have been a borderline case.'

'And the sequel, you were about to say?'

'Eh? Oh, the sequel. I'm coming to that. Not that there are many rhymes to "Loch Lomond." Got to be fair to the chap, I suppose. Yes, the sequel. Well, right on top of this, Connie comes back with your daughter. She's charming.'

'I have not met Lady Constance.'

'You daughter, I mean.'

'Oh, very. Her name is Gwendoline.'

'So she told us. But that didn't stop Horace from going up to her and calling her Polly.'

'Polly?'

'Polly. "Why, hullo, Polly!" were his exact words.'

Lord Ickenham reflected.

'The conclusion that suggests itself is that he had mistaken her for a girl called Polly.'

'Exactly. The very thought that flashed on me. Well, you can imagine that that made me realize that matters were grave. One

bloomer of that sort—yes. But when it happens twice in two minutes, you begin to fear the worst. I've always been uneasy about
Horace's mental condition, ever since he had measles as a boy and
suddenly shot up to the height of about eight foot six. It stands to
reason a chap's brain can't be all that way from his heart and still
function normally. Look at the distance the blood's got to travel.
Well, here we are,' said the Duke, as they passed through the great
front door that stood hospitably open. 'Hullo, where's everybody?
Dressing, I suppose. You'll be wanting to go to your room. I'll take
you there. You're in the Red Room. The bathroom's at the end of
the passage. What was I saying? Oh, yes. I said I began to fear the
worst. I reasoned the whole thing out. A chap can't be eight foot six
and the son of my late brother and expect to carry on as if nothing
had happened. Something's bound to give. I remembered what he
had told me about thinking he had seen Baxter at the Ball, and it
suddenly struck me like a blow that he must have developed—I
don't know what you call it, but I suppose there's some scientific
term for it when a feller starts seeing things.'

'You mean a sublunary medulla oblongata diathesis.'

'Very possibly. I can see now why that girl broke off the engagement. She must have realized that he had got this—whatever it
was you said, and decided it wasn't good enough. No girl wants a
potty husband, though it's dashed hard not to get one nowadays.
Here's your room. I wish you would see what you can do for the
boy. Can't you examine him or something?'

'I shall be delighted to examine him. Just give me time to have
a bath, and I will be at his disposal.'

'Then I'll send him to you. If there's anything to be done for
him, I'd be glad if you would do it. What with him and Bosham
and Emsworth and that whistling feller, I feel as if I were living in
a private asylum, and I don't like it.'

The Duke stumped off, and Lord Ickenham, armed with his
great sponge Joyeuse, made his way to the bathroom. He had just
got back from a refreshing dip, when there was a knock at the door
and Horace entered. And, having done so, he stood staring dumbly.

Horace Davenport's face had two features that called for attention. From his father he had inherited the spacious Dunstable nose; from his mother, a Hilsbury-Hepworth, the large, fawnlike eyes which distinguish that family. This nose, as he gazed at Lord Ickenham, was twitching like a rabbit's, and in the eyes behind their tortoiseshell-rimmed spectacles there was dawning slowly a look of incredulous horror. It was as if he had been cast for the part of Macbeth and was starting to run through the Banquo's ghost scene.

The events of the evening had come as a great shock to Horace. Firmly convinced for some time past that his Uncle Alaric was one of England's outstanding schizophrenic cases, a naturally nervous disposition had led him to look on the latter's mental condition as something which might at any moment spread to himself, like a cold in the head. The double hallucination which he had so recently experienced, coming on top of the delusion he had had about seeing Baxter at the Ball, had rendered him apprehensive in the last degree, and he had welcomed the suggestion that he should get together with Sir Roderick Glossop for a quiet talk.

And now, so all his senses told him, he was suffering yet another hallucination. In the bathrobed figure before him, he could have sworn that he was gazing at his late *fiancée's* uncle, the Earl of Ickenham.

Yet this was the Red Room, and in the Red Room he had been specifically informed, Sir Roderick Glossop was to be found. Moreover, in the other's demeanour there was no suggestion of recognition, merely a courteous air of mild enquiry.

After what seemed an age-long pause, he managed to speak.

'Sir Roderick Glossop?'

'Yes.'

'Er—my name's Davenport.'

'Of course, yes. Come in, my dear fellow. You won't mind if I dress while we are talking? I haven't left myself too much time.'

Horace watched him with a dazed eye as he dived with boy-ish animation into a studded shirt. The grey head, popping out a moment later at shirt's end, gave him a renewed sense of shock, so intensely Ickenhamian was it in every respect.

A sudden feeble hope came to him that this time there might be a simple explanation. It might prove to be one of those cases of extraordinary physical resemblance of which you read in the papers.

'I—er—I say,' he asked, 'do you by any chance know a man named Lord Ickenham?'

'Lord Ickenham?' said Lord Ickenham, springing into dress trousers like a trained acrobat. 'Yes. I've met him.'

'You're amazingly like him, aren't you?'

Lord Ickenham did not reply for a moment. He was tying his tie, and on these occasions the conscientious man anxious to give of his best at the dinner-table rivets his attention on the task in hand. Presently the frown passed from his face, and he was his genial self again.

'I'm afraid I missed that. You were saying—'

'You and Lord Ickenham look exactly alike, don't you?'

His companion seemed surprised.

'Well, that's a thing nobody has ever said to me before. Con-sidering that Lord Ickenham is tall and slender—while I am short and stout . . .'

'Short?'

'Quite short.'

'And stout?'

'Extremely stout.'

A low gulp escaped Horace Davenport. It might have been the expiring gurgle of that feeble hope. The sound caused his compan-ion to look at him sharply, and as he did so his manner changed.

'You really must forgive me,' he said. 'I fear I missed the point of what you have been saying. Inexcusable of me, for your uncle gave me your case history. He told me how in the hall this evening you mistook my daughter and nephew for old acquaintances, and there was something about thinking that a man you saw at some Ball in London was his secretary Mr Baxter. Was that the first time this sort of thing happened?'

'Yes.'

'I see. The delusion metabolis came on quite suddenly, as it so often does. Can you suggest anything that might account for it?'

Horace hesitated. He shrank from putting his secret fears into words.

'Well, I was wondering . . .'

'Yes?'

'Is loopiness hereditary?'

'It can be, no doubt.'

'Noses are.'

'True.'

'This beezer of mine has come down through the ages.'

'Indeed?'

'So what I was wondering was, if a chap's got a dotty uncle, is he bound to catch it?'

'I would not say it was inevitable. Still . . . How dotty is your uncle?'

'Quite fairly dotty.'

'I see. Had your father any such structural weakness?'

'No. No, he was all right. He collected Japanese prints,' said Horace, with an afterthought.

'He didn't think he *was* a Japanese print?'

'Oh, no. Rather not.'

'Then that is all right. I feel sure that there need be no real anxiety. I am convinced that all that we are suffering from is some minor nervous lesion, brought about possibly by worry. Have we been worried lately?'

The question seemed to affect Horace Davenport much as it might have affected Job. He stared at his companion as at one who does not know the half of it.

'Have we!'

'We have?'

'You bet we have.'

'Then what we need is a long sea voyage.'

'But, dash it, we're a rotten sailor. Would you mind awfully if we got a second opinion?'

'By all means.'

'The other chap might simply tell us to go to Bournemouth or somewhere.'

'Bournemouth would be just as good. We came here in our car, did we not? Then directly after dinner I advise that we steal quietly off, without going through the strain of saying good-bye to any-one, and drive to London. Having reached London, we can pack anything that may be necessary and go to Bournemouth and stay there.'

'And you think that that will put us right?'

'Unquestionably.'

'And one other point. Would there be any medical objection to just one good, stiff, energetic binge in London? You see,' said Hor-ace, with a touch of apology, 'we do rather feel, what with one thing and another, as if we wanted taking out of ourself at the moment.'

Lord Ickenham patted his shoulder.

'My dear boy, it is what any member of my profession would advise. Do we by any chance know a beverage called May Queen? Its full name is "To-morrow'll be of all the year the maddest, merriest day, for I'm to be Queen of the May, mother, I'm to be Queen of the May." A clumsy title, generally shortened for purposes of ordinary conversation. Its foundation is any good, dry champagne, to which is added liqueur brandy, armagnac, kummel, yellow chartreuse and old stout, to taste. It is a good many years since I tried it myself, but I can thoroughly recommend it to alleviate the deepest despondency. Ah!' said Lord Ickenham, as a mellow booming rose from below. 'Dinner. Let us be going down. We do not want to be late for the trough our first night at a house, do we? Creates a bad impression.'

I T had been Lord Ickenham's intention, directly dinner was over, to seek out his nephew Pongo with a view to giving him a bracing pep talk. But a lengthy conference with his hostess delayed him in the drawing-room, and it was only after the subject of the Duke had been thoroughly threshed out between them that he was able to tear himself away. He found the young man eventually in the billiard-room, practicing solitary cannons.

Pongo's demeanour at dinner had been such as to cause concern to an uncle and a fellow-conspirator. Solomon in all his glory, arrayed for the banquet, could not have surpassed him in splendour, but there is no question that he would have looked happier. Pongo's tie was right, and his shirt was right, and his socks were right, and the crease in his trousers was a genuine feast for the eye, but his resemblance to a fox with a pack of hounds and a bevy of the best people on its trail, which had been so noticeable all through the day, had become more pronounced than ever.

It was the cheerful, stimulating note, accordingly, that Lord Ickenham now set himself to strike. This wilting object before him was patently in need of all the cheer and stimulation he could get.

'Well, my young ray of sunshine,' he said, 'I can see by our expression that we are feeling that everything is going like a breeze. I hear you put it across Horace properly.'

Pongo brightened momentarily, as a veteran of Agincourt might have done at the mention of the name of Crispian.

'Yes, I put it across old H. all right.'

'You did indeed. You appear to have conducted yourself with admirable *sang-froid*. I am proud of you.'

'But what's the use?' said Pongo, subsiding into gloom once more. 'It can't last. Even a goop like Horace, though nonplussed for the moment, is bound to start figuring things out and arriving at the nub. Directly he sees you—'

'He has seen me.'

'Oh, my gosh! What happened?'

'We had a long and interesting conversation, and I am happy to be able to report that he is leaving immediately for Bournemouth, merely pausing in London on his way, like some butterfly alighting on a flower, in order to get pickled to the tonsils.'

Pongo, listening attentively to the *précis* of recent events, seemed grudgingly pleased.

'Well, that's something, I suppose,' he said. 'Getting Horace out of the place is better than nothing.'

His tone pained Lord Ickenham.

'You appear still moody,' he said reproachfully. 'I had supposed that my narrative would have had you dancing about the room, clapping your little hands. Is it possible that you are still finding Lady Constance a source of anxiety?'

'And that man Baxter.'

Lord Ickenham waved a cue in airy scorn of his hostess and the spectacled secretary.

'Why do you bother about Connie and Baxter? A gorilla could lick them both. What has she been doing to you?'

'She hasn't been doing anything, exactly. She's been quite matey, as a matter of fact. But my informants were right. She is the sort of woman who makes you feel that, no matter how suave her manner for the nonce, she is at heart a twenty-minute egg and may start functioning at any moment.'

Lord Ickenham nodded.

'I know what you mean. I have noticed the same thing in volcanoes, and the head mistress of my first kindergarten was just like that. It is several years, of course, since I graduated from the old place, but I can remember her vividly. The sweet, placid face . . . the cooing voice . . . but always, like some haunting strain in a piece of music, that underlying suggestion of the sudden whack over the knuckles with a ruler. Why did Baxter jar upon you?'

'He kept asking me questions about my methods of work.'

'Ah, the two secs getting together and swapping shop. I thought that might happen.'

'Then I wish you had warned me. That bird gives me the creeps.'

'He struck you as sinister, did he? I have felt the same thing myself. Our conversation on the platform left me not altogether satisfied in my mind about that young man. It seemed to me that during my explanations with reference to the poor fellow on the train who thought he was Sir Roderick Glossop I detected a certain dryness in his manner, a subtle something that suggested that, lacking our friend Bosham's Norman blood, he was equally deficient in that simple faith which the poet ranks even more highly. If you ask me, my dear Pongo, Baxter suspects.'

'Then I'm jolly well going to get out of this!'

'Impossible. Have you forgotten that Polly has to fascinate the Duke and will be lost without you beside her to stimulate and encourage? Where's your chivalry? A nice figure you would have cut at King Arthur's Round Table.'

He had found the talking point. Pongo said Yes, there was something in that. Lord Ickenham said he had known that Pongo would arrive at that conclusion, once he had really given his keen brain to the thing.

'Yes,' he said, 'we have set our hands to the plough, and we cannot sheathe the sword. Besides, I shall require your help in snitching the pig. But I was forgetting. You are not abreast of that side of our activities, are you? Emsworth has a pig. The Duke wants it. Emsworth would like to defy him, but dare not, owing to that twist in the other's character which leads him, when defied on any premises, to give those premises the works with a poker. So, on my advice, he is resorting to strategy. I have promised him that we will remove the animal from its sty, and you will then drive it across country to Ickenham, where it can lie low till the danger is past.'

It was not often that Pongo Twistleton disarranged his hair, once he had brushed it for the evening, but he did so now. Such was his emotion that he plunged both hands through those perfect waves.

'Ha!'

'I keep asking you not to say "Ha!" my boy.'

'So that's the latest, is it? I'm to become a blasted pig's chauffeur, am I?'

'A brilliant summing-up of the situation. Flaubert could not have put it better.'

'I absolutely and definitely refuse to have anything to do with the bally scheme.'

'That is your last word?'

'Specifically.'

'I see. Well, it's a pity, for Emsworth would undoubtedly have rewarded you with a purse of gold. Noblesse would have obliged. He has the stuff in sackfuls, and this pig is the apple of his eye. And you could do with a purse of gold just now, could you not?'

Pongo started. He had missed this angle of the situation.

'Oh! I didn't think of that.'

'Start pondering on it now. And while you are doing so,' said Lord Ickenham, 'I will show you how billiards should be played. Watch this shot.'

He had begun to bend over the table, a bright eye fixed on the object ball, when he glanced round. The door had opened, and he was aware of something like a death ray playing about his person.

Rupert Baxter was there, staring at him through his spectacles.

· · ·

To most people at whom the efficient Baxter directed that silent, steely, spectacled stare of his there was wont to come a sudden malaise, a disposition to shuffle the feet and explore the conscience guiltily: and even those whose consciences were clear generally quailed a little. Lord Ickenham, however, continued undisturbed.

'Ah, my dear Baxter. Looking for me?'

'I should be glad if you could spare me a moment.'

'Something you want to talk to me about?'

'If you have no objection.'

'You have not come to consult me in my professional capacity, I trust? We have not been suffering from delusions, have we?'

'I never suffer from delusions.'

'No, I should imagine not. Well, come on in. Push off, Basil.'

'He can remain,' said Baxter sombrely. 'What I have to say will interest him also.'

It seemed to Pongo, as he withdrew into the farthest corner of the room and ran a finger round the inside of his collar, that if ever he had heard the voice of doom speak, he had heard it then. To him there was something so menacing in the secretary's manner that he marvelled at his uncle's lack of emotion. Lord Ickenham, having scattered the red and spot balls carelessly about the table, was now preparing to execute a tricky shot.

'Lovely evening,' he said.

'Very. You had a pleasant walk, I hope?'

'That is understating it. Ecstatic,' said Lord Ickenham, making a dexterous cannon, 'would be a better word. What with the pure air, the majestic scenery, the old gypsy feeling of tramping along the high road and the Duke's conversation, I don't know when I have enjoyed a walk more. By the way, the Duke was telling me that there had been a little friction on your arrival. He said he had handed you the two weeks' notice because Horace Davenport told him that he had seen you at a Ball in London.'

'Yes.'

'Everything satisfactory now, I hope?'

'Quite. He discovered that he had been misinformed, and apologized. I am continuing in his employment.'

'I'm glad. You wouldn't want to lose a job like that. A man can stick on a lot of side about being secretary to a Duke. Practically as good as being a Duke himself. I am afraid Basil here has no such excuse for spiritual uplift. Just an ordinary secretary—Basil.'

'A very peculiar one, I should have said.'

'Peculiar? In what respect? In the words of the bridegroom of Antigua, is it manners you mean or do you refer to his figuah?'

'He seems ignorant of the very rudiments of his work.'

'Yes, I fear poor Basil would strike a man like you as something of an amateur. He has not had your wide experience. You were Lord Emsworth's secretary once, were you not?'

'I was.'

A flush deepened the swarthiness of Rupert Baxter's cheek. He had been Lord Emsworth's secretary several times, and on each occasion his employer, aided by the breaks, had succeeded in throwing him out. He did not care to be reminded of these flaws in a successful career.

'And before that?'

'I was with Sir Ralph Dillingworth, a Yorkshire baronet.'

'Yours has been a very steady rise in the social scale,' said Lord Ickenham admiringly. 'Starting at the bottom with a humble baronet—slumming, you might almost call it—you go on to an earl and then to a duke. It does you credit.'

'Thank you.'

'Not at all. I think I've heard of Dillingworth. Odd sort of fellow, isn't he?'

'Very.'

'There was some story about him shooting mice in the drawing-room with an elephant gun.'

'Yes.'

'Painful for the family. For the mice, too, of course.'

'Most.'

'They should have called me in.'

'They did.'

'I beg your pardon?'

'I say they did.'

'I don't remember it.'

'I am not surprised.'

Rupert Baxter was sitting back in his chair, tapping the tips of his fingers together. It seemed to Pongo, watching him pallidly from afar, that if he had had a different-shaped face and had not worn spectacles he would have looked like Sherlock Holmes.

'It was unfortunate for you that I should have met the real Sir Roderick. When I saw him on the train, he had forgotten me, of course, but I knew him immediately. He has altered very little!'

Lord Ickenham raised his eyebrows.

'Are you insinuating that I am not Sir Roderick Glossop?'

'I am.'

'I see. You accuse me of assuming another man's identity, do you, of abusing Lady Constance's hospitality by entering her house under false pretences? You deliberately assert that I am a fraud and an impostor?'

'I do.'

'And how right you are, my dear fellow!' said Lord Ickenham. 'How right you are.'

Rupert Baxter continued to tap his fingertips together and to project through his spectacles as stern a glare as they had ever been called upon to filter, but he was conscious as he did so of a certain sense of flatness. Unmasked Guilt, in his opinion, should have taken it rather bigger than this man before him appeared to be doing. Lord Ickenham was now peering at himself in the mirror and fiddling with his moustache. He may have been feeling as if the bottom of his world had dropped out, but he did not look it.

'I don't know who you are—'

'Call me Uncle Fred.'

'I will not call you Uncle Fred!' said Rupert Baxter violently.

He restored his composure with a glance at Pongo. There, he felt, was Unmasked Guilt looking as Unmasked Guilt should look.

'Well, there you are,' he resumed, becoming calmer. 'The risk you run, when you impersonate another man, is that you are apt to come up against somebody to whom his appearance is familiar.'

'Trite, but true. Do you like me with my moustache like that? Or like this?'

Rupert Baxter's impatient gesture seemed to say that he was Nemesis, not a judge in a male beauty contest.

'Perhaps it would interest you now,' he said, 'to hear about the local train service.'

'Is there a milk train?' asked Pongo, speaking for the first time.

'I expect so,' said Baxter, giving him a cold look, 'but probably you would prefer to take the eight-twenty in the morning.'

Lord Ickenham seemed puzzled.

'You speak as if you were under the impression that we were leaving.'

'That is my impression.'

'You are not going to respect our little secret, then?'

'I intend to expose you immediately.'

'Even if I assure you that we did not come here after the spoons, but rather to do two loving hearts a bit of good?'

'Your motives do not interest me.'

Lord Ickenham gave his moustache a thoughtful twirl.

'I see. You are a hard man, Baxter.'

'I do my duty.'

'Not always, surely? How about the toot in London?'

'I don't understand you.'

'So you won't talk? Still, you know you went to that Ball at the Albert Hall. Horace Davenport saw you there.'

'Horace!'

'Yes, I admit that at the moment what Horace says is not evidence. But why is it not evidence, Baxter? Simply because the Duke, after seeing him make what appeared to be two bad shots at identifying people this evening, assumes that he must also have been mistaken in thinking that he saw you at the Ball. He supposes that his young relative is suffering from hallucinations. But if you denounce me, my daughter and nephew will testify that they really are the persons he supposed them to be, and it will become clear to the Duke that Horace is not suffering from hallucinations and that when he says he saw you at the Ball he did see you at the Ball. Then where will you be?'

He paused, and in the background Pongo revived like a watered flower. During this admirably lucid exposition of the state of affairs, there had come into his eyes a look of worshipping admiration which was not always there when he gazed at his uncle.

'At-a-boy!' he said reverently. 'It's a dead stymie.'

'I think so.'

Rupert Baxter's was one of those strong, square jaws which do not readily fall, but it had undeniably wavered, as if its steely muscles were about to relax. And though he hitched it up, there was dismay in the eyes behind the spectacles.

'It doesn't follow at all!'

'Baxter, it must follow as the night the day.'

'I shall deny—'

'What's the use? I have not known the Duke long, but I have known him long enough to be able to recognize him as one of those sturdy, tenacious souls, the backbone of England, who when they have once got an idea into their fat heads are not to be induced to relinquish it by any denials. No, if you do not wish to imperil the cordial relations existing between your employer and yourself, I would reflect, Baxter.'

'Definitely,' said Pongo.

'I would consider.'

'Like billy-o.'

'If you do, you will perceive that we stand or fall together. You cannot unmask us without unmasking yourself. But whereas we, unmasked, merely suffer the passing embarrassment of being thrown out by strong-armed domestics, you lose that splendid post of yours and have to go back to mixing with baronets. And how do you know,' said Lord Ickenham, 'that next time it would even be a baronet? It might be some bounder of a knight.'

He placed a kindly hand on the secretary's arm, and led him to the door.

'I really think, my dear fellow,' he said, 'that we had better pursue a mutual policy of Live and Let Live. Let our motto be that of the great Roi Pausole—*Ne nuis pas à ton voisin*. It is the only way to get comfortably through life.'

He closed the door. Pongo drew a deep breath.

'Uncle Fred,' he said, 'there have been times, I don't mind admitting, when I have viewed you with concern—'

'You mean that afternoon down at Valley Fields?'

'I was thinking more of our day at the Dog Races.'

'Ah, yes. We did slip up a little there.'

'But this time you have saved my life.'

'My dear boy, you embarrass me. A mere nothing. It is always my aim to try to spread sweetness and light.'

'I should describe that bird as baffled, wouldn't you?'

'Baffled as few secretaries have ever been, I think. We can look upon him, I fancy, as a spent force. And now, my boy, if you will excuse me, I must leave you. I promised the Duke to drop in on him for a chat round about ten o'clock.'

12

IN supposing that their heart-to-heart talk would cause Rupert Baxter to abandon his intention of making a public exposure of his machinations, Lord Ickenham had been correct. In his assumption that he had rendered the man behind the steel-rimmed spectacles a spent force, however, he had erred. Baxter's hat was still in the ring. At Blandings Castle he had a staunch ally in whom he could always confide, and it was to her boudoir that he made his way within five minutes of leaving the billiard-room.

'Could I speak to you for a moment, Lady Constance?'

'Certainly, Mr Baxter.'

'Thank you,' said the secretary, and took a seat.

He had found Lady Constance in a mood of serene contentment. In the drawing-room over the coffee she had had an extended interview with that eminent brain-specialist, Sir Roderick Glossop, and his views regarding the Duke, she was pleased to find, were in complete accord with her own. He endorsed her opinion that steps must be taken immediately, but assured her that only the simplest form of treatment was required to render His Grace a man who, if you put an egg into his hand, would not know what to do with it.

And she had been running over in her mind a few of his most soothing pronouncements and thinking what a delightful man he was, when in came Baxter. And within a minute, for he was never a man to beat about the bush and break things gently, he had wrecked her peace of mind as thoroughly as if it had been a sitting-room and he her old friend with a whippy-shafted poker in his hand.

'Mr Baxter!' she cried.

From anyone else she would have received the extraordinary statement which he had just made with raised eyebrows and a shrivelling stare. But her faith in this man was the faith of a little child. The strength of his personality, though she had a strong personality herself, had always dominated her completely.

'Mr BAX-ter!'

The secretary had anticipated some such reaction on her part. This spasm of emotion was what is known in the motion-picture world as 'the quick take 'um,' and in the circumstances he supposed that it was inevitable. He waited in stern silence for it to expend itself.

'Are you sure?'

A flash of steel-rimmed spectacles told her that Rupert Baxter was not a man who made statements without being sure.

'He admitted it to me personally.'

'But he is such a charming man.'

'Naturally. Charm is the chief stock-in-trade of persons of that type.'

Lady Constance's mind was beginning to adjust itself to the position of affairs. After all, she reflected, this was not the first time that impostors had insinuated themselves into Blandings Castle. Her nephew Ronald's chorus-girl, to name one instance, had arrived in the guise of an American heiress. And there had been other cases. Indeed, she might have felt justified in moments of depression in yielding to the gloomy view that her visiting list consisted almost exclusively of impostors. There appeared to be something about Blandings Castle that attracted impostors as catnip attracts cats.

'You say he admitted it?'

'He had no alternative.'

'Then I suppose he has left the house?'

Something of embarrassment crept into Rupert Baxter's manner. His spectacles seemed to flicker.

'Well, no,' he said.

'No?' cried Lady Constance, amazed. Impostors were tougher stuff than she had supposed.

'A difficulty has arisen.'

It is never pleasant for a proud man to have to confess that scoundrels have got him in cleft sticks, and in Rupert Baxter's manner as he told his tale there was nothing of relish. But painful though it was, he told it clearly.

'To make anything in the nature of an overt move is impossible. It would result in my losing my post, and my post is all important to me. It is my intention ultimately to become the Duke's man of affairs, in charge of all his interests. I hope I can rely on you to do nothing that will jeopardize my career.'

'Of course,' said Lady Constance. Not for an instant did she contemplate the idea of hindering this man's rise to the heights. Nevertheless, she chafed. 'But is there nothing to be done? Are we to allow this person to remain and loot the house at his leisure?'

On this point, Rupert Baxter felt that he was in a position to reassure her.

'He is not here with any motive of robbery. He has come in the hope of trapping Horace Davenport into marriage with that girl.'

'What!'

'He virtually said as much. When I told him that I knew him to be an impostor, he said something flippant about not having come after the spoons but because he was trying to do what he described as "a bit of good to two loving hearts." His meaning escaped me at the time, but I have now remembered something which had been hovering on the edge of my mind ever since I saw these people at Paddington. I had had one of those vague ideas

one gets that I had seen this girl before somewhere. It has now
come back to me. She was at that Ball with Horace Davenport.
One sees the whole thing quite clearly. In London, presumably,
she was unable to make him commit himself definitely, so she has
followed him here in the hope of creating some situation which
will compel him to marry her.'

The fiendish cunning of the scheme appalled Lady Constance.

'But what can we do?'

'I myself, as I have explained, can do nothing. But surely a hint
from you to the Duke that his nephew is in danger of being lured
into a disastrous marriage—'

'But he does not know it is a disastrous marriage.'

'You mean that he is under the impression that the girl is the
daughter of Sir Roderick Glossop, the brain specialist? But even so.
The Duke is a man acutely alive to the existence of class distinctions, and I think that as a wife for his nephew he would consider
the daughter of a brain specialist hardly—'

'Oh, yes,' said Lady Constance, brightening. 'I see what you
mean. Yes, Alaric is and always has been a perfect snob.'

'Quite,' said Baxter, glad to find his point taken. 'I feel sure that
it will not be difficult for you to influence him. Then I will leave
the matter in your hands.'

The initial emotion of Lady Constance, when she found herself
alone, was relief, and for a while nothing came to weaken this
relief. Rupert Baxter, as always, seemed in his efficient way to have
put everything right and pointed out with masterly clearness the
solution of the problem. There was, she felt, as she had so often
felt, nobody like him.

But gradually, now that his magnetic personality was no longer
there to sway her mind, there began to steal over her a growing
uneasiness. Specious though the theory was which he had put forward, that the current instalment of impostors at Blandings Castle
had no designs on the castle's many valuable contents but were

bent simply on the task of getting Horace Davenport into a morning coat and sponge-bag trousers and leading him up the aisle, she found herself less and less able to credit it.

To Lady Constance's mind, impostors were not like that. Practical rather than romantic, as she saw it, they preferred jewellery to wedding bells. They might not actually disdain the 'Voice That Breathed O'er Eden,' but in their scale of values it ran a very poor second to diamond necklaces.

She rose from her chair in agitation. She felt that something must be done, and done immediately. Even in her alarm, of course, she did not consider the idea of finding Rupert Baxter and trying to argue him out of his opinions. One did not argue with Rupert Baxter. What he said, he said, and you had to accept it. Her desire was to buttonhole some soothingly solid person who would listen to her and either allay her fears or suggest some way of staving off disaster. And it so happened that Blandings Castle housed at that moment perhaps the most solid person who had ever said 'Yoicks' to a foxhound.

In the hope that he would also prove soothing, she hurried from the room in quest of her nephew, Lord Bosham.

Rupert Baxter, meanwhile, feeling in need of fresh air after the mental strain to which he had been subjected, had left the house and was strolling under the stars. His wandering feet had taken him to that velvet lawn which lay outside the Garden Suite. There, pacing up and down, brow knitted and hands clasped behind back, he gave himself up to thought.

His admission to Lady Constance that there was nothing which he himself could do in this situation which called so imperiously for decisive action had irked Rupert Baxter and wounded his self-esteem. That remark of Pongo's, moreover, about a dead stymie still rankled in his bosom like a poisoned dart. He was not accustomed to being laid dead stymies by the dregs of the underworld. Was there, he asked himself, no method by which he could express his personality, no means whereby he could make his presence felt? He concentrated on the problem exercising his brain vigorously.

It often happens that great brains, when vigorously exercised, find a musical accompaniment of assistance to their activities. Or, putting it another way, thinkers, while thinking, frequently whistle. Rupert Baxter did, selecting for his purpose a melody which had always been a favourite of his—the 'Bonny Bonny Banks of Loch Lomond.'

If he had been less preoccupied, he would have observed that at about the fourth bar a certain liveliness had begun to manifest itself behind the French window which he was passing. It opened softly, and a white-moustached head peered furtively out. But he was preoccupied, and consequently did not observe it. He reached the end of the lawn, ground a heel into the immemorial turf and turned. Starting his measured walk anew, he once more approached the window.

He was now singing. He had a pleasant tenor voice.

'You take the high road
And I'll take the low road,
And I'll be in Scotland a-FORE ye.
For I and my true love
Will never meet again—'

The starlight gleamed on a white-moustached figure.

'On the bonny bonny BANKS of Loch LO—'

Something whizzed through the night air . . . crashed on Rupert Baxter's cheek . . . spread itself in sticky ruin . . .

And simultaneously there came from the Garden Suite the sudden, sharp cry of a strong man in pain.

• • •

It was perhaps half an hour after he had left it that Lord Ickenham returned to the billiard-room. He found Pongo still there, but no longer alone. He had been joined by Lord Bosham, who had suggested a hundred up, and Lord Ickenham found the game nearing its conclusion, with Pongo, exhilarated by recent happenings, performing prodigies with the cue. He took a seat, and with a decent respect for the amenities waited in silence until the struggle was over.

Lord Bosham resumed his coat.

'Jolly well played, sir,' he said handsomely, a gallant loser. 'Jolly good game. Very jolly, the whole thing.' He paused, and looked at Lord Ickenham enquiringly. The latter had clicked his tongue and was shaking his head with an air of rebuke. 'Eh?' he said.

'It was simply that the irony of the thing struck me,' explained Lord Ickenham. 'Tragedy has been stalking through this house: doctors have been telephoned for, sick rooms made ready, cool compresses prepared: and here are you two young men carelessly playing billiards. Fiddling while Rome burns is about what it amounts to.'

'Eh?' said Lord Bosham again, this time adding a 'What?' to lend the word greater weight. He found him cryptic.

'Somebody ill?' asked Pongo. 'Not Baxter?' he went on, a note of hope in his voice.

'I would not say that Baxter was actually ill,' said Lord Ickenham, 'though no doubt much bruised in spirit. He got an egg on the left cheek-bone. But soap and water will by now have put this right. Far more serious is the case of the Duke. It was he who threw the egg, and overestimating the limberness of what is known in America, I believe, as the old soup-bone, he put his shoulder out. I left him drinking barley-water with his arm in a sling.'

'I say!' said Lord Bosham. 'How dashed unpleasant for him.'

'Yes, he didn't seem too elated about it.'

'Still,' argued Pongo, pointing out the bright side, 'he got Baxter all right?'

'Oh, he got him squarely. I must confess that my respect for the Duke has become considerably enhanced by to-night's exhibition of marksmanship. Say what you will, there is something fine about our old aristocracy. I'll bet Trotsky couldn't hit a moving secretary with an egg on a dark night.'

A point occurred to Lord Bosham. His was rather a slow mind, but he had a way of getting down to essentials.

'Why did old Dunstable bung an egg at Baxter?'

'I thought you might want to know that. Events moved towards the big moment with the inevitability of Greek tragedy. There appears to be a member of the gardening staff of Blandings Castle who has a partiality for the "Bonny Bonny Banks of Loch Lomond," and he whistles and sings it outside the Duke's window, with the result that the latter has for some time been lying in wait for him with a basket of eggs. To-night, for some reason which I am unable to explain, Baxter put himself on as an understudy. The Duke and I were in the Garden Suite, chatting of this and that, when he suddenly came on the air and the Duke, diving into a cupboard like a performing seal, emerged with laden hands and started to say it with eggs. I should have explained that he has a rooted distaste for that particular song. I gather that his sensitive ear is offended by that rather daring rhyme—"Loch Lomond" and "afore ye." Still, if I had given the matter more thought, I would have warned him. You can't throw eggs at his age without—'

The opening of the door caused him to suspend his remarks. Lady Constance came in. Her sigh of relief as she saw Lord Bosham died away as she perceived the low company he was keeping.

'Oh!' she said, surveying his foul associates with unconcealed dislike, and Pongo, on whom the first full force of her gaze had been turned, shook like a jelly and fell backwards against the billiard-table.

Lord Ickenham, as usual, remained suave and debonair.

'Ah, Lady Constance. I have just been telling the boys about the Duke's unfortunate accident.'

'Yes,' said Lord Bosham. 'It's true, is it, that the old bird has bust a flipper?'

'He has wrenched his shoulder most painfully,' assented Lady Constance, with a happier choice of phrase. 'Have you finished your game, Bosham? Then I would like to speak to you.'

She led her nephew out, and Lord Ickenham looked after her thoughtfully.

'Odd,' he said. 'Surely her manner was frigid? Did you notice a frigidity in her manner, Pongo?'

'I don't know about her manner. Her eye was piping hot,' said Pongo, who was still quivering.

'Warm eye, cold manner. . . . This must mean something. Can Baxter have been blowing the gaff, after all? But no, he wouldn't dare. I suppose it was just a hostess's natural reaction to having her guests wrench themselves asunder and involve her in a lot of fuss with doctors. Let us dismiss her from our thoughts, for we have plenty of other things to talk about. To begin with, that pig-snitching scheme is off.'

'Eh?'

'You remember I outlined it to you? It was to have started with you driving Emsworth's pig to Ickenham and ended with him gratefully pressing purses of gold into your hand, but I'm afraid it is not to be. The Duke's stranglehold on Emsworth, you will recall, was the fact that if the latter did not obey his lightest word he would wreck the home with a poker. This accident, of course, has rendered him incapable of any serious poker-work for some time to come, and Emsworth, seizing his advantage like a master-strategist, has notified him that he cannot have the pig. So he no longer wishes it snitched.'

Pongo had listened to this exposition with mixed feelings. On the whole, relief prevailed. A purse of gold would undoubtedly have come in uncommonly handy, but better, he felt, to give it a miss than to pass a night of terror in a car with a pig. Like so many sensitive young men, he shrank from making himself conspicuous, and only a person wilfully blind to the realities of life could deny that you made yourself dashed conspicuous, driving pigs across England in cars.

'Well,' he said, having considered, 'I could have used a purse of gold, but I don't know that I'm sorry.'

'You may be.'

'What do you mean?'

'Another complication has arisen, which is going to make it a little difficult for us to linger here and look about at our leisure for ways of collecting cash.'

'Oh, my gosh, what's wrong now?'

'I would not say that there was anything *wrong*. This is just an additional obstacle, and one welcomes obstacles. They put one on one's mettle and bring out the best in one.'

Pongo danced a step or two.

'Can't you tell me what has happened?'

'I will tell you in a word. You know Polly's minstrel boy. The poet with a punch.'

'What about him?'

'He will shortly be with us.'

'What?'

'Yes, he's joining the troupe. When we were alone together, after the tumult and the shouting had died and the captains and kings—I allude to Emsworth, Connie and the doctor—had departed, the Duke confided in me that he was going to show Emsworth what was what. That pig, he said, had been definitely promised to him, and if Emsworth thought he could double-cross him, he was dashed well mistaken. He intends to steal the pig, and has sent for Ricky Gilpin to come and do it. In my presence, he dictated a long telegram to the young man, commanding his instant presence.'

'But if Ricky comes here and meets Miss Pott, we shall be dished. You can't fool a hardheaded bird like that the way we did Horace.'

'No. That is why I called it an obstacle. Still, he will not actually be in residence at the castle. The Duke's instructions to him were to take a room at the Emsworth Arms. He may not meet Polly.'

'A fat chance!'

'Pretty obese, I admit. Still, we must hope for the best. Pull yourself together, my dear Pongo. Square the shoulders and chuck out the chest. Sing like the birdies sing—Tweet, tweet-tweet, tweet-tweet.'

'If you're interested in my plans, I'm going to bed.'

'Yes, do, and get a nice rest.'

'Rest!'

'You think you may have some difficulty in dropping off? Count sheep.'

'Sheep! I shall count Baxters and Lady Constances and loony uncles. Ha!' said Pongo, withdrawing.

Lord Ickenham took up a cue and gave the white ball a pensive tap. He was a little perplexed. The reference to Baxter and Lady Constance he could understand. It was the allusion to loony uncles that puzzled him.

Lady Constance Keeble was a gifted *raconteuse*. She had the knack of telling a story in a way that left her audience, even when it consisted of a nephew who had to have the He-and-She jokes in the comic papers explained to him, with a clear grasp of what she was talking about. After a shaky start, Lord Bosham followed her like a bloodhound. Long before she had finished speaking, he had gathered that what Blandings Castle was overrun with was impostors, not mice.

His first words indicated this.

'What ho!' he said. 'Impostors!'

'Impostors!' said Lady Constance, driving it home.

'What ho, what ho!' said Lord Bosham, giving additional proof that he was alive to the gravity of the situation.

A silence followed. Furrows across his forehead and a tense look on his pink face showed that Lord Bosham was thinking.

'Then, by Jove,' he said, 'this bird is the bird, after all! I thought for a while,' he explained, 'that he couldn't be the bird, but now you've told me this it's quite clear he must be the bird. The bird in the flesh, by Jingo! Well, I'm dashed!'

Lady Constance was very seldom in the mood for this sort of thing, and to-night after the nervous strain to which she had been subjected she was less in the mood for it than ever.

'What *are* you talking about, George?'

'This bird,' said Lord Bosham, seeing that he had not made himself clear. 'It turns out he was the bird, after all.'

'Oh, George!' Lady Constance paused for an instant. It was a hard thing that she was going to say, but she felt she must say it. 'Really, there are times when you are exactly like your father!'

'The confidence-trick bird,' said Lord Bosham, annoyed at her slowness of comprehension. 'Dash it, you can't have forgotten me telling you about the suave bimbo who got away with my wallet in Park Lane.'

Lady Constance's fine eyes widened.

'You don't mean—?'

'Yes, I do. That's just what I do mean. Absolutely. When I met him at the station, the first thing I said to myself was "What ho, the bird!" Then I said to myself: "What ho, no, not the bird." Because you had told me he was a big bug in the medical world. But now you tell me he isn't a big bug in the medical world—'

Lady Constance brought her hand sharply down on the arm of her chair.

'This settles it! Mr Baxter was wrong.'

'Eh?'

'Mr Baxter thinks that the reason these people have come here is that they are trying to trap Horace Davenport into marrying the girl. I don't believe it. They are after my diamond necklace. George, we must act immediately!'

'How?' asked Lord Bosham, and for the second time since their conference had begun Lady Constance was struck by the resemblance of his thought-processes to those of a brother whom she had often wanted to hit over the head with a blunt instrument.

'There is only one thing to do. We must—'

'But half a jiffy. Aren't you missing the nub? If you know these bounders are wrong 'uns, why don't we just whistle up the local police force?'

'We can't. Do you suppose I did not think of that? It would mean that Mr Baxter would lose his position with Alaric.'

'Eh? Why? What? Which? Wherefore? Why would Baxter lose his posish?'

It irked Lady Constance to be obliged to waste valuable time in order to explain the position of affairs, but she did it.

'Oh, ah?' said Lord Bosham, enlightened. 'Yes, I see. But couldn't he get another job?'

'Of course he could. But he was emphatic about wishing to continue in Alaric's employment, so what you suggest is out of the question. We must—'

'I'll tell you one thing. I don't intend to be far away from my gun these next few days. This is official.'

Lady Constance stamped her foot. It was not an easy thing for a sitting woman to do impressively, but she did it in a way that effectually silenced a nephew who in his boyhood had frequently been spanked by her with the back of a hairbrush. Lord Bosham, who had intended to speak further of his gun, of which he was very fond, desisted.

'Will you please not keep interrupting me, George! I say there is only one thing to do. We must send for a detective to watch these people.'

'Why, of course!' Like his younger brother, Frederick Threepwood, now over in the United States of America selling the dog-biscuits manufactured by the father of his charming wife, Lord Bosham was a great reader of thrillers, and anything about detectives touched a ready chord in him. 'That's the stuff! And you know just the man, don't you?'

'I?'

'Wasn't there a detective here last summer?'

Lady Constance shuddered. The visit of the person to whom he alluded had not passed from her memory. Sometimes she thought it never would. Occasionally in the late afternoon, when the vitality is low and one tends to fall a prey to strange, morbid fancies, she had the illusion that she was still seeing that waxed moustache of his.

'Pilbeam!' she cried. 'I would rather be murdered in my bed than have that man Pilbeam in the house again. Don't you know any detectives?'

'Me? No. Why should I know any . . . By Jove, yes, I do, though,' said Lord Bosham, inspired. 'By Jingo, now I come to think of it, of course I do. That man of Horace's.'

'What man of Horace's?'

Lord Bosham dissembled. Belatedly, he had realized that he was on the verge of betraying confidences. Horace, he recalled when unburdening his soul during their drive from London, had sworn him to the strictest secrecy on the subject of his activities as an employer of private investigators.

'Well, when I say he was a man of Horace's, of course, I'm sort of speaking loosely. He was a fellow Horace told me about that a friend of his engaged to—to—er—do something or other.'

'And did he do it?'

'Oh, yes, he did it.'

'He is competent, then?'

'Oh, most competent.'

'What is his name?'

'Pott. Claude Pott.'

'Do you know his address?'

'I expect it would be in the book.'

'Then go and speak to him now. Tell him to come down here immediately.'

'Right ho,' said Lord Bosham.

13

THE Duke's decision, on receiving Lord Emsworth's ultimatum regarding the Empress of Blandings, to mobilize his nephew Ricky and plunge immediately into power politics was one which would have occasioned no surprise to anybody acquainted with the militant traditions of his proud family. It was this man's father who had twice cut down the barbed wire fence separating the garden of his villa in the South of France from the local golf links. His grandfather, lunching at his club, had once rubbed the nose of a member of the committee in an unsatisfactory omelette. The Dukes of Dunstable had always been men of a high and haughty spirit, swift to resent affronts and institute reprisals—the last persons in the world, in short, from whom you could hope to withhold pigs with impunity.

His shoulder, thanks to the prompt treatment it had received, had soon ceased to pain him. Waking next morning, he found himself troubled physically by nothing worse than an uncomfortable stiffness. But there was no corresponding improvement in his spiritual condition. Far into the night he had lain brooding on Lord Emsworth's chicanery, and a new day brought no relief. The bitterness still persisted, and with it the grim determination to fight for his rights.

At lunch-time a telegram came from his nephew saying that he was catching the five o'clock train, and at ten o'clock on the following morning, after another wakeful night, he summoned his secretary, Rupert Baxter, and bade him commandeer a car from the castle garage and drive him to the Emsworth Arms. He arrived there at half-past ten precisely, and a red-haired, thickset, freckled young man came bounding across the lounge to greet him.

Between Horace Davenport and his cousin Alaric Gilpin there was nothing in the nature of a family resemblance. Each had inherited his physique from his father, and the father of Ricky Gilpin had been an outsize gentleman with a chest like an all-in-wrestler's. This chest he had handed down to his son, together with enough muscle to have fitted out two sons. Looking at Ricky, you might be a little surprised that he wrote poetry, but you had no difficulty in understanding how he was able to clean up coster-mongers in Covent Garden.

But though externally as intimidating as ever and continuing to give the impression of being a young man with whom no prudent person would walk down a dark alley, Ricky Gilpin on this April morning was feeling a sort of universal benevolence towards all created things. A child could have played with him, and the cat attached to the Emsworth Arms had actually done so. Outwardly tough, inwardly he was a Cheeryble Brother.

There is nothing that so braces a young man in love as a statement on the part of the girl of his dreams, after events have occurred which have made him think her ardour has begun to cool, that he is the only man for her, and that though she may have attended dances in the company of Zulu warriors the latter are to be looked on as the mere playthings of an idle hour. Polly Pott's assurance after that scene at the Bohemian Ball that Horace Davenport was a purely negligible factor in her life had affected Ricky profoundly. And on top of that had come his uncle's telegram.

That telegram, he considered, could mean only one thing. He was about to be afforded the opportunity of placing him under an obliga-tion—of putting him in a position, in short, where he could scarcely fail to do the decent thing in return. The Duke's attitude in the matter of sympathy and support for that onion soup project would, he felt, be very different after he had been helped out of whatever difficulty it was that had caused him to start dispatching S.O.S.'s.

It was a buoyant and optimistic Ricky Gilpin who had caught the five o'clock train to Market Blandings on the previous afternoon, and it was a gay and effervescent Ricky Gilpin who now bounded forward with a hamlike hand outstretched. Only then did he observe that his relative's right arm was in a sling.

'Good Lord, Uncle Alaric,' he cried, in a voice vibrant with dismay and concern, 'have you hurt yourself? I'm so sorry. What a shame! How absolutely rotten! How did it happen?'

The Duke snorted.

'I put my shoulder out, throwing an egg at my secretary.'

Many young men, on receipt of this information, would have said the wrong thing. Ricky's manner, however, was perfect. He placed the blame in the right quarter.

'What the dickens was he doing, making you throw eggs at him?' he demanded indignantly. 'The man must be an ass. You ought to sack him.'

'I'm going to, directly we've had our talk. It was only this morning that I found out he was the feller. Ever since I came here,' explained the Duke, 'there's been a mystery man whistling the "Bonny Bonny Banks of Loch Lomond" day in and day out on the lawn outside my room. Got on my nerves. Beastly song.'

'Foul.'

'I wasn't going to stand it.'

'Quite right.'

'I laid in eggs.'

'Very sensible.'

'To throw at him.'

'Of course.'

'Last night, there he was again with his "You take the high road" and all the rest of it, and I loosed off. And this morning Connie comes to me and says I ought to be ashamed of myself for behaving like that to poor Mr Baxter.'

'What an absolutely imbecile thing to say! Who is this fathead?'

'Emsworth's sister. Lord Emsworth. Blandings Castle. I'm staying there. She's potty, of course.'

'Must be. Any balanced woman would have seen in a second that you had right on your side. It seems to me, Uncle Alaric,' said Ricky, with warmth, 'that you have been subjected to a campaign of deliberate and systematic persecution, and I'm not surprised that you decided to send for me. What do you want me to do? Throw some more eggs at this man Baxter? Say the word, and I start to-day.'

If his arm had not been in a sling, the Duke would have patted his nephew on the back. He was conscious of a keen remorse for having so misjudged him all these years. Ricky Gilpin might have his faults—one looked askance at that habit of his of writing poetry—but his heart was sound.

'No,' he said. 'After to-night there won't be any Baxter to throw eggs at. I sacked him a couple of days ago, and with foolish kindheartedness took him back, but this time it's final. What I've come to talk to you about is this pig.'

'What pig would that be?'

'Emsworth's. And there's another high-handed outrage!'

Ricky was not quite able to follow the trend of his uncle's remarks.

'They've been setting the pig on you?' he asked, groping.

'Emsworth promised to give it to me.'

'Oh, I see.'

'Nothing down in writing, of course, but a gentleman's agreement, thoroughly understood on both sides. And now he says he won't.'

'What!' Ricky had not thought that human nature could sink so low. 'You mean he intends to go back on his sacred word? The man must be a louse of the first water.'

The Duke was now quite certain that he had been all wrong about this splendid young man.

'That's how it strikes you, eh?'

'It is how it would strike any right-thinking person. After all, one has a certain code.'

'Exactly.'

'And one expects other people to live up to it.'

'Quite.'

'So I suppose you want me to pinch this pig for you?' said Ricky.

The Duke gasped. His admiration for his nephew had now reached boiling point. He had been expecting to have to spend long minutes in tedious explanation. It was not often, he felt, that you found in the youth of to-day such lightning intelligence combined with so fine a moral outlook.

'Precisely,' he said. 'When you're dealing with men like Emsworth, you can't be too nice in your methods.'

'I should say not. Anything goes. Well, how do I set about it? I shall require some pointers, you know.'

'Of course, of course, of course. You shall have them. I have been giving this matter a great deal of thought. I lay awake most of last night—'

'What a shame!'

'—and before I went to sleep I had my plan of campaign mapped out to the last detail. I examined it this morning, and it seems to me flawless. Have you a pencil and a piece of paper?'

'Here you are. I'll tear off the top page. It has a few rough notes for a ballade on it.'

'Thanks. Now then,' said the Duke, puffing at his moustache under the strain of artistic composition, 'I'll draw a map for you. Here's the castle. Here's my room. It's got a lawn outside it. Lawn,' he announced, having drawn something that looked like a clumsily-fried egg.

'Lawn,' said Ricky, looking over his shoulder. 'I see.'

'Now along here, round the end of the lawn, curves the drive. It curves past a thick shrubbery—that's at the farther side of the lawn—and then curves past a meadow which adjoins the kitchen garden. In this meadow,' said the Duke, marking the spot with a cross, 'is the sty where the pig resides. You see the strategic significance of this?'

'No,' said Ricky.

'Nor did I,' admitted the Duke handsomely, 'till I was brushing my teeth this morning. Then it suddenly flashed on me.'

'You have an extraordinarily fine brain, Uncle Alaric. I've sometimes thought you would have made a great general.'

'Look at it for yourself. Anybody removing that pig from its sty could dive into the shrubbery with it, thus securing excellent cover, and the only time he would be in danger of being observed would be when he was crossing the lawn to my room. And I propose to select a moment for the operation when there will be no eye-witnesses.'

Ricky blinked.

'I don't quite follow that, Uncle Alaric. You aren't going to keep the animal in your room?'

'That is exactly what I am going to do. It's on the ground floor, with serviceable French windows. What simpler than to bring the pig in through these windows and lodge it in the bathroom?'

'What, and keep it there all night?'

'Who said anything about night? It enters the bathroom at two o'clock in the afternoon. Use your intelligence. At two o'clock in the afternoon everyone's at lunch. Butler, footmen and so forth, all in the dining-room. Maids of all descriptions, their work in the bedrooms completed during the morning, in the kitchen or the housekeeper's room or wherever they go. And the pig-man, I happen to know, off having his dinner. The coast is clear. A thousand men could steal a thousand pigs from the piggeries of Blandings Castle at two o'clock in the afternoon, and defy detection.'

Ricky was impressed. This was unquestionably G.H.Q. stuff. 'Throughout the afternoon,' continued the Duke, 'the pig remains in the bathroom, and continues to do so till nightfall. Then—'

'But, Uncle Alaric, somebody's sure to go into the bathroom before that. Housemaids with clean towels. . . .'

The Duke swelled belligerently.

'I'd like to see anybody go into my bathroom, after I've issued orders that they're not to. I shall stay in my room all through the day, refusing admittance to one and all. I shall have my dinner there on a tray. And if any dashed housemaid thinks she's going to muscle in with clean towels, she'll soon find herself sent off with a flea in her ear. And during dinner you will return. You will have a car waiting here'—he prodded the sketch map with a large thumb—'where the road curves along the bushes at the end of the lawn. You will remove the pig, place it in the car and drive it to my house in Wiltshire. That is the plan I have evolved. Is there anything about it you don't understand?'

'Not a thing, Uncle Alaric!'

'And you think you can do it?'

'On my head, Uncle Alaric. It's in the bag. And may I say, Uncle Alaric, that I don't believe there's another man in England who could have thought all that out as you have done. It's genius.'

'Would you call it that?'

'I certainly would.'

'Perhaps you're right.'

'I know I'm right. It's the most extraordinary exhibition of sheer ice-cold brainwork that I've ever encountered. What did you do in the Great War, Uncle Alaric?'

'Oh, this and that. Work of national importance, you know.'

'I mean, they didn't put you on the Staff?'

'Oh, no. Nothing of that sort.'

'What waste! What criminal waste! Thank God we had a Navy.'

The most delightful atmosphere now prevailed in the lounge of the Emsworth Arms. The Duke said it was extremely kind of Ricky to be so flattering. Ricky said that 'flattering' was surely hardly the word, for he had merely given a frank opinion which would have been the opinion of anybody who recognized genius when they came across it. The Duke said would Ricky have a drink? Ricky, thanking him profusely, said it was a bit early. The Duke asked Ricky if he had been writing anything lately. Ricky said not just lately, but he had a sonnet coming out in the *Poetry Review* next month. Dashed interesting things, sonnets, said the Duke, and asked if Ricky had regular hours for sitting at his desk or did he wait for an inspiration. Ricky said he found the policy that suited him best was to lurk quietly till an idea came along and then jump out and land on the back of its neck with both feet. The Duke said that if somebody offered him a million pounds he himself would be incapable of writing a sonnet. Ricky said Oh, it was just a knack—not to be compared with work that took real, hard thinking, and gave as an instance of such work the planning out of campaigns for stealing pigs. To do that said Ricky, a fellow really had to have something.

There was, in fact, only one word to describe what was in progress in that dim lounge—the word 'Love-feast.' And it was a thousand pities, therefore, that Ricky should have proceeded, as he now did, to destroy the harmony.

Poets, as a class, are business men. Shakespeare describes the poet's eye as rolling in a fine frenzy from heaven to earth, from earth to heaven, and giving to airy nothing a local habitation and a name, but in practice you will find that one corner of that eye is generally glued on the royalty returns. Ricky was no exception. Like all poets, he had his times of dreaminess, but an editor who sent him a cheque for a pound instead of the guinea which had been agreed upon as the price of his latest *morceau* was very little older before he found a sharp letter on his desk or felt his ear burning at what was coming over the telephone wire. And now, having accepted this commission and discussed it in broad outline, he was anxious to get the terms settled.

'By the way, Uncle Alaric,' he said.

'Hey?' said the Duke, who had been interrupted in what promised to be rather a long story about a man he had known in South Africa who had once written a limerick.

Ricky, though feeling that this sort of negotiation would have been better placed in the hands of one's agent, was resolute.

'There's just one small point,' he said. 'Would you rather give me your cheque before I do the job, or after?'

The cosy glow which had been enveloping the Duke became shot through by a sudden chill. It was as if he had been luxuriating in a warm shower-bath, and some hidden hand had turned on the cold tap.

'My cheque? What do you mean, my cheque?'

'For two hundred and fifty pounds.'

The Duke shot back in his chair, and his moustache, foaming upwards as if a gale had struck it, broke like a wave on the stern and rockbound coast of the Dunstable nose. A lesser moustache, under the impact of that quick, agonized expulsion of breath, would have worked loose at the roots. His recent high opinion of his nephew had undergone a sharp revision. Though there were many points on which their souls would not have touched, he was at one with Mr Pott in his dislike of parting with money. Only a man of very exceptional charm could have retained his esteem after asking him for two hundred and fifty pounds.

'What the devil are you talking about?' he cried. Ricky was looking anxious, like one *vis-à-vis* with a tiger and not any too sure that the bars of the cage are to be depended on, but he continued resolute.

'I am taking it for granted that you will now let me have the money to buy that onion soup bar. You remember we discussed it in London a few days ago. At that time five hundred was the price, but the man has since come down to two hundred and fifty, provided the cash is in his hands by the end of the week. The most convenient thing for me, of course, would be if you would write out a cheque now. Then I could mail it to him this morning and he would get it first thing to-morrow. Still, suit yourself about that. Just so long as I get the money by Friday—'

'I never heard anything so dashed absurd in my life!'

'You mean you won't give me two hundred and fifty pounds?'

'Of course I mean I won't give you two hundred and fifty

pounds,' said the Duke, recovering his moustache and starting to chew it. 'Gah!' he said, summing up.

The love-feast was over.

A tense silence fell upon the lounge of the Emsworth Arms.

'I thought I had heard the last of that silly nonsense,' said the Duke, breaking it. 'What on earth do you want with an onion soup bar?'

It was perhaps the memory of how close they had been to one another only a few brief minutes back—two of the boys kidding back and forth about the Sonnet question, as you might say—that decided Ricky to be frank with his uncle. He was conscious as he spoke that frankness is a quality that can be overdone and one which in the present case might lead to disagreeable consequences, but some powerful argument had to be produced if there was to be a change for the better in the other's attitude. And there was just a chance—Mr Pott in his Silver Ring days would probably have estimated it at 100–8—that what he was about to say would touch the man's heart. After all, the toughest specimens were sometimes melted by a tale of true love.

'I want to get married,' he said.

If the Duke's heart was touched, his rugged exterior showed no sign of it. His eyes came out of his head like a prawn's, and once more his moustache foamed up against his breakwater of a nose.

'Married?' he cried. 'What do you mean, married? Don't be an ass.'

Ricky had started the day with a tenderness towards all created things, and this attitude he had hoped to be able to maintain. But he could not help feeling that Providence, in creating his Uncle Alaric, was trying him a little high.

'I never heard such nonsense in my life. How the devil can you afford to get married? You've got about twopence a year which your mother left you, and I don't suppose you make enough out of those sonnets of yours to keep you in cigarettes.'

'That's why I want to buy this onion soup bar.'

'And a nice fool you would look, selling onion soup.'

With a strong effort, Ricky succeeded in making no comment on this. It seemed to him that silence was best. Galling though it was to allow his companion to score debating points, it was better than to close all avenues leading to an appeasement with a blistering repartee. At the moment, moreover, he could not think of a blistering repartee.

The Duke's moustache was rising and falling like seaweed on an ebb tide.

'And a nice fool I'd look, going about trying to explain away a nephew who dished soup out of a tureen. It's been bad enough having to tell my friends you write poetry. "What's that nephew of yours doing these days?"' the Duke proceeded, giving an imitation of an enquiring friend with—for some reason—a falsetto voice. '"The Guards? Diplomatic Service? Reading for the Bar?" "No," I tell them. "He's writing poetry," and there's an awkward silence. And now you want me to have to spread it about that you've become a blasted soup-dispenser. Gah!'

A deep flush had spread itself over Ricky's face. His temper, always a little inclined to be up and doing, had begun to flex its muscles like an acrobat about to do a trick.

'As for this idea of yours of getting married . . . Why do you want to get married? Hey? Why?'

'Oh, just to score off the girl. I dislike her.'

'What!'

'Why do you think I want to get married? Why do people usually want to get married? I want to get married because I've found the most wonderful girl in the world, and I love her.'

'You said you disliked her.'

'I was merely trying to be funny.'

The Duke took in a mouthful of moustache, chewed it for a moment, seemed dissatisfied with the flavour and expelled it again with another forceful puff.

'Who is she?'

'Nobody you know.'

'Well, who's her father?'

'Oh, nobody special.'

A sudden, sinister calm fell upon the Duke, causing his manner to resemble that of a volcano which is holding itself in by sheer will-power.

'You don't need to tell me any more. I see it all. The wench is a dashed outsider.'

'She is not!'

'Don't argue with me. Well, that settles it. Not a penny do you get from me.'

'All right. And not a pig do you get from me.'

'Hey?'

The Duke was taken aback. It was seldom that he found himself in the position of having to deal with open mutiny in the ranks. Indeed, the experience had never happened to him before, and for an instant he was at a loss. Then he recovered himself, and the old imperious glare returned to his bulging eyes.

'Don't take that tone with me, young man.'

'Not one single, solitary porker do you set your hands on,' said Ricky. 'My price for stealing pigs is two hundred and fifty pounds per pig per person, and if you don't wish to meet my terms, the deal is off. If, on the other hand, you consent to pay this absurdly moderate fee for a very difficult and exacting piece of work, I on my side am willing to overlook the offensive things you have said about a girl you ought to think yourself honoured to have the chance of welcoming into the family.'

'Stop talking like a damned fool. She's obviously the scum of the earth. The way a man's nephews get entangled with the dregs of the human species is enough to give one apoplexy. I absolutely forbid you to marry this female crossing-sweeper.'

Ricky drew a deep breath. His face was like a stormy sky, and his eyes bored into his uncle like bradawls.

'Uncle Alaric,' he said, 'your white hairs protect you. You are an old man on the brink of the tomb—'

The Duke started.

'What do you mean, on the brink of the tomb?'

'On the brink of the tomb,' repeated Ricky firmly. 'And I am not going to shove you into it by giving you the slosh on the jaw which you have been asking for with every word you have uttered. But I would just like to say this. You are without exception the worst tick and bounder that ever got fatty degeneration of the heart through half a century of gorging food and swilling wine wrenched from the lips of a starving proletariat. You make me sick. You poison the air. Good-bye, Uncle Alaric,' said Ricky, drawing away rather ostentatiously. 'I think that we had better terminate this interview, or I may become brusque.'

With a parting look of a kind which no nephew should have cast at an uncle, Ricky Gilpin strode to the door and was gone. The Duke remained where he sat. He felt himself for the moment incapable of rising.

It is bad enough for a man of imperious soul to be defied by a beardless boy, and his nephew's determination, in face of his opposition, to cling to the ballet girl or whatever she might be with whom he had become entangled would have been in itself enough to cause a temporary coma. But far more paralysing was the reflection that in alienating Ricky Gilpin he had alienated the one man who could secure the person of the Empress for him. Pig-kidnappers do not grow on every bush.

The Duke of Dunstable's mind was one of those which readily fall into the grip of obsessions, and though reason now strove to convince him that there were prizes in life worth striving for beside the acquisition of a pig, he still felt that only that way lay happiness and contentment. He was a man who wanted what he wanted when he wanted it, and what he wanted now was the Empress of Blandings.

A cold voice, speaking at his side, roused him from his reverie.

'Pardon me, your Grace.'

'Hey? What's the matter?'

Rupert Baxter continued to speak coldly. He was feeling bleakly hostile towards this old image. He disliked people who threw eggs at him. Nor was he the man to allow himself to be softened by any sportsmanlike admiration for a shot which had unquestionably been a very creditable one, showing great accuracy of aim under testing conditions.

'A policeman has just informed me that I must move the car from the inn door.'

'He has, has he? Well, tell him from me that he's a blasted officious jack-in-office.'

'With your Grace's permission, I propose to drive it round the corner.'

The Duke did not speak. A sudden, flaming inspiration had come to him.

'Hey, you,' he said. 'Sit down.'

Rupert Baxter sat down. The Duke eyed him closely, and felt that his inspiration had been sound. The secretary, he observed, had a strong, well-knit frame, admirably suited for the performance of such feats as the removal of pigs from their sties. A moment before, he had been feeling that, Ricky having failed him, he would seek in vain for an assistant to do the rough work. And now, it seemed, he had found him. From this quarter he anticipated no defiance. He was well aware of the high value which Rupert Baxter placed upon his job.

'Ever done any pig-stealing?' he asked.

'I have not,' said Rupert Baxter coldly.

'Well, you start to-day,' said the Duke.

14

IT was at about three o'clock that afternoon that the Market
Blandings station cab (Ed. Robinson, propr.) turned in at the
gates of Blandings Castle and started creakily up the long drive.
And presently Mr Pott, seated in its smelly interior, was setting
eyes for the first time on the historic home of the Earls of
Emsworth.

His emotions, as he did so, differed a good deal from those of
the ordinary visitor in such circumstances. Claude Pott was a real-
ist, and this tended to colour his outlook. Where others, getting
their initial glimpse of this last stronghold of an old order, usually
admired the rolling parkland and the noble trees or thrilled with
romantic awe as they thought of what sights those grey walls must
have seen in the days when knights were bold, he merely felt that
the owner of a place like this must unquestionably have what it
takes to play Persian Monarchs.

Mr Pott, like Ricky, had arrived at Market Blandings in good
spirits. Lord Bosham's telephone call, coming through just as he
was dropping off to sleep, had at first inclined him to peevishness.
But when he discovered that he was talking to a client, and not only
to a client but a client who was inviting him to Blandings Castle,
he had become sunny to a degree. And this sunniness still lingered.

Ever since he had made Lord Emsworth's acquaintance,
Claude Pott had been sighing for a closer intimacy with one whom

his experienced eye had classified immediately as the king of the mugs. There, he had felt, went one literally designed by Nature to be a good man's opponent at Persian Monarchs, and the thought that they had met and parted like ships that pass in the night was very bitter to him. And now he was being asked to come to Lord Emsworth's home and, what was more, was being paid for coming.

Little wonder that life looked rosy to Claude Pott. And he was still suffused with an optimistic glow, when the cab drew up at the front door and he was conducted by Beach, the butler, to the smoking-room, where he found a substantial, pink young man warming a solid trouser-seat in front of a cheerful fire.

'Mr Claude Pott, m'lord,' announced Beach, and withdrew with just that touch of aloofness in his manner which butlers exhibit when they would prefer not to be held responsible for peculiar visitors.

The pink young man, on the other hand, was cordiality itself.

'Hullo, Pott. So here you are, Pott, what? Fine. Splendid. Excellent. Capital. Take a seat, dear old clue-collector. My name's Bosham. I'm by way of being Lord Emsworth's son. To refresh your memory, I'm the bird who rang you up.'

Mr Pott found himself unable to speak. The sight of his employer had stirred him to his depths.

Up till now, he had regarded Lord Emsworth as the most promising claim that any prospector for ore could hope to stake out, but one glance at the latter's son told him that he had been mistaken. This was the mug of a good man's dreams. For a long instant he stood staring silently at Lord Bosham with the same undisguised interest which stout Cortez had once displayed when inspecting the Pacific. It is scarcely exaggerating to say that Mr Pott was feeling as if a new planet had swum into his ken.

Lord Bosham, too, after that opening speech of welcome, had fallen into a thoughtful silence. Like so many men who have done their business on the mail-order system, he was reflecting, now that the parcel had been unwrapped, that it would have been more prudent to have inspected the goods before purchasing. It seemed to him, as it had seemed to Pongo Twistleton on a former occasion, that if this rummy object before him was a detective, his whole ideas about detectives would have to be revised from the bottom up.

'You *are* the right Pott?' he said.

Mr Pott seemed to find a difficulty in helping him out. The question of the rightness or wrongness of Potts appeared to be one on which he was loth to set himself up as an authority.

'The private investigator, I mean. The bloodstain-and-magnifying-glass bloke.'

'My card,' said Pott, who had been through this sort of thing before.

Lord Bosham examined the card, and was convinced.

'Ah,' he said. 'Fine. Well, going back to what I was saying, here you are, what?'

'Yes, sir.'

'I was expecting you yesterday.'

'I'm sorry, Lord B. I'd have come if I could. But the boys at the Yard just wouldn't let me.'

'What yard would that be?'

'Scotland Yard.'

'Oh, ah, of course. You work for them, do you?' said Lord Bosham, feeling that this was more the stuff.

'When they get stuck, they generally call me in,' said Pott nonchalantly. 'This was a particularly tough job.'

'What was it?'

'I can't tell you that,' said Mr Pott, 'my lips being sealed by the Official Secrets Act, of which you have doubtless heard.'

Lord Bosham felt that his misgivings had been unworthy. He remembered now that quite a number of the hottest detectives on his library list had been handicapped—or possibly assisted—by a misleading appearance. Buxton Black in *Three Dead at Mistleigh Court* and Drake Denver in *The Blue Ribbon Murders* were instances that sprang to the mind. The former had looked like a prosperous solicitor, the latter like a pleasure-loving young man about town. What Mr Pott looked like he could not have said on the spur of the moment, but the point was that it didn't matter.

'Well, let's get down to it, shall we?'

'I should be glad to have a brief outline of the position of affairs.'

'Brief?' Lord Bosham looked dubious. 'I'm not so sure about that. As a matter of fact, bloodhound, it's rather a long and intricate story. But I'll cut it as short as I can. Do you know what impostors are?'

'Yes, sir.'

'Well, we've got them in the house. That's the nub of the thing. Three of them—count 'em! Three!—all imposting away like the dickens.'

'H'm.'

'You may well say "H'm." It's a most exasperating state of affairs, and I don't wonder my aunt's upset. Not nice for a woman, feeling that every time she goes to her room to fetch a handkerchief or what not she may find the place littered with bounders rifling her jewel-case.'

'Are these impostors male?'

'Two of them are. The third, in sharp contra-distinction, is female. And speaking of her brings us to what you will probably find it convenient to register in your mind as the Baxter Theory. Do you register things in your mind, or do you use a notebook?'

'Is Baxter an impostor?'

'No,' said Lord Bosham, with the air of one being fair. 'He's a gosh-awful tick with steel-rimmed spectacles, but he's not an impostor. He's the Duke's secretary, and his theory is that these blighters are here not for what they can pouch, but in order to lure the Duke into allowing his nephew to marry the girl. Ingenious, of course, but in my opinion there is nothing to it and you may dismiss it absolutely. They are after the swag. Well, when I tell you that one of them played the confidence trick on me a couple of days ago, you will be able to estimate the sort of hell-hounds they are. Write them down in your notebook, if you use a notebook, as men who will stick at nothing.'

Mr Pott was beginning to feel fogged. If anything emerged clearly from this narrative, it seemed to him that it was the fact that the entire household was fully aware of the moral character of these miscreants. And yet they were apparently being given the run of the house and encouraged to make themselves at home.

'But if you know that these individuals are here with criminal intent—'

'Why don't we have them led off with gyves upon their wrists? My dear old cigar-ash inspector, it's what I'd give my eye-teeth to do, but it can't be done. You wouldn't understand, if I explained for an hour, so just take it at this, that no—what's that word beginning with "o"?'

'What word beginning with "o"?'

'That's what I'm asking you. Opal? Oval? Ha! Got it! Overt. You must just accept the fact that no overt act can be contemplated, because it would lead to consequences which we don't' want led to. When I say "we," I speak principally for my aunt. Personally, I don't care if Baxter loses his job to-morrow.'

Mr Pott gave it up.

'I don't follow you, Lord B.'

'I thought you wouldn't. Still, you've grasped the salient fact that the place is crawling with impostors?'

Mr Pott said he had.

'Then that's all right. That's all you really need to know. Your job is to keep an eye on them. See what I mean? You follow them about watchfully, and if you see them dipping into the till, you shout "Hoy!" and they cheese it. That's simple enough? Fine,' said Lord Bosham. 'Capital. Excellent. Splendid. Then you can start in at once. And, by the way, you'd like something in the nature of a retaining fee, what?'

Mr Pott said he would, and his employer suddenly began to

spray bank-notes like a fountain. It was Lord Bosham's prudent practice, when he attended a rural meeting, as he proposed to do on the morrow, to have plenty of ready cash on his person.

'Call it a tenner?'

'Thank you, Lord B.'

'Here you are, then.'

Mr Pott's eyes were glistening a little, as he trousered the note.

'You've got a lot of money there, Lord B.'

'And I may need it before to-morrow's sun has set. It's the first day of the Bridgeford races, where I usually get skinned to the bone. Very hard to estimate form at these country meetings. You interested in racing?'

'I was at one time a turf commissioner, operating in the Silver Ring.'

'Good Lord! Were you really? My young brother Freddie was a partner in a bookie's firm once. His father-in-law made him give it up and go over to America and peddle dog-biscuits. Absorbing work.'

'Most.'

'I expect you miss it, don't you?'

'I do at times, Lord B.'

'What do you do for amusement these days?'

'I like a quiet little game of cards.'

'So do I.' Lord Bosham regarded this twin soul with a kindly eye. Deep had spoken to deep. 'Only the trouble is, it's a dashed difficult thing for a married man to get. You a married man?'

'A widower, Lord B.'

'I wish you wouldn't keep saying "Lord B." It sounds as if you had been starting to call me something improper and changed your mind. Where was I? Oh, yes. When I'm at home, I don't get a chance of little games of cards. My wife objects.'

'Some wives are like that.'

'All wives are like that. You start out in life a willing, eager

sportsman, ready to take anybody on at anything, and then you
meet a girl and fall in love, and when you come out of the ether you
find not only that you are married but that you have signed on for
a lifetime of bridge at threepence a hundred.'

'Too true,' sighed Mr Pott.

'No more friendly little games with nothing barred except biting
and bottles.'

'Ah!' said Mr Pott.

'We could do far worse,' said Lord Bosham, 'while we're waiting for these impostors to get up steam, than have a friendly little
game now.'

'As your lordship pleases.'

Lord Bosham winced.

'I wish you wouldn't use that expression. It was what counsel for
the defence kept saying to the judge at my breach-of-promise case,
every time the latter ticked him off for talking out of his turn. So
don't do it, if you don't mind.'

'Very good, your lordship.'

'And don't call me "your lordship," either. I hate all this formal-
ity. I like your face . . . well, no, that's overstating it a bit . . . put it
this way, I like your personality, bloodhound, and feel that we shall
be friends. Call me Bosham.'

'Right ho, Bosham.'

'I'll ring for some cards, shall I?'

'Don't bother to do that, Bosham. I have some.'

The sudden appearance of a well-thumbed pack from the
recesses of Mr Pott's costume seemed to interest Lord Bosham.

'Do you always go about with a pack of cards on you?'

"When I travel. I like to play solitaire in the train.'

'Do you play anything else?'

'I am fond of Snap.'

'Yes, Snap's a good game.'

'And Animal Grab.'

'That's not bad, either. But I can tell you something that's better than both.'

'Have—' said Mr Pott.

'Have you—' said Lord Bosham.

'Have you ever—' said Mr Pott.

'Have you ever,' concluded Lord Bosham, 'heard of a game called Persian Monarchs?'

Mr Pott's eyes rolled up to the ceiling, and for an instant he could not speak. His lips moved silently. He may have been praying.

'No,' he said, at length. 'What is it?'

'It's a thing I used to play a good deal at one time,' said Lord Bosham, 'though in recent years I've dropped it a bit. As I say, a married man of the right sort defers to his wife's wishes. If she's around. But now she isn't around, and it would be interesting to see if the old skill still lingers.'

'It's a pretty name,' said Mr Pott, still experiencing some trouble with his vocal chords. 'Is it difficult to learn?'

'I could teach it you in a minute. In its essentials it is not unlike Blind Hooky. Here's the way it goes. You cut a card, if you see what I mean, and the other fellow cuts a card, if you follow me. Then if the card you've cut is higher than the card the other fellow has cut, you win. While, conversely, if the card the other fellow's cut is higher than the card you've cut, he wins.'

He shot an anxious glance at Mr Pott, as if wondering if he had been too abstruse. But Mr Pott appeared to have followed him perfectly.

'I think I see the idea,' he said. 'Anyway, I'll pick it up as I go along. Come on, my noble sportsman. Follow the dictates of your heart and fear nothing. Roll, bowl or pitch! Ladies half-way and all bad nuts returned! If you don't speculate, you can't accumulate.'

'You have a rummy way of expressing yourself,' said Lord Bosham, 'but no doubt your heart is in the right place. Start ho, Pott?'

'Start ho, Bosham!'

• • •

Twilight had begun to fall, the soft mysterious twilight of an English spring evening, when a rotund figure came out of the front door of Blandings Castle and began to walk down the drive. It was Claude Pott, private investigator, on his way to the Emsworth Arms to have a couple. The beer, he knew, was admirable there. And if it should seem strange that one so recently arrived in Market Blandings was in possession of this local knowledge, it may be explained that his first act on alighting from the station cab had been to canvass Ed. Robinson's views on the matter. Like some canny explorer in the wilds, Mr Pott, on coming to a strange place, always made sure of his drink supply before doing anything else.

Ed. Robinson, a perfect encyclopædia on the subject in hand, had been fluent and informative. But while he had spoken with a generous warmth of the Wheatsheaf, the Waggoner's Rest, the Beetle and Wedge, the Stitch in Time, the Blue Cow, the Blue Boar, the Blue Dragon and the Jolly Cricketers, for he was always a man to give credit where credit was due, he had made it quite clear where his heart lay, and it was thither that Mr Pott was now proceeding.

He walked slowly, with bowed head, for he was counting tenpound notes. And it was because his head was bowed that he did not immediately observe the approach of his old friend Lord Ickenham, who was coming with springy steps along the drive towards him. It was only when he heard a surprised voice utter his name that he looked up.

Lord Ickenham had been for an afternoon ramble, in the course of which he had seen many interesting objects of the country-side, but here was one which he had not expected to see, and in his eyes as he saw it there was no welcoming glow. Claude Pott's advent, he could not but feel, added another complication to an already complicated situation. And even a man who holds that complications lend spice to life may legitimately consider that enough is enough.

'Mustard!'

'Coo! Lord I.!'

'What on earth are you doing in the middle of Shropshire, Mustard?'

Mr Pott hesitated. For a moment, it seemed that professional caution was about to cause him to be evasive. Then he decided that so ancient a crony as his companion deserved to enjoy his confidence.

'Well, it's a secret, Lord I., but I know you won't let it go any further. I was sent for.'

'Sent for? By Polly?'

'Polly? She's not here?'

'Yes, she is.'

'I thought she was at your country seat.'

'No, she's at this country seat. Who sent for you?'

'A member of the aristocracy residing at Blandings Castle. Name of Bosham. He rang me up night before last, engaging my professional services. Seems there's impostors in the place, and he wants an eye kept on them.'

For the first time since George, Viscount Bosham, had come into his life, Lord Ickenham began to feel a grudging respect for that young man's intelligence stealing over him. It was clear that he had formed too low an estimate of this adversary. In lulling suspicion as he had done on the station platform by looking pink and letting his mouth hang open, while all the time he was planning to send for detectives, the other had acted, he was forced to confess, with a shrewdness amounting to the snaky.

'Does he, by Jove?' he said, giving his moustache a thoughtful twirl.

'Yes, I'm to take up my residence as an unsuspected guest and keep my eyes skinned to see that they don't walk off with the *objets d'art.*'

'I see. What did he tell you about these impostors? Did he go into details?'

'Not what you would call details. But he told me there was three of them—two *m*, one *f*.'

'Myself, my nephew Pongo and your daughter Polly.'

'Eh?'

'The impostors to whom Bosham refers are—reading from right to left—your daughter Polly, my nephew Pongo and myself.'

'You're pulling my leg, Lord I.'

'No.'

'Well, this beats me.'

'I thought it might. Perhaps I had better explain.'

Before starting to do so, however, Lord Ickenham paused for a moment in thought. He had just remembered that Mr Pott was not an admirer of Ricky Gilpin and did not approve of his daughter's desire to marry that ineligible young man. He also recalled that Polly had said that it was her father's hope that she would succumb to the charms of Horace Davenport. It seemed to him, therefore, that if Mr Pott's sympathy for and co-operation in their little venture was to be secured, it would be necessary to deviate slightly from the actual facts. So he deviated from them. He was a man who was always ready to deviate from facts when the cause was good.

'Polly,' he began, 'is in love with Horace Davenport.'

Mr Pott's eyes widened to saucerlike dimensions, and such was his emotion that he dropped a ten-pound note. Lord Ickenham picked it up, and looked at it with interest.

'Hullo! Somebody been leaving you a fortune, Mustard?'

Mr Pott smirked.

'Tantamount to that, Lord I. Young Bosham—and a nice young fellow he is—was teaching me to play Persian Monarchs.'

'You seem to have cleaned up.'

'I had beginner's luck,' said Mr Pott modestly.

'How much did you get away with?'

'Two hundred and fifty I make it. He had a system which involved doubling up when he lost.'

'That will make a nice little dowry for Polly. Help her to buy her trousseau.'

'Eh?'

'But I shall be coming back to that later. For the moment, I will be putting you *au courant* with the position of affairs at Blandings Castle. The key to the whole business, the thing you have to grasp at the outset, is that Polly is in love with Horace Davenport.'

'When you told me that, you could have knocked me down with a feather. I thought the one she was in love with was young Gilpin.'

'Oh, that? A mere passing flirtation. And even if it had been anything deeper, his behaviour at that Ball would have quenched love's spark.'

'Love's what?'

'Spark.'

'Oh, spark? Yes, that's right, too,' said Mr Pott, beginning to get the whole thing into perspective. 'Cursing and swearing and calling her names, all because she went to a dance with somebody, such as is happening in our midst every day. Seems he'd told her not to go. A nice way to carry on with a girl of spirit. What right has he to get bossy and tell my dear daughter what she can do and what she can't do? Who does he think he is? Ben Bolt?'

'Ben who?'

'Bolt. Bloke with the girl called Sweet-Alice-With-Hair-So-Brown who laughed with delight at his smile and trembled with fear at his frown. Does he expect my dear daughter to do that? Coo! Whoever heard of such a thing? Is this Greece?'

Lord Ickenham weighed the question.

'Not that I know of. Why?'

'I didn't mean Greece,' said Mr Pott, correcting himself with some annoyance. 'I meant Turkey, where women are kept in subjection and daren't call their souls their own. If Polly hadn't got a sweet nature, she'd have hit him with a bottle. But she's her mother's daughter.'

'Whose daughter did you expect her to be?'

'You don't apprehend my meaning, Lord I.,' said Mr Pott patiently. 'I meant that she takes after her dear mother in having a sweet nature. Her dear mother had the loving kindness of an angel or something, and so has Polly. That's what I meant. Her dear mother wouldn't hurt a fly, nor would Polly hurt a fly. I've seen her dear mother take a fly tenderly in her hand—'

Lord Ickenham interrupted. He would have liked to hear all about the late Mrs Pott and the insect kingdom, but time was getting on.

'Suppose we shelve the subject of flies for the moment, shall we, Mustard? Let us get back to Horace Davenport. As I was saying, he is the man Polly has got her eye on. And he loves her just as she loves him. He came down here the day after that dance, and we came the day after, following him.'

'Why?'

'It's quite simple. You know who Horace is, Mustard. The nephew and heir of the Duke of Dunstable.'

'Ah!' said Mr Pott, and seemed about to bare his head.

'And we have come here in the humble capacity of impostors because it is essential, if there is to be a happy ending, that Polly shall fascinate the Duke and set him thinking that she is the ideal girl to marry his nephew and heir. This Duke is tough, Mustard. He nails his collar to the back of his neck to save buying studs. Horace has been scared to death of him since infancy, and would never have the nerve to marry unless he first put up the All Right sign. Before Polly can walk up the aisle with Horace Davenport, the Duke has got to be worked on lovingly and patiently. And I cannot impress it upon you too emphatically that you must keep yourself in the background, Mustard. Polly is supposed to be my daughter.'

In a few well-chosen words Lord Ickenham sketched out the position of affairs. Mr Pott, when he had finished, seemed inclined to be critical.

'Seems a roundabout way of doing things,' he complained. 'Why couldn't she have come here as my daughter?'

'Well, it just happened to work out the other way,' said Lord Ickenham tactfully. 'Too late to do anything about it now. But you understand?'

'Oh, I understand.'

'I knew you would. Nobody has ever disparaged your intelligence, though I have known people to be a bit captious about that habit of yours of always cutting the ace. And that brings me back to what I was saying just now. This money you've taken off Bosham. Kiss it good-bye, Mustard.'

'I don't follow you, Lord I.'

'I want you to give me that money, my dear old friend—'

'What!'

'—and I will hand it over to Polly as her wedding portion. I know, I know,' said Lord Ickenham sympathetically. 'You've no need to tell me that it will be agony. I can see the thought searing your soul. But there comes a time in every man's life, Mustard, when he has to decide whether to do the fine, generous thing or be as the beasts that perish. Put yourself in Polly's place. The child must have her little bit of stuff, to make her feel that she is not going empty-handed to the man she loves. Her pride demands it.'

'Yes, but hoy—!'

'And think how you have always watched over her with a father's tender care. Did she have measles as a child?'

'Yes, she had measles, but that's not the point—'

'It is the point, Mustard. Throw your mind back to the picture of her lying there, flushed and feverish. You would have given all you possessed to help her then. I see your eyes are wet with tears.'

'No, they aren't.'

'Well, they ought to be.'

'I don't approve of a young girl having a lot of money. I wouldn't mind giving her a tenner.'

'Pah!'

'Yes, but two hundred and fifty—'

'A trifle compared with your peace of mind. If you fail her now, you will never have another happy moment. It would be criminal to allow a sensitive girl like Polly to get married without a penny in her pocket. You're a man of the world, Mustard. You know what buying a trousseau means. She will need two of everything. And can you subject her to the degradation of going and touching her future husband for those intimate articles of underclothing which a nice girl shrinks from naming when there are gentlemen present? Compel her to do so, and you leave a scar on her pure soul which the years may hide but which will always be there.'

Mr Pott shuffled his feet.

'She needn't tell him what she wants the money for.'

'For Heaven's sake, Mustard, don't try to evade the issue. Of course, she would have to tell him what she wanted the money for. A girl can't be whispering in the twilight with the man she loves and suddenly introduce a demand for two hundred and fifty pounds as a sort of side issue. She will have to get right down to it and speak of camisoles and slips. Are you going to force her to do that? It will not make very pleasant reading in your Biography, my dear chap. As I see it,' said Lord Ickenham gravely, 'you are standing at the cross-roads, Mustard. This way lies happiness for Polly, peace of mind for you . . . that way, self-scorn for you, misery for her. Which road will you take? I seem to picture your late wife asking herself the same question. I can see her up there now . . . watching . . . waiting . . . all agog . . . wondering if you are going to do the square thing. Don't disappoint her, Mustard.'

Mr Pott continued to shuffle his feet. It was plain that in one sense he was touched, but not so certain that he intended to be in another.

'How about a nice twenty?'

'All or nothing, Mustard, all or nothing. Dash it, it's not as if the money would be lost. You can always take it off Horace at Persian Monarchs after the honeymoon.'

Mr Pott's face lit up with a sudden glow that made it for a moment almost beautiful.

'Coo! That's right, isn't it?'

'It seems to me to solve the whole difficulty.'

'Of course I can. Here you are, Lord I.'

'Thank you, Mustard. I knew you would not fail. And now, if you will excuse me, I will be going and taking a bath. In the course of my rambles I seem to have got quite a lot of Shropshire on my person. The moment I have removed it, I will find Polly and tell her the good news. You will never regret this, my dear fellow.'

In this prediction, Lord Ickenham was wrong. Mr Pott was regretting it rather keenly. He was not the man to see two hundred and fifty pounds pass from his possession without a pang, and already a doubt had begun to creep over him as to whether the transaction could, as his companion had so jauntily suggested, be looked on as merely a temporary loan. Long before he reached Market Blandings he had begun to wonder if he could really rely on Horace Davenport. It takes two to play Persian Monarchs, and it might be that Horace would prove to be one of those odd, unpleasant people who have no fondness for the game. He had sometimes met them on race trains.

However, there is always something stimulating in the doing of a good deed, and Claude Pott, as he entered the private bar of the Emsworth Arms, could have been written down as on the whole a reasonably happy man. He was at any rate sufficiently uplifted to be in a mood for conversation, and it was with the idea of initiating a feast of reason and a flow of soul that he addressed the only other occupant of the bar, a thick-set young man seated at its shadowy end.

'Nice day,' he said.

His fellow-customer turned, revealing himself as Ricky Gilpin.

15

RICKY had come to the private bar in search of relief for his bruised soul, and he could have made no wiser move. Nothing can ever render the shattering of his hopes and the bringing of his dream castles to ruin about his ears really agreeable to a young man, but the beer purveyed by G. Ovens, proprietor of the Emsworth Arms, unquestionably does its best. The Ovens home-brewed is a liquid Pollyanna, for ever pointing out the bright side and indicating silver linings. It slips its little hand in yours, and whispers 'Cheer up!' If King Lear had had a tankard of it handy, we should have had far less of that 'Blow, winds, and crack your cheeks!' stuff.

On Ricky it acted like magic. Hours of brooding over that interview with his Uncle Alaric had brought him into the bar a broken man. At the moment of Mr Pott's entry, he was once more facing the future with something like fortitude.

Money, the beer pointed out, was not everything. 'Look at it this way,' it argued. 'It's absurd to say there aren't a hundred ways by which a smart and enterprising young fellow can get enough money to marry on. The essential thing about this marrying business is not money, but the girl. If the girl's all right, everything's all right. It's true that at the moment you're down among the wines and spirits a bit financially, but what of it? Polly's still there, loving you just as much as ever. And something is sure to turn up.'

And now Mr Pott had turned up. And at the sight of him it was as if the scales had suddenly fallen from Ricky Gilpin's eyes.

Until this moment, the idea of trying to secure the purchase price of the onion soup bar from Claude Pott had never occurred to him. But when you examined it, what an obvious solution it seemed. Mr Pott was Polly's father. He had once rescued Mr Pott from an infuriated mob. That Mr Pott should supply the money to ensure Polly's happiness and repay that old debt was one of the things that one recognizes as dramatically right.

'Why, hullo, Mr Pott!' he said.

The affection in his voice was quite untinged with surprise. A ready explanation of the other's presence here had presented itself. He assumed he had come for the Bridgeford races, of which he had been hearing so much since his arrival in Market Blandings. But if he was not surprised to see Mr Pott, Mr Pott was extremely surprised to see him.

'Young Gilpin! What are you doing here?'

'My uncle sent for me. He's staying at Blandings Castle, a couple of miles down the road. He wanted to see me on a business matter.'

Mr Pott was aghast.

'You mean you're going to the castle?'

'No. My uncle came down here this morning to discuss the thing, but it fell through. I'm leaving for London this evening.'

Mr Pott breathed again. The thought of this young man coming blundering into the delicate web of intrigue at Blandings Castle had appalled him.

'You're here for the races, of course?'

'That's right,' said Mr Pott, grateful for the suggestion.

'Where are you staying?'

'In the vicinity.'

'Have some of this beer. It's good.'

'Thanks,' said Mr Pott. 'Thanks.'

Until his guest had been supplied with the refreshment, Ricky did not speak again. All his life he had been sturdy and independent, and it embarrassed him to have to ask a comparative stranger for money. This diffidence, with an effort, he overcame. Stranger or no stranger, he reminded himself, Claude Pott would most certainly have spent several weeks in hospital but for the prowess of Alaric Gilpin.

'Mr Pott.'

'Sir?'

'There's something I would like a word with you about, Mr Pott.'

'Oh?'

'Are you fond of onion soup?'

'No.'

'Well, lots of people are. And in this connection I want to put a business proposition up to you.'

'Ah?'

Ricky took a sip of G. Ovens's home-brewed. It had not escaped him that his companion's manner was reserved. Mr Pott's eyes seemed always to be covered by a protective layer of film. Now, it was as if another layer had been superimposed.

'I don't know if Polly has happened to mention to you, Mr Pott, that I have the opportunity of buying one of these onion soup bars? You've probably noticed them round Piccadilly Circus way.'

'I seem to remember her talking about it.'

'Enthusiastically, I expect. They coin money. Gold mines, every one of them. The one I'm speaking of belongs to an American friend of mine. He has offered to let me have it for two hundred and fifty pounds.'

The mention of that exact sum caused Mr Pott to wince a little, as if an exposed nerve had been touched. He was still unable to make up his mind about Horace Davenport as a sportsman with a taste for Persian Monarchs. Sometimes he could see him reaching out to cut from the pack. Sometimes he could not. The future was wrapped in mist.

'That's a lot of money,' he said.

Ricky was amazed.

'A lot of money? For a going concern right in the heart of London's onion-soup-drinking belt? He's simply giving it away. But he's homesick for New York, and would like to sail to-morrow, if he could. Well, that's the position. He says I can have this going concern for two hundred and fifty, provided I give him the money by the end of the week. And let me tell you, Mr Pott, the potentialities of that bar are stupendous. I've stood there night after night and watched the bottle-party addicts rolling up with their tongues out. It was like a herd of buffaloes stampeding for a water-hole.'

'Then you'd better give him his two hundred and fifty.'

'I would, if I had it. That's exactly the point I was coming to. Can you lend me the money?'

'No.'

'You can have any interest you like.'

'No, sir. Include me out.'

'But you can't say you haven't got it.'

'I have got it, and more. I've got it in cash in my pocket now, on account of the Clothes Stakes I ran at the Drones Club Tuesday.'

'Then why—?'

Mr Pott drained the remains of his tankard, but the noble brew had no mellowing effect. He might have been full of lemonade.

'I'll tell you why. Because if I give it you, you'll go and talk my dear daughter into marrying you. Polly's easily led. She's like her mother. Anything to make people happy. You'd tell her the tale, and she'd act against her better judgment. And then,' said Mr Pott, 'the bitter awakening.'

'What do you mean, the bitter awakening? Polly loves me.'

'What makes you think that?'

'She told me so.'

'That was just being civil. Love you? Coo! What would she want to love you for? If I were a girl, I wouldn't give you one little rose from my hair.'

'You haven't got any hair.'

'There is no occasion to be personal,' said Mr Pott stiffly. 'And hair's not everything, let me tell you. There's been a lot of fellows that found themselves wishing they'd been more like me in that respect. Absolom, for one. And you're wilfully missing the point of my remarks, which is that if I was a girl and had hair and there was a rose in it and you asked me for that rose, I wouldn't give it to you. Because, after all, young G., what are you? Just a poet. Simply a ruddy ink-slinger, that's you. Polly can do better.'

'I'm sorry you dislike me—'

'It's not disliking. It's disapproving of in the capacity of a suitor for my dear daughter's hand. There's nothing fundamentally wrong with you, young G.—I'll admit you've got a sweet left hook—but you aren't an om seerioo. A French term,' explained Mr Pott, 'meaning a fellow that's going to get on in the world and be able to support a sweet girl as a sweet girl ought to be supported. If you were an om seerioo, you wouldn't be wasting your time messing about writing poetry.'

Ricky was telling himself that he must be calm. But calmness was a thing that did not come readily to him in trying circumstances.

'My dear daughter ought to marry a man of substance. This Horace Davenport, now. . . .'

'Horace!'

'It's all very well to say "Horace!" in that tone of voice. He's the nephew of a Duke,' said Mr Pott reverently.

'Well, if we're being snobs, so am I the nephew of a Duke.'

'Ah, but your Ma hadn't the stuff, and Horace's Pa had. That's where the difference comes in. The way I got the story, your Ma married beneath her. Too late to regret it now, of course.'

'The thing I regret is that you won't listen to reason.'

'I haven't heard any yet.'

There was a silence. Mr Pott would have liked another tankard of home-brew, but the way things seemed to be shaping, it appeared probable that he would have to pay for it himself.

'Mr Pott,' said Ricky, 'I saved your life once.'

'And on that last awful day when we all have to render account it will be duly chalked up to you on the credit side. Though, as a matter of fact,' said Mr Pott nonchalantly, 'I've no doubt I could have handled those fellows all right myself.'

The muscles inherited from his robust father stood out on Ricky's cheek-bones.

'I hope you will have many more opportunities of doing so,' he said.

Mr Pott seemed wounded.

'That's a nasty thing to say.'

'It was meant to be. Because,' said Ricky, becoming frank, 'if ever there was a pot-bellied little human louse who needed to have the stuffing kicked out of him and his remains jumped on by strong men in hobnailed boots, it is you, Mr Pott. The next time I see a mob in the street setting on you, I shall offer to hold their coats and stand by and cheer.'

Mr Pott rose.

'Ho! If that's the sort of nasty mind you have, I don't wonder she prefers Horace.'

'May I ask where you got the idea that she prefers Horace?'

'I got it by seeing her that night he took her to the Ball. There was a look in her eyes that made me think right away that she was feeling he was her Prince Charming. And this has since been confirmed by a reliable source.'

Ricky laughed.

'Would it interest you to know,' he said, 'that Polly has promised me that she will never see Horace again?'

'It wouldn't interest me in the slightest degree,' retorted Mr Pott. 'Because I happen to know that she's seeing him regular.'

Whether it was excusable in the circumstances for Ricky at this point to tell Mr Pott that he was lying in his teeth, and that only the fact of his being an undersized little squirt whom no decent man would bring himself to touch with a barge pole saved him from having his neck wrung, is open to debate. Mr Pott, who thought not, drew himself up stiffly.

'Young G.,' he said, 'I will wish you a very good afternoon. After that crack, I must decline to hold any association with you. There is such a thing as going too far, and you have gone it. I will take my refreshment elsewhere.'

He went off to the Jolly Cricketers to do so, and for some moments Ricky continued to sit over his tankard. Now that the first spasm of indignation had spent itself, he was feeling more amused than wrathful. The lie had been so clumsy, so easily seen through. He blamed himself for ever having allowed it to annoy him.

If there was one thing certain in an uncertain world, it was that Polly was as straight as a die. How she came to be so with a father like that constituted one of the great mysteries, but there it was. The thought of Polly cheating was inconceivable.

With a glowing heart, Ricky Gilpin rose and walked down the passage that led to the back door of the inn. He felt he wanted air. After having had Mr Pott in it, the bar struck him as a little close.

The garden of the Emsworth Arms runs down to the river, and is a pleasant, scented place on a spring evening. Ricky wished that he could linger there, but he was intending to catch the late after-noon express back to London, and he still had his packing to do. He turned regretfully, and he had just reached the inn, when from somewhere in its interior there came a disembodied voice.

'Hullo,' it was saying. 'Hullo.'

Ricky halted, amazed. There was only one man in the world who said 'Hullo' with just that lilting bleat.

'Hullo . . . Polly?'

Ricky Gilpin's heart seemed to leap straight up into the air twid-dling its feet, like a Russian dancer. He had sometimes wondered how fellows in the electric chair must feel when the authorities turned on the juice. Now he knew.

'Hullo? Polly? Polly, old pet, this is Horace. Yes, I know. Never mind all that. I've got to see you immediately. Of course it's impor-tant. Matter of life and death. So drop everything like the sweet angel you are, and come along. Meet me at the castle gate, out in the road. I don't want anybody to see us. Eh? What? Yes. All right. I've got my car. I'll be there before you are.'

A red-haired bombshell burst into the lounge of the Emsworth Arms. There, in the corner near the window, stood the telephone, but the speaker had gone. And from outside in the street there came the sound of a car.

Ricky Gilpin leaped to the door. A rakish Bingley was moving off up the High Street, a long, thin, familiar figure at its wheel.

For an instant, he contemplated shouting. Then, perceiving that there was a better way, he ran, sprang and flung himself on to the Bingley's stern.

Horace Davenport, all unconscious that he had taken aboard a stowaway, pressed his foot on the accelerator and the Bingley gathered speed.

Lord Ickenham, much refreshed after his bath, had left his room, and begun to search through Blandings Castle for Polly. Unable to find her, he sought information from Pongo, whom he discovered in the smoking-room staring silently at nothing. The burden of life was weighing on Pongo Twistleton a good deal just now.

'Ah, my boy. Seen Polly anywhere?'

Pongo roused himself from his thoughts.

'Yes, I saw her . . .'

He broke off. His eyes had started from their sockets. He had just observed what it was that the other was holding in his hand.

'My gosh! Money?'

'Yes.'

'How much?'

'Two hundred and fifty pounds.'

'Oh, my golly! Where did you get it?'

'From—you will scarcely credit this—Mustard Pott.'

'What!'

'Yes. Mustard, it will astound you to hear, has just arrived at the castle in his professional capacity, sent for by Bosham to watch our movements. I seem to have dismissed Bosham as a force too lightly. He appears to have seen through my well-meant attempt to convince him that I was not the man who got away with his wallet and to have decided to seek assistance. A dashed deep young man. He took me in completely. What led him to select Mustard from London's myriad sleuths is more than I can tell you. I can only suppose that he must have heard of him from Horace. At any rate, he's here, and he has not been idle. Within half an hour of his arrival, he took this nice round sum off Bosham at Persian Monarchs, and I, after wrestling with him as the angel wrestled with Jacob, have taken it off him.'

Pongo was quivering in every limb.

'But this is stupendous! This is definitely the happy ending, with the maker's name woven into every yard. I had a feeling all along that you would pull it off sooner or later. Good old Uncle Fred! You stand alone. There is none like you, none. Gimme!'

Lord Ickenham perceived that his nephew was labouring under a misapprehension. Regretfully he put him straight.

'Alas, my boy, this is not for you.'

'What do you mean?'

'It is earmarked for Polly. It is the purchase price of that onion soup bar, which will enable her to marry the man she loves. I'm sorry. I can appreciate what a blow this must be for you. All I can say by way of apology is that her need is greater than yours.'

There was the right stuff in Pongo Twistleton. It had seemed to him for an instant that the world was tumbling about him in rending chaos, but already his finer self had begun to take command of things. Yes, he felt—yes, it was better thus. Agony though it was to think that he was not going to get his hooks on the boodle, it was a not unpleasant agony. His great love demanded some such sacrifice.

'I see what you mean,' he said. 'Yes, something in that.'

'Where is she?'

'I think she's gone to Market Blandings.'

'What would she be going to Market Blandings for?'

'Ah, there you have me. But I was on the terrace having a cigarette not long ago and she came out, hatted and booted, and gave the impression, when questioned, that that was where she was heading.'

'Well, go after her and bring the sunlight into her life.'

The idea did not seem immediately attractive to Pongo.

'It's four miles there and back, you know.'

'Well, you're young and strong.'

'Why don't you go?'

'Because Age has its privileges, my boy. My ramble having left me a little drowsy, I propose to snatch a few winks of sleep in my room. I often say there is nothing so pleasant as a nap in front of a crackling fire in a country-house bedroom. Off you go.'

Pongo did not set out with enthusiasm, but he set out, and Lord Ickenham made his way to his room. The fire was bright, the armchair soft, and the thought of his nephew trudging four miles along the high road curiously soothing. It was not long before the stillness was broken by a faint, musical noise like a kettle singing on the hob.

But these good things do not last. A little sleep, a little slumber, a little folding of the hands in sleep, and along comes somebody shaking us by the shoulder.

Lord Ickenham, sitting up, found that the person shaking his shoulder was Horace Davenport.

16

HE rose courteously. To say that the sight of this unexpected apparition had left him feeling completely at his ease would be to present the facts incorrectly. For an instant, indeed, his emotions had been practically identical with those of the heroine of a pantomime when the Demon King suddenly pops up out of a trap at her elbow in a cascade of red fire. But his nervous system was under excellent control, and there was nothing in his manner to indicate how deeply he had been stirred.

'Ah, good evening, good evening!' he said. 'Mr Davenport, is it not? Delighted to see you. But what are we doing here? I thought we had decided to go and take a rest cure at Bournemouth. Did something happen to cause us to change our mind?'

'Hoy!' said Horace.

He had raised a protesting hand. His eyes were the eyes of one who has passed through the furnace, and he was vibrating gently, as if he had swallowed a small auxiliary engine.

'I beg your pardon?'

'That "we" stuff. Cut it out. Not in the mood.'

Something seemed to tell Lord Ickenham that this was not the delightfully receptive Horace Davenport of their previous meeting, but he persevered.

'My dear fellow, of course. I'm sorry if it annoyed you. Just one of those professional mannerisms one slips into. Most of my patients seem to find it soothing.'

'They do, do they? You and your bally patients!'

The undisguised bitterness with which the young man spoke these words confirmed Lord Ickenham in his view that there had been a hitch somewhere. However, he continued to do his best.

'I beg your pardon?'

'Don't keep begging my pardon. Though, my gosh,' said Horace shrilly, 'you jolly well ought to. Pulling my leg like that. It may interest you to learn that I know all.'

'Indeed?'

'Yes. You're not Sir Roderick Glossop.'

Lord Ickenham raised his eyebrows.

'That is a very odd statement to make. I confess I do not like the sound of it. It suggests a feverishness. Tell me, do we—'

'Will you stop it! Listen. You're Valerie's Uncle Fred. I've met someone who knows Glossop, and have had him described to me in pitiless detail.'

Lord Ickenham was a man who could accept the inevitable. He might not like it, but he could accept it.

'In that case, as you suggest, it is perhaps hardly worth while to try to keep up the innocent deception. Yes, my dear fellow, you are perfectly right. I am Valerie's Uncle Fred.'

'And it was Pongo Twistleton and Polly Pott that I met in the hall that time. It wasn't a—what's the word? A nice thing that was you three blisters did to me, making me think I was off my rocker. I realize now that there was absolutely nothing wrong with me at all.'

'No doubt you are feeling much relieved.'

'What I'm feeling, if you want to know, is considerably incensed and pretty dashed shirty.'

'Yes, I can appreciate your emotion, and I can only say that I am sorry. It went to my heart to do it, but it was military necessity.

You were in the way, and had to be removed by such means as lay to hand. Let me explain what we are all doing, visiting Blandings Castle incognito like this. Believe me, it was no idle whim that brought us here. We are hoping that Polly may succeed in winning the Duke's heart, without him knowing who she is, thus paving the way for her marriage to your cousin Ricky. You know that pumpkin-headed old man's views on class distinctions. If Ricky told him that he wanted to marry a girl of dubious origin—and I defy anyone to think of an origin more dubious than dear old Mustard—he would forbid the banns without hesitation. We are trying to put something over by stealth, and we could not trust your open, honest nature not to give the show away.'

Horace's just wrath gave way momentarily to bewilderment.

'But I thought Ricky and Polly had split up.'

'Far from it. It is true that after that affair at the Ball there was a temporary rift, but Polly's womanly tact smoothed the thing over. He is once more one hundred per cent the devout lover.'

'Then why does he want to murder me?'

'He doesn't.'

'He does, I tell you.'

'You're thinking of someone else.'

'I'm not thinking of someone else. I found him on the back of my car just now, and he distinctly stated that he was going to tear me into little shreds and strew me over the local pasture land.'

'On the back of your car, did you say?'

'Yes. As I climbed down from the front, he climbed down from the back and made a dive at me.'

'I appear not to be abreast of the Stop Press situation,' said Lord Ickenham. 'You had better tell me your story—one, I can see, that promises to be fraught with interest.'

For the first time, Horace brightened. It was plain that some pleasing thought had occurred to him.

'It's going to interest you, all right. Yes, by Jove, you're going to sit up and take notice, believe me. A pretty nasty spot you're in. The curse has come upon me, said the Lady of Shalott. What, what?'

Lord Ickenham found him obscure.

'You speak in riddles, my boy. A little less of the Delphic Oracle. Let your Yea be Yea and your Nay be Nay.'

'All right. If you want the thing in a nutshell, then, Valerie is in full possession of the facts concerning your goings-on, and is coming here to-morrow at the latest.'

Here was something Lord Ickenham had not anticipated. And though it was his habit to present on all occasions an impassive front to the blows of Fate, he started perceptibly, and for an instant his jaunty moustache seemed to droop.

'Valerie? Coming here?'

'I thought that would touch you up.'

'Not at all. I am always glad to see my dear niece, always. You have run into her again, then?'

Horace's manner became more friendly. He was still resentful of the trick that had been played upon him and by no means inclined to accept as an adequate excuse for it the plea of military necessity, but he found it impossible not to admire this iron man.

'I met her at a restaurant last night. I had gone there in pursuance of that idea we discussed of having the binge of a lifetime before tooling off to Bournemouth. You remember agreeing with me that it would be a good thing to go on a binge?'

'Ah, yes. So I did.'

'You also recommended me to steep myself in a beverage called May Queen.'

'That's right. The binge-goer's best friend. Did you like it?'

'Well, yes and no. Peculiar stuff. For a while it makes you feel as if you were sitting on top of the world. But, as you progress, a great sorrow starts to fill you. Quart One—fine. Joy reigning supreme and blue birds singing their little hearts out. The moment you're well into Quart Two, however, the whole situation alters. You find yourself brooding on what a rotten world this is and what a foul time you're having in it. The outlook darkens. Tears spring to the eyes. Everything seems sad and hopeless.'

'This is most interesting. In my day, I never went into the thing as thoroughly as you appear to have done. One-Pint Ickenham, they used to call me.'

'And I had just reached this second stage, when who should come in but Valerie, accompanied by an elderly female who looked as if she might have something to do with breeding Pekinese. They sat down, and the next thing I knew, I had squashed in between them and was telling Valerie how miserable I was.'

'This must have interested her companion.'

'Oh, it did. She seemed absorbed. A decent old bird, at that. I owe everything to her. As soon as she got the hang of the situation, she started advocating my cause in the most sporting fashion. Valerie, I should mention, wasn't frightfully sympathetic at the outset. Her manner was cold and proud, and she kept telling me to take my elbow out of her lap. But this fine old geezer soon altered all that. It seemed that there had been a similar tragedy in her own life, and she told us all about it.'

'You revealed the facts about your broken engagement to this Pekinese-breeder, then?'

'Oh, rather. Right away. There's something about this May Queen of yours that seems to break down one's reserve, if you know what I mean. And when I had given her a full synopsis, she related her story. Something to do with once long ago loving a bloke dearly and quarrelling with him about something and him turning on his heel and going to the Federated Malay States and marrying the widow of a rubber planter, all because she had been too proud to speak the little word that would have fixed everything. And years afterwards there arrived a simple posy of white violets, together with a slip of paper bearing the words: "It might have been."'

'Moving.'

'Very. I cried buckets. She then leaned across me and told Valerie that the quality of mercy was not strained but dropped like something or other on something I didn't catch. I couldn't quite follow it all, but the effects were excellent. I saw Valerie's eye soften, and a tear stole into it. The next moment, we were locked in a close embrace.'

'And then?'

'Well, the long evening wore on, so to speak. The female Pekinese told us more about her Federated Malay Stater, and I went on crying, and Valerie started crying, too, and presently the Peke was also weeping freely, and it was at about this time that the head waiter came up and suggested that we should take our custom elsewhere. So we all went back to my flat and had eggs and bacon. And it was while I was doling out the dishfuls that I suddenly remembered that I was a loony and so had no right to marry a sweet girl. I mentioned this to Valerie, and then the whole story came out.'

'I see.'

'The Peke, it appeared, knew Sir Roderick Glossop well, her cousin Lionel having been treated by him for some form of loopiness, and her description of the man made it clear that you couldn't be him. So it seemed pretty obvious that you must be you.'

'Remorseless reasoning.'

'And when I speculated as to your motives for leading me up the garden path, Valerie snorted a bit and said it was plain that you were up to some kind of hell in this ancient pile and had wanted to get me out of the way. Which you admit to have been the case. She's a most intelligent girl.'

'Most. I have sometimes thought that it would be an admirable thing if she were to choke.'

'And the outcome of the whole affair was that she went down to Ickenham this morning, just to make sure you weren't on the premises—her intention, having ascertained this, being to breeze along here and expose you to one and all. And I saw that what I had got to do was make an early start and get here before she did. Because you see, though all is forgiven and forgotten between us, so to speak, and love has, as it were, come into its own again, there is just one small catch, that she seems a bit curious about Polly.'

'You mean about your relations with her?'

'Yes. She said in rather a sinister way that she supposed Polly was a very pretty girl, and my statement to the effect that she was a plain little thing whom I had taken to the Ball purely out of pity was none too cordially received. Her manner struck me as that of a girl who intended to investigate further.'

'So your desire to have her arrive here and meet Polly and see what she really looks like is slight?'

'Almost nil,' confessed Horace frankly. 'As soon as I could manage it, therefore, I drove here in the car to tell Polly to clear out while there was yet time.'

'Very shrewed.'

'I 'phoned her from the Emsworth Arms, arranging a meeting at the castle gate. I then hopped into the car and went there. And conceive my astonishment when, alighting from the prow, I observed Ricky alighting from the stern.'

'It must have given you a start.'

'It did. A flying start. I was off like a jack rabbit. And after I had gone about three-quarters of a mile, touching the ground perhaps twice in the process, I found myself outside the castle and stopped and reviewed the situation. And I saw that having missed Polly, the best thing I could do was to get hold of you. I knew which your room was, of course, and I sneaked up with the idea of waiting till you came to dress for dinner. That I should have found you first crack out of the box like this is the one bit of goose I have experienced in the course of a sticky evening.'

'You wish me, I take it, to find Polly and tell her not to be among those present when Valerie arrives?'

'Exactly.'

'She shall be removed. Indeed, I rather think that none of us will be here to welcome the dear girl. I remember telling my nephew Pongo not long ago that the Twistletons do not clear out, but there are exceptions to the rule. If Valerie were in a position to report to G.H.Q. that she had found me at Blandings Castle posing as a brain specialist, the consequences might well be such as would stagger humanity. But if I am gone before she gets here, it seems to me that I am up against nothing that stout denial will not cover. So rest assured, my boy, that I will lose no time in collecting my young associates, and you shall drive us back to London in your car. Unlike the Arabs, who paused to fold their tents before silently stealing away, we will not even stop to pack.'

'But how can I get at the car? I left Ricky standing guard over it.'

'I think I shall be able to adjust your little trouble with Ricky satisfactorily. My first move shall be to go and explain things to him. I would suggest that you remain here till my return. If you prefer to hide in the cupboard in case your uncle happens to look in, by all means do so. Make yourself quite at home.'

The evening was cool and fragrant and a soft wind whispered in the trees, as Lord Ickenham made his way down the drive. Despite the peril that loomed, his mood was serene. He was sorry to be obliged to leave Blandings Castle, which he had found a pleasant spot full of interesting personalities, but he could see that the time had come to move on. And, after all, he reflected, his work was done. Polly had her money, Pongo had been promised his, and the Empress was safe from the Duke's clutching hand. There was really, he felt, nothing to keep him. All he had to do now was to speak a few soothing words to this explosive young poet of Polly's, and an agreeable episode might be considered closed.

He was about half-way to the castle gate when he heard the

sound of footsteps. A small figure was coming towards him through the dusk.

'Polly?'

'Hullo.'

It seemed to Lord Ickenham that there was a flat note in the girl's usually musical voice, and as he halted beside her he detected in her bearing a listlessness which struck him as odd.

'What's the matter?'

'Nothing.'

'Don't be evasive, child. The visibility may not be good, but I can see that you are drooping like a tired flower. Your depression is almost Pongoesque. Come on, now, what has happened?'

'Oh, Uncle Fred!'

'Hullo! Here, I say! Dash it, what's all this about?'

It was some moments later that Polly drew away, dabbing at her eyes.

'I'm sorry. I've been making a fool of myself.'

'Nothing of the kind. A good cry is what we all want at times. I shall recommend it to Pongo. I think I can guess what is wrong. I take it that you have been having a talk with your young man. You went to meet Horace at the gate, and found Ricky. And from your manner, I gather that the plugugly rather than the poet was uppermost in him.'

'He was awful. Not that you can blame him.'

'Of course not, bless his heart, the little pet.'

'I mean, I can understand how he must have been feeling. I had promised I would never see Horace again, and there I was, sneaking off to him.'

'Don't be so infernally broadminded, child. Why the devil shouldn't you see Horace as often as you like? What right has this sweet-singing baboon to tell you whom you shall see and whom you shan't see? What happened?'

'He raved and yelled at me. He said everything was over.'

'So he did a couple of days ago, after that Ball. But you smoothed him down.'

'I couldn't this time.'

'Did you try?'

'No. I lost my temper, and started being as beastly as he was.'

'Good girl.'

'It was horrible. He hated me.'

'Do you hate him?'

'Of course I don't.'

'You mean that in spite of everything you love him still?'

'Of course I do.'

'Women are amazing. Well, I'll soon fix things. I'm on my way to interview him now.'

'It won't be any use.'

'That's what they said to Columbus. Don't you worry, my dear. I can handle this. I know my potentialities, and sometimes they absolutely stun me. Are there no limits, I ask myself, to the powers of this wonder-man? I am still completely unable to comprehend why you should want the chap, but if you do you must have him.'

He walked on, and coming presently to the gate found the Bingley standing at the roadside. Pacing up and down in its vicinity like a tiger at feeding-time he perceived a sturdy figure.

'Mr Gilpin, I presume?' he said.

17

So many disturbing things had happened to Ricky Gilpin in the course of this April day that it is scarcely to be wondered at that his mood was not sunny. In a world congested with dukes and Potts and Horace Davenports and faithless girls, it is only an exceptionally philosophical man who can preserve his amiability unimpaired, and Ricky had never been that. He scowled darkly. He did not know who this elegant stranger was, but he was prepared to dislike him.

'Who are you?'

'My name is Ickenham.'

'Oh?'

'I see that it is familiar. No doubt Polly has spoken of me?'

'Yes.'

'Then in reciprocal spirit I will now speak of Polly.'

A quiver passed through Ricky Gilpin's solid body.

'No, you won't. I've finished with her.'

'Don't say that.'

'I do say that.'

Lord Ickenham sighed.

'Youth, Youth! How it flings away its happiness like a heedless child,' he said, and, pausing for a moment to think what heedless children flung away, added 'blowing bubbles and throwing them idly into the sunlit air. Too bad, too bad. Shall I tell you a little story, Mr Gilpin?'

'No.'

'Years ago'—it would have taken a better man than Ricky to stop Lord Ickenham telling stories—'I loved a girl.'

'You haven't by any chance seen Horace Davenport, have you?'

'Loved her dearly.'

'If you do, tell him it's no use his skulking away. I intend to wait here for weeks, if necessary.'

'We quarrelled over some trivial matter. Bitter recriminations ensued. And finally she swept out of the room and married a rubber planter.'

'Sooner or later he will have to present himself and be torn into little pieces.'

'And years afterwards there arrived a simple posy of white violets, together with a slip of paper bearing the words: "It might have been." Tragic, eh? If you will allow an old man to advise you, Mr Gilpin—an old man who has suffered—an old man who threw away his happiness just because he was too proud to speak the little word that—'

There was a metallic clang. Ricky Gilpin appeared to have kicked the fender of the car.

'Listen,' he said. 'I may as well tell you at once that you're wasting your time. I know Polly sent you to try to talk me round—'

'Sent me to talk you round? My dear fellow! You little know that proud girl.'

Lord Ickenham paused. Ricky had moved into the golden pool spread by the headlights, and for the first time he was able to see him as more than an indistinct figure in the dusk.

'Tell me,' he said, 'was your father a chap named Billy Gilpin? In some Irish regiment?'

'His name was William, and he was in the Connaught Rangers. Why?'

'I thought so. You're the living spit of him. Well, now I know that, I'm not so surprised that you should have been behaving in this idiotic way. I used to know your father, and I wish I had five pounds for every time I've sat on his head in bars and restaurants in a painstaking effort to make him see reason. Of all the fly-off-the-handle asses that ever went about with a chip on the shoulder, taking offence at the merest trifles—'

'We won't discuss my father. And if you're suggesting that it's the merest trifle, the girl who's supposed to love you going and hob-nobbing with Horace Davenport after she had promised—'

'But, my dear boy, don't you understand that it was precisely because she loved you that she did hobnob with Horace? . . . Let me explain, and if when I have finished you are not bathed in shame and remorse, you must be dead to all human feeling. In the first place, nothing but her love for you could have dragged her to that Ball at the Albert Hall. You don't suppose a girl enjoys being seen in public with a fellow wearing the costume of a Zulu warrior and tortoiseshell-rimmed spectacles, do you? Polly went to that Ball because she was prepared to endure physical and spiritual agony in order to further your interest. It was her intention to catch Horace in mellow mood and plead with him to advance you the sum which you require for that onion soup bar of yours.'

'What!'

'For weeks she had been sedulously sweetening him by giving him dancing lessons, and that night was to have marked the cul-mination of the enterprise. She was hoping to be able to come to you and tell you that the weary waiting was over and that you and she could get married and live happy ever after, dishing out onion soup to the blotto survivors of bottle-parties. By your headstrong conduct you ruined her plans that night. A girl can't try to bor-row money from a man while he's being taken off to Marlborough Street Police Station. Her instinct tells her that he will not be in the mood. So she had to wait for another opportunity. Learning that Horace was expected here, she came, too. She met him. She got the money—'

'She—what?'

'Certainly. It's in her possession now. She was bringing it to you.'

'But how did she know I was here?'

For perhaps a third of a split second this question had Lord Ickenham in difficulties.

'Woman's intuition,' he suggested.

'But—'

'Well, there it is,' said Lord Ickenham bluffly. 'What does it matter how she knew you were here? Suffice it that she did know, and she came running to you with the money in her hand like a child about to show some cherished treasure. And you—what did you do? You behaved like a cad and a scoundrel. I'm not surprised that she feels she has had a lucky escape.'

'Oh, my gosh! Does she?'

'That is what she was saying when I saw her just now. And I don't blame her. There can be no love without trust, and a pretty exhibition of trustfulness you gave, did you not?'

To Horace Davenport, could he have seen it at this moment, Ricky Gilpin's face would have come as a revelation. He would scarcely have been able to believe that those incandescent eyes had it in them to blink so sheepishly, or that that iron jaw could have sagged so like a poorly set blancmange. The future Onion Soup King was exhibiting all the symptoms of one who has been struck on the back of the head with a sock full of wet sand.

'I've made a fool of myself,' he said, and his voice was like the earliest pipe of half-awakened birds.

'You have.'

'I've mucked things up properly.'

'I'm glad you realize it.'

'Where is Polly? I must see her.'

'I wouldn't advise it. You don't appear to understand what it means, behaving to a girl of spirit as you have behaved to Polly. She's furious with you. It would be madness to see her. There is only one thing you can do. When are you returning to London?'

'I had meant to catch the evening train.'

'Do so. Polly will be back at her home shortly. As soon as she arrives, go and buy her chocolates—lots of chocolates—and send them round with a grovelling note.'

'I will.'

'You might then plead for an interview. And when I say plead, I mean plead.'

'Of course.'

'If you display a sufficiently humble and contrite spirit, I see no reason for you to despair. She was fond of you once, and it may be that she will grow fond of you again. I will talk to her and do what I can for you.'

'That's awfully kind of you.'

'Not at all. I would like to do a good turn for the son of an old friend. Good evening, Gilpin, my boy, and remember . . . chocolates—humble, remorseful chocolates—and plenty of them.'

It was perhaps fortunate that Pongo Twistleton was not present when his uncle, rejoining Polly, concluded the recital of what had passed between Ricky Gilpin and himself, for there ensued an emotional scene which would have racked him to the foundations of his being.

'Well, there you are,' said Lord Ickenham, at length. 'That is how matters stand, and all you have to do is sit tight and reap the strategic advantages. I'm glad I told him to send you chocolates. I don't suppose a rugged he-man like that would ever dream of giving a girl chocolates in the ordinary course of things. He struck me as a fellow lacking in the softer social graces.'

'But why wouldn't you let him see me?'

'My dear child, it would have undone all the good work I had accomplished. You would have flung yourself into his arms, and he would have gone on thinking he was the boss. As it is, you have got that young man just where you want him. You will accept his chocolates with a cool reserve which will commit you to nothing, and eventually, after he has been running round in circles for some weeks, dashing into his tailors' from time to time for a new suit of sackcloth and ashes and losing pounds in weight through mental anguish, you will forgive him—on the strict understanding that this sort of thing must never occur again. It doesn't do to let that dominant male type of chap think things are too easy.'

Polly frowned. In a world scented with flowers and full of soft music, these sentiments jarred upon her.

'I don't see why it's got to be a sort of fight.'

'Well, it has. Marriage is a battlefield, not a bed of roses. Who said that? It sounds too good to be my own. Not that I don't think of some extraordinarily good things, generally in my bath.'

'I love Ricky.'

'And very nice, too. But the only way of ensuring a happy married life is to get it thoroughly clear at the outset who is going to skipper the team. My own dear wife settled the point during the honeymoon, and ours has been an ideal union.'

Polly halted abruptly.

'It's all nonsense. I'm going to see him.'

'My dear, don't.'

'Yes.'

'You'll regret it.'

'I won't.'

'Think of all the trouble I've taken.'

'I do, and I can't tell you how grateful I am, Uncle Fred. You've been wonderful. You've picked me up out of the mud and changed the whole world for me. But I can't treat Ricky like that. I'd hate myself. I don't care if he does go on thinking he's the boss. So he is, and I like it!'

Lord Ickenham sighed.

'Very well, if that's the way you feel. "His fair large front and eye sublime declared Absolute rule." If that's the sort of thing you want, I suppose it's no use arguing. If you are resolved to chuck away a heaven-sent opportunity of putting this young man in his place, go ahead, my dear, and God bless you. But you can't see him now. He has gone to catch his train. You must wait till to-morrow.'

'But it's such ages. Couldn't I send him a telegram?'

'No,' said Lord Ickenham firmly. 'There are limits. At least preserve a semblance of womanly dignity. Why not get Horace to drive you to London to-night in his car?'

'Would he, do you think? He's had one long drive already to-day.'

'It is his dearest wish to have another, provided you are at his side. Pongo and I can come on in the morning by that eight-twenty-five train of which everybody speaks so highly.'

'But are you leaving, too?'

'We are. Get Horace to tell you all about it. You will find him in my bedroom. If you don't see him, look in the cupboard. I, meanwhile, must be getting in touch with Pongo and communicating the arrangements to him. The news that we are flitting should please him. For some reason, Pongo has not been happy at Blandings Castle. By the way, did you meet him?'

'Yes. As I was coming back after seeing Ricky.'

'Good. I was only wondering if you had got that money all right.'

'He did offer me some money, but I gave it back to him.'

'Gave it back?'

'Yes. I didn't want it.'

'But, my good child, it was the purchase price of the onion soup bar. Your wedding portion!'

'I know. He told me.' Polly laughed amusedly. 'But I had just had that frightful row with Ricky, and we had parted for ever, and I was thinking of drowning myself, so I didn't want a wedding portion. Will you tell him I should like it, after all.'

Lord Ickenham groaned softly.

'You would not speak in that airy, casual way, if you knew the circumstances. Informing Pongo that you would like it, after all, is not going to be the pleasant task you seem to think it. I dare say that with the aid of anaesthetic and forceps I shall eventually be able to extract the money from the unhappy young blighter, but there will be a nasty, hacking sound as he coughs up. Still, you may rely on me to protect your interests, no matter what the cost. I will bring the stuff round to the Pott home to-morrow afternoon. And now run along and find Horace. I know he would appreciate an early start.'

'All right. Uncle Fred, you're an angel.'

'Thank you, my dear.'

'If it hadn't been for you—'

Once more Lord Ickenham found his arms full and behaved with a warmth far greater than one of his nephew's austere views would have considered either necessary or suitable. Then he was alone, and Polly a voice in the darkness, singing happily as she went on her way.

It was some ten minutes later that Lord Ickenham, sauntering along the high road in the direction of Market Blandings, heard another voice, also singing happily. He recognized it with a pang. It was not often that Pongo Twistleton cast off his natural gloom in order to carol like a lark, and the thought that it was for him to wipe this unaccustomed melody from the lips of a young man of whom he was very fond was not an agreeable one.

'Pongo?'

'Hullo, Uncle Fred. I say, what a lovely evening!'

'Very.'

'The air! The stars! The scent of growing things!'

'Quite. Er—Pongo, my boy, about that money.'

'The money you gave me to give to Miss Pott? Oh, yes—I was going to tell you about that. I offered it to her, but she would have none of it.'

'Yes—But—'

'She told me that owing to her having parted brass rags with Ricky, she had no need of it.'

'Precisely. But since then—'

'So I trousered it, and toddled along to Market Blandings, and breezed into the post office, and shoved two hundred quid into an envelope addressed to George Budd and fifty into an envelope addressed to Oofy Prosser and sent them off, registered. So all is now well. The relief,' said Pongo, 'is stupendous.'

It was not immediately that Lord Ickenham spoke. For some moments he stood fingering his moustache and gazing at his nephew thoughtfully. He was conscious of a faint resentment against a Providence which was unquestionably making things difficult for a good man.

'This,' he said, 'is a little awkward.'

'Awkward?'

'Yes.'

'How do you mean? It seems to me . . .'

Pongo's voice trailed away. A hideous thought had come to him.

'Oh, my aunt! Don't tell me she's changed her mind and wants the stuff, after all?'

'I fear so.'

'You mean she's made it up with Ricky?'

'Yes.'

'And needs this money to get married on?'

'Exactly.'

'Oh, my sainted bally aunt!'

'Yes,' said Lord Ickenham, 'it is awkward. No getting away from that. I told Ricky the money was actually in her possession, and he went off to catch his train with golden visions of soup-swilling multitudes dancing before his eyes. I told Polly I would bring her the stuff to-morrow, and she went off singing. It is not going to be pleasant to have to reveal the facts. Disappointment will be inevitable.'

'Would it be any good to ring up Budd and Oofy and ask them to give the money back?'

'No.'

'No, I suppose not. Then what?'

Lord Ickenham's face brightened. He had seen that all was not lost. That busy brain was seldom baffled for long.

'I have it! Mustard!'

'Eh?'

'Mustard Pott. He must handle this for us. Obviously, what we must do is unleash Mustard once more. I think he may be a little annoyed when he learns that his former donation, instead of ensuring the happiness of a loved daughter, has gone to ease the financial difficulties of a comparative stranger like yourself, but I have no doubt that a few minutes of my eloquence will persuade him to forget his natural chagrin and have another pop.'

'At Bosham?'

'Not at Bosham. People who play Persian Monarchs with Mustard in the afternoon are seldom in a frame of mind to play again in the evening. Emsworth is the man.'

'Old Emsworth? Oh, I say, dash it!'

Lord Ickenham nodded.

'I know what you mean. You feel that one ought to draw the line at nicking a kindly host, with whose bread and meat we are bursting, and considering the thing as a broad general proposition I agree with you. It will undoubtedly tarnish the Ickenham escutcheon, and I wish it hadn't got to be done. But in a crisis like this one must sink one's finer feelings. I don't believe I told you, did I, that your sister Valerie is expected here shortly?'

'What!'

'So Horace informs me, and you may look on him as a reliable source. This means that we have got to get out of here by tomorrow's eight-twenty-five train without fail, so you will see that we cannot loiter and dally, if we are to secure funds for Polly. It is not a question of asking ourselves "Is it right to take it off Emsworth?" and "Are we ethically justified in skinning this good old man?" but rather "Has he got it?" And he has. Emsworth, therefore, shall give us of his plenty, and I will be going along now and putting the thing in train. I will look in at your room later and report.'

18

I T was a sombre, preoccupied Pongo Twistleton who dressed for
dinner that night in the small apartment which had been allotted
to him on the second floor. As a rule, the process of transforming
himself from the chrysalis of daytime to the shimmering butterfly
of night was one that gave him pleasure. He liked the soothing
shave, the revivifying bath, the soft crackle of the snowy shirt-
front and the general feeling that in a few minutes he would be
giving the populace an eyeful. But tonight he was moody and
distrait. His lips were tight, and his eyes brooded. Even when he
tied his tie, he did it without any real animation.

The news that his sister was on her way to join the little circle
at Blandings Castle had shaken him a good deal. It had intensified
in him the sensation, which he had been experiencing ever since
his arrival, of being beset by perils and menaced by bad citizens.
A cat in a strange alley, with an eye out for small boys with bricks,
would have understood how he felt. And this nervous apprehension would alone have been enough to take his mind off his toilet.

But far more powerful than apprehension as an agent for
wrecking his mental peace was remorse. Ever since he had fallen
in love at first sight with Polly Pott, he had been dreaming that
an occasion might arise which would enable him to make some
great sacrifice for her sake. He had pictured himself patting her
little hand, as she thanked him brokenly for that astounding act

of nobility. He had seen himself gazing down into her eyes with one of those whimsical, twisted, Ronald Colman smiles. He had even gone so far as to knock together a bit of dialogue for the scene—just in case—starting 'There, there, little girl, it was nothing. All I want is your happiness' and getting even more effective as it went on.

And what had actually happened was that, unless her Persian-Monarchs-playing father intervened and saved the situation at the eleventh hour, he had ruined her life. It takes an unusually well-tied tie to relieve a mind tottering under a reflection like that, and his, he found, looking in the mirror, was only so-so. Indeed, it seemed to him to fall so far short of the ideal that he was just about to scrap it and start another, when the door opened and Lord Ickenham came in.

'Well?' cried Pongo eagerly.

Then his heart sank far beyond what a few moments before he had supposed to have been an all-time low. One glance at his uncle's face was enough to tell him that this was no exultant bearer of glad tidings who stood before him.

Lord Ickenham shook his head. There was a gravity in his manner that struck a nameless chill.

'The United States Marines have failed us, my boy. The garrison has not been relieved, the water supply is giving out, and the savages are still howling on the outskirts. In other words, Mustard has let us down.'

Pongo staggered to a chair. He sat down heavily. And some rough indication of his frame of mind may be gathered from the fact that he forgot to pull the knees of his trousers up.

'Wouldn't he take it on?'

'He would, and did. As I had anticipated, there was a certain huffiness at first, but I soon talked him round and he assented to the plan, saying in the most sporting spirit that all I had got to do was to provide Emsworth, and he would do the rest. He pulled out his pack of cards and fingered it lovingly, like some grand old warrior testing the keenness of his blade before a battle. And at this moment Emsworth entered.'

Pongo nodded heavily.

'I see where you're heading. Emsworth wouldn't play?'

'Oh yes, he played. This is a long and intricate story, my boy, and I think you had better not interrupt too much, or it will be dinner-time before we can get down to the agenda.'

'What agenda?'

'I have a scheme or plan of action which I propose to place before you in due course. Meanwhile, let me relate the sequence of events. As I say, Emsworth entered, and it was plain from his manner that he was in the grip of some strong emotion. His eyes goggled, his pince-nez were adrift and he yammered at me silently for a while, as is his habit when moved. It then came out that his pig had been stolen. He had gone down to refresh himself with an after-tea look at it, and it was not there. Its sty was empty, and its bed had not been slept in.'

'Oh?'

'I should have thought you could have found some more adequate comment on a great human tragedy than a mere "Oh?"' said Lord Ickenham reprovingly. 'Youth is very callous. Yes, the pig had been stolen, and Emsworth's suspicions immediately leaped, of course, to the Duke. He was considerably taken aback when I pointed out that the latter could scarcely be the guilty person, seeing that he had been in his room all the afternoon. He retired there immediately after lunch, and was not seen again. And he could not have gone out into the garden through his bedroom window, because we find that Baxter was sitting on the lawn from one-thirty onwards. You may recall that Baxter was not with us at lunch. It appears that he had a slight attack of dyspepsia and decided to skip the meal. He testifies that Dunstable did not emerge. The thing, therefore, becomes one of the great historic mysteries, ranking with the Man in the Iron Mask and the case of the *Mary Celeste*. One seeks in vain for a solution.'

Pongo, who had been listening to the narrative with growing impatience, denied this.

'I don't. I don't give a single, solitary damn. Dash all pigs, is the way I look at it. You didn't come here to talk about pigs, did you? What happened about Pott and the card game?'

Lord Ickenham apologized.

'I'm sorry. I'm afraid we old fellows have a tendency to ramble on. I should have remembered that your interest in the fortunes of Emsworth's pig is only tepid. Well, I suggested to Emsworth that what he wanted was to take his mind off the thing, and that an excellent method of doing this would be to play cards. Mustard said that curiously enough he happened to have a pack handy, and the next moment they had settled down to the game.'

Lord Ickenham paused, and drew his breath in reverently.

'It was a magnificent exhibition. Persian Monarchs at its best. I never expect to witness a finer display of pure science than Mustard gave. He was playing for his daughter's happiness, and the thought seemed to inspire him. Generally, I believe, on these occasions, it is customary to allow the mug to win from time to time as a sort of gesture, but it was clear that Mustard felt that in a crisis like this old-world courtesy would be out of place. Ignoring the traditions, he won every coup, and when they had finished Emsworth got up, thanked him for a pleasant game, said that it was fortunate that they had not been playing for money or he might have lost a considerable sum, and left the room.'

'Oh, my gosh!'

'Yes, it was a little disconcerting. Mustard tells me he was once bitten by a pig, but I doubt if even on that occasion—high spot in his life though it must have been—he can have been more overcome by emotion. For about five minutes after Emsworth's departure, all he could do was to keep saying in a dazed sort of way that this had never happened to him before. One gets new experiences. And then suddenly I saw his face light up, and he seemed to revive like a watered flower. And, looking round, I found that the Duke had come in.'

'Ah!'

Lord Ickenham shook his head.

'It's no good saying "Ah!" my boy. I told you at the beginning that this story hadn't a happy ending.'

'The Duke wouldn't play?'

'You keep saying that people wouldn't play. People always play when Mustard wants them to. He casts a sort of spell. No, the Duke was delighted to play. He said that he had had a boring afternoon, cooped up in his room, and that now he was out for a short breather a game of Persian Monarchs was just what he would enjoy. He said that as a young man he had been very gifted at the pastime. I saw Mustard's eyes glisten. They sat down.'

Lord Ickenham paused. He seemed to be torn between the natural desire of a raconteur to make the most of his material and a humane urge to cut it short and put his nephew out of his suspense. The latter triumphed.

'Dunstable's claim to excellence at the game was proved to the hilt,' he said briefly. 'Mark you, I don't think Mustard was at his best. That supreme effort so short a while before had left him weak and listless. Be that as it may, Dunstable took three hundred pounds off him in ten minutes.'

Pongo was staring.

'Three hundred pounds?'

'That was the sum.'

'In ready money, do you mean?'

'Paid right across the counter.'

'But if he had all that on him, why didn't he give it to Miss Pott?'

'Ah, I see what you mean. Well, Mustard is a peculiar chap in some ways. It is difficult enough to get him to part with his winnings. Not even for a daughter's sake would he give up his working capital. One dimly understands his view-point.'

'I don't.'

'Well, there it is.'

'And now what do we do?'

'Eh? Oh, now, of course, we nip into the Duke's room and pinch the stuff.'

That strange nightmare feeling which had grown so familiar to Pongo of late came upon him again. He presumed he had heard aright—his uncle's enunciation had been beautifully clear—but it seemed incredible that he could have done so.

'Pinch it?'

'Pinch it.'

'But you can't pinch money.'

'Dashed bad form, of course, I know. But I shall look upon it as a loan, to be paid back at intervals—irregular intervals—each instalment accompanied by a posy of white violets.'

'But, dash it—'

'I know what you are thinking. To that highly-trained legal mind of yours it is instantly clear that the act will constitute a tort or misdemeanour, if not actual barratry or socage in fief. But it has got to be done. Polly's need is paramount. I remember Mustard saying once, apropos of my affection for Polly, that I seemed to look on her more like a daughter than a whatnot, and he was right. I suppose my feelings towards her are roughly those of Emsworth towards his pig, and when I have the chance to ensure her happiness I am not going to allow any far-fetched scruples to stand in my way. I am a mild, law-abiding man, but to make that kid happy I would willingly become one of those fiends with hatchet who seem to spend their time slaying six. So, as I say, we will pinch the stuff.'

'You aren't proposing to lug me into this?'

Lord Ickenham was astounded.

'Lug you? What an extraordinary expression. I had naturally supposed that you would be overjoyed to do your bit.'

'You don't get me mixed up in this sort of game,' said Pongo firmly. 'Dog Races, yes. Crashing the gate at castles, right. Burglary, no.'

'But, my dear boy, when you reflect that but for you Polly would have all the money she needs—'

'Oh, golly!'

Once more, remorse had burst over Pongo like a tidal wave. In the agitation of the moment, he had forgotten this aspect of the affair. He writhed with shame.

'You mustn't overlook that. In a sense, you are morally bound to sit in.'

'That's right.'

'Then you will?'

'Of course. Rather.'

'Good. I knew you would. You shouldn't pull the old man's leg, Pongo. For a minute I thought you were serious. Well, I am relieved, for your co-operation is essential to the success of the little scheme I have roughed out. What sort of voice are you in these days? Ah, but I remember. When we met in the road, you were warbling like a nightingale. I mistook you for Lily Pons. Excellent.'

'Why?'

'Because it will be your task—your simple, easy task—I will attend to all the really testing work—to flit about the lawn outside Dunstable's window, singing the "Bonny Bonny Banks of Loch Lomond".'

'Eh? Why?'

'You do keep saying "Why?" don't you. It is quite simple. Dunstable, for some reason, is keeping closely to his room. Our first move must be to get him out of it. Even a novice to burglary like myself can see that if you are proposing to ransack a man's room for money, it is much pleasanter to do it when he is not there. Your rendering of Loch Lomond will lure him out. We know how readily he responds to that fine old song. I see your role in this affair as a sort of blend of Lorelei and Will-o'-the-Wisp. You get Dunstable out with your siren singing, and you keep him out by flitting ahead of him through the darkness. Meanwhile, I sneak in and do the needful. No flaws in that?'

'Not so long as nobody sees you.'

'You are thinking of Baxter? Quite right. Always think of everything. If Baxter sees us slip away on some mysterious errand, his detective instincts will undoubtedly be roused. But I have the situation well in hand. I shall give Baxter a knock-out drop.'

'A what?'

'Perhaps you are more familiar with it under the name of Mickey Finn.'

'But where on earth are you going to get a knock-out drop?'

'From Mustard. Unless his whole mode of life has changed since I used to know him, he is sure to have one. In the old days, he never moved without them. When he was running that club of his, it was only by a judicious use of knock-out drops that he was able to preserve order and harmony in his little flock.'

'But how do you propose to make him take it?'

'I shall find a way. He would be in his room now, I imagine?'

'I suppose so.'

'Then after paying a brief call on Mustard I will look in on him and enquire after his dyspepsia. You may leave all this side of the thing to me with every confidence. Your duties will not begin till after dinner. Zero hour is at nine-thirty sharp.'

It was plain to Lord Ickenham, directly he thrust his unwanted society on him a few minutes later, that Rupert Baxter was far from being the stern, steely young fellow of their previous encounters. The message, conveyed by Beach the butler to Lady Constance shortly after noon, that Mr Baxter regretted he would be unable to lunch to-day had been no mere ruse on the secretary's part to enable him to secure the solitude and leisure essential to the man who is planning to steal pigs. The effect of his employer's assignment had been to induce a genuine disorder of the digestive organs. There is always a weak spot in the greatest men. With Baxter, as with Napoleon, it was his stomach.

He had felt a little better towards evening, but now the thought that there lay before him the fearful ordeal of removing the

Empress from her temporary lodging in the Duke's bathroom to the car which was to convey her to her new home had brought on another and an even severer attack. At the moment of Lord Ickenham's entry, wild cats to the number of about eighteen had just begun to conduct a free-for-all in his interior.

It was not to be expected, therefore, that he should beam upon his visitor. Nor did he. Ceasing for an instant to massage his waistcoat, he glared in a manner which only the dullest person could have failed to recognize as unfriendly.

'Well?' he said, between clenched teeth.

Lord Ickenham, who had not expected cordiality, was in no way disconcerted by his attitude. He proceeded immediately to supply affability enough for two, which was the amount required.

'I just dropped in,' he explained, 'to make enquiries and offer condolences. You will have been thinking me remiss in not coming before, but you know how it is at a country house. Distractions all the time. Well, my dear fellow, how are you? A touch of the collywobbles, I understand. Too bad, too bad. We all missed you at lunch, and there was a great deal of sympathy expressed—by myself, of course, no less than the others.'

'I can do without your sympathy.'

'Can any of us do without sympathy, Baxter, even from the humblest? Mine, moreover, takes a practical and constructive form. I have here,' said Lord Ickenham, producing a white tablet, 'something which I guarantee will make you forget the most absorbing stomach-ache. You take it in a little water.'

Baxter regarded the offering suspiciously. His knowledge of impostors told him that they seldom act from purely altruistic motives. Examine an impostor's act of kindness, and you see something with a string attached to it.

And suddenly there came to him, causing him momentarily to forget bodily anguish, an exhilarating thought.

Rupert Baxter had no illusions about his employer. He did not suppose that the gruff exterior of the Duke of Dunstable hid a heart of gold, feeling—correctly—that if the Duke were handed a heart of gold on a plate with watercress round it, he would not know what it was. But he did credit him with an elementary sense of gratitude, and it seemed to him that after he, Baxter, had carried through with success the perilous task of stealing a pig on his behalf, the old hound could scarcely sack him for having attended a fancy-dress Ball without permission. In other words, this man before him, beneath whose iron heel he had been supposing himself to be crushed, no longer had any hold over him and could be defied with impunity.

'I see you have a tumbler there. I place the tablet in it—so. I fill with water—thus. I stir. I mix. And there you are. Drink it down, and let's see what happens.'

Baxter waved away the cup with a sneer.

'You are very kind,' he said, 'but there is no need to beat about the bush. It is obvious that you have come here in the hope of getting round me—'

Lord Ickenham looked pained.

'Yours is a very suspicious nature, Baxter. You would do well to try to overcome this mistrust of your fellow-men.'

'You want something.'

'Merely to see you your old bonny self again.'

'You are trying to conciliate me, and I know why. You have begun to wonder if the hold you suppose yourself to have over me is quite as great as you imagined.'

'Beautifully expressed. I like the way you talk.'

'Let me tell you at once that it is not. You have no hold over me. Since our conversation in the billiard-room, the whole situation has altered. I have been able to perform a great service for my employer, with the result that I am no longer in danger of being dismissed for having gone to that Ball. So I may as well inform you here and now that it is my intention to have you turned out of the house immediately. Ouch!' said Baxter, rather spoiling the effect of a dignified and impressive speech by clutching suddenly at his midriff.

Lord Ickenham eyed him sympathetically.

'My dear fellow, something in your manner tells me you are in pain. You had better drink that mixture.'

'Get out!'

'It will do you all the good in the world.'

'Get out!'

Lord Ickenham sighed.

'Very well, since you wish it,' he said and, turning, collided with Lord Bosham in the doorway.

'Hullo!' said Lord Bosham. 'Hullo-ullo-ullo! Hullo-ullo-ullo-ullo-ullo!'

He spoke with a wealth of meaning in his voice. There was, he felt, something pretty dashed sinister about finding the villain of the piece alone with Baxter in his room like this. An acquaintance with mystery thrillers almost as comprehensive as his brother Freddie's had rendered him familiar with what happened when these chaps got into rooms. On the thin pretext of paying a formal call, they smuggled in cobras and left them there to do their stuff. 'Well, good afternoon,' they said, and bowed themselves out. But the jolly old cobra didn't bow itself out. It stuck around, concealed in the curtain.

'Hullo!' he added, concluding his opening remarks. 'Want anything?'

'Only dinner,' said Lord Ickenham.

'Oh?' said Lord Bosham. 'Well, it'll be ready in a minute. What was that bird after?' he asked tensely, as the door closed.

Baxter did not reply for a moment. He was engaged in beating his breast, like the Wedding Guest.

'I kicked him out before he could tell me,' he said, as the agony abated. 'Ostensibly, his purpose in coming was to bring me something for my indigestion. A tablet. He put it in that glass. What he was really leading up to, of course, was a request that I would refrain from exposing him.'

'But you can't expose him, can you? Wouldn't you lose your job?'

'There is no longer any danger of that.'

'You mean, even if he tells old Dunstable that you were out on a bender that night, you won't get the boot?'

'Precisely.'

'Then now I know where I stand! Now the shackles have fallen from me, and I am in a position to set about these impostors as impostors should be set about. That's really official, is it?'

'Quite. Ouch!'

'Anguish?'

'Oo!'

'If I were you,' said Lord Bosham, 'I'd drink the stuff the blighter gave you. There's no reason why it shouldn't prove efficacious. The fact that a chap is an impostor doesn't necessarily mean that he can't spot a good stomach-ache cure when he sees one. Down the hatch with it, my writhing old serpent, with a hey nonny nonny and a hot cha-cha.'

Another twinge caused Baxter to hesitate no longer. He saw that the advice was good. He raised the glass to his lips. He did not drain it with a hey nonny nonny, but he drained it.

It was then too late for him to say 'Hey, nonny nonny,' even if he had wished to.

Down in the hall, like a hound straining at the leash, Beach the butler stood with uplifted stick, waiting for the psychological moment to beat the gong. Lady Constance, as she came downstairs, caught a glimpse of him over the banisters, but she was not accorded leisure to feast her eyes on the spectacle, for along the corridor to her left there came a galloping figure. It was her nephew, Lord Bosham. He reached her, seized her by the wrist and jerked her into an alcove. Accustomed though she was to eccentricity in her nephews, the action momentarily took her breath away.

'Gee-ORGE!' she cried, finding speech.

'Yes, I know, I know. But listen.'

'Are you intoxicated?'

'Of course I'm not. What a dashed silly idea. Much shaken, but sober to the gills. Listen, Aunt Connie. You know those impostors? Impostors A, B, and C? Well, things are getting hot. Impostor A has just laid Baxter out cold with a knock-out drop.'

'What! I don't understand.'

'Well, I can't make it any simpler. That is the bedrock fact. Impostor A has just slipped Baxter a Mickey Finn. And what I'm driving at is, that if these birds are starting to express themselves like this, it means something. It means that tonight's the night. It signifies that whatever dirty work they are contemplating spring-ing on this community will be sprung before to-morrow's sun has risen. Ah!' said Lord Bosham, with animation, as the gong boomed out below. 'Dinner, and not before I was ready for it. Let's go. But mark this, Aunt Connie, and mark it well—the moment we rise from the table, I get my good old gun, and I lurk! I don't know what's up, and you don't know what's up, but that something is up sticks out a mile, and I intend to lurk like a two-year-old. Well, I mean to say, dash it,' said Lord Bosham, with honest heat, 'we can't have this sort of thing, what? If impostors are to be allowed to go chucking their weight about as if they'd bought the place, matters have come to a pretty pass!'

19

A T twenty minutes past nine, the Duke of Dunstable, who had
dined off a tray in his room, was still there, waiting for his coffee
and liqueur. He felt replete, for he was a good trencherman and
had done himself well, but he was enjoying none of that sensation
of mental peace which should accompany repletion. Each moment
that passed found him more worried and fretful. The failure of
Rupert Baxter to report for duty was affecting him much as their
god's unresponsiveness once affected the priests of Baal. Here it
was getting on for goodness knew what hour, and not a sign of him.
It would have pained the efficient young secretary, now lying on
his bed with both hands pressed to his temples in a well-meant but
unsuccessful attempt to keep his head from splitting in half, could
he have known the black thoughts his employer was thinking of
him.

The opening of the door, followed by the entry of Beach bearing a tray containing coffee and a generous glass of brandy, caused
the Duke to brighten for an instant, but the frown returned to his
brow as he saw that the butler was not alone. The last thing he
wanted at a time like this was a visitor.

'Good evening, my dear fellow. I wonder if you could spare me
a moment?'

It was about half-way through dinner that the thought had
occurred to Lord Ickenham that there might be an easier and

more agreeable method than that which he had planned of obtaining from the Duke the money which he was, as it were, holding in trust for Polly. He had not developed any weak scruples about borrowing it on the lines originally laid down, but the almost complete absence of conversation at the dinner-table had given him time to reflect, and the result of this reflection had been to breed misgivings.

Success in the campaign which he had sketched out would depend—he had to face it—largely on the effectiveness of his nephew Pongo's performance of the part assigned to him, and he feared lest Pongo, when it came to the pinch, might prove a broken reed. You tell a young man to stand on a lawn and sing the 'Bonny Bonny Banks of Loch Lomond', and the first thing you know he has forgotten the tune or gone speechless with stage fright. Far better, it seemed to him, to try what a simple, straightforward appeal to the Duke's better feelings would do—and, if that failed, to have recourse to the equally simple and straightforward Mickey Finn.

That glass of brandy there would make an admirable receptacle for the sedative, and he had taken the precaution, while tapping Mr Pott's store, to help himself to a couple of the magic tablets, one of which still nestled in his waistcoat pocket.

'It's about that money you won from that man—Pott is his name, I believe—this evening,' he went on.

The Duke grunted guardedly.

'I have been talking to him, and he is most distressed about it.'

The Duke grunted again, scornfully this time, and it seemed to Lord Ickenham that an odd sort of echo came from the bathroom. He put it down to some trick of the acoustics.

'Yes, most distressed. It seems that in a sense the money was not his to gamble with.'

'Hey?' The Duke seemed interested. 'What do you mean? Robbed a till or something, did he?'

'No, no. Nothing like that. He is a man of the most scrupulous honesty. But it was a sum which he had been saving up for his daughter's wedding portion. And now it has gone.'

'What do you expect me to do about it?'

'You wouldn't feel inclined to give it back?'

'Give it back?'

'It would be a fine, generous, heart-stirring action.'

'It would be a fine, potty, fatheaded action,' corrected the Duke warmly. 'Give it back, indeed! I never heard of such a thing.'

'He is much distressed.'

'Let him be.'

It began to be borne in upon Lord Ickenham that in planning to appeal to the Duke's better feelings he had omitted to take into his calculations the fact that he might not have any. With a dreamy look in his eye, he took the tablet from his pocket and palmed it thoughtfully.

'It would be a pity if his daughter were not able to get married,' he said.

'Why?' said the Duke, a stout bachelor.

'She is engaged to a fine young poet.'

'Then,' said the Duke, his face beginning to purple – the Dunstables did not easily forget—'she's jolly well out of it. Don't talk to me about poets! The scum of the earth.'

'So you won't give the money back?'

'No.'

'Reflect,' said Lord Ickenham. 'It is here, in this room—is it not?'

'What's that got to do with it?'

'I was only thinking that there it was—handy—and all you would have to do would be to go to the drawer . . . or cupboard . . .'

He paused expectantly. The Duke maintained a quiet reserve.

'I wish you would reconsider.'

'Well, I won't.'

'The quality of mercy,' said Lord Ickenham, deciding that he could not do better than follow the tested methods of Horace's Pekinese breeder, 'is not strained—'

'The what isn't?'

'The quality of mercy. It droppeth as the gentle rain from heaven upon the place beneath. It is twice blessed—'

'How do you make that out?'

'It blesseth him that gives and him that takes,' explained Lord Ickenham.

'Never heard such rot in my life,' said the Duke. 'I think you're potty. Anyhow, you'll have to go now. I'm expecting my secretary at any moment for an important conference. You haven't seen him anywhere, have you?'

'I had a few words with him before dinner, but I have not seen him since. He is probably amusing himself somewhere.'

'I'll amuse him, when I see him.'

'No doubt he has been unable to tear himself away from the fascinations of the backgammon board or the halma table. Young blood!'

'Young blood be blowed.'

'Ah, that will be he, no doubt.'

'Eh?'

'Someone knocked.'

'I didn't hear anything.'

The Duke went to the door and opened it. Lord Ickenham stretched a hand over the brandy glass and opened it. The Duke came back.

'Nobody there.'

'Ah, then I was mistaken. Well, if you really wish me to go, I will be leaving you. If you don't feel like making the splendid gesture I proposed, there is no more to be said. Good night, my dear fellow,' said Lord Ickenham, and withdrew.

It was perhaps a minute after he had taken his departure that Mr Pott entered the corridor.

Of all the residents of Blandings Castle who had been doing a bit of intensive thinking during dinner—and there were several—Claude Pott was the one who had been thinking hardest.

And the result of his thoughts had been to send him hastening to the Duke's room. It was his hope that he would be able to persuade him to play a hand or two of a game called Slippery Joe.

The evening's disaster had left Mr Pott not only out of pocket and humiliated, but full of the liveliest suspicion. How the miracle had been accomplished, he was unable to say, but the more he brooded over the Duke's triumph, the more convinced did he become that he had been cheated and hornswoggled. Honest men, he told himself, did not beat him at Persian Monarchs, and he blamed himself for having selected a game at which it was possible, apparently, for an unscrupulous opponent to put something over. Slippery Joe was open to no such objection. Years of experience had taught him that at Slippery Joe he could always deal himself an unbeatable hand.

He was just about to turn the corner leading to the Garden Suite, hoping for the best, when the Duke came round it, travelling well, and ran into him.

For some moments after Lord Ickenham had left him, the Duke of Dunstable had remained where he sat, frowning peevishly. Then he had risen. Distasteful and even degrading though it might be to go running about after secretaries, there seemed nothing for it but to institute a search for the missing Baxter. He hastened out, and the first thing he knew he was colliding with the frightful feller.

Then he saw that it was not the frightful feller, after all, but another feller, equally frightful—the chap with the wedding-portion daughter, to wit—a man for whom, since listening to Lord Ickenham's remarks, he had come to feel a vivid dislike. He was not fond of many people, but the people of whom he was least fond were those who wanted to get money out of him.

'Gah!' he said, disentangling himself.

Mr Pott smiled an ingratiating smile. It was only a sketchy one, for he had had to assemble it in a hurry, but such as it was he let the Duke have it.

'Hullo, your Grace,' he said.

'Go to hell,' said the Duke and, these brief civilities concluded, stumped off and was lost to sight.

And simultaneously a thought came to Mr Pott like a full-blown rose, flushing his brow.

Until this moment, Mr Pott's only desire had been to recover his lost money through the medium of a game of Slippery Joe. He now saw that there was a simpler and less elaborate way of arriving at the happy ending. Somewhere in the Duke's room there was three hundred pounds morally belonging to himself, and the Duke's room was now unoccupied. To go in and help himself would be to avoid a lot of tedious preliminaries.

Though stout of build, he could move quickly when the occasion called for speed. He bounced along the passage like a rubber ball. Only when he had reached his destination did he find that he need not have hurried. Preoccupied the Duke might have been, but he had not been too preoccupied to remember to lock his door.

The situation was one that might have baffled many men, and for an instant it baffled Mr Pott completely. Then, his native ingenuity asserting itself, he bethought him that the door was not the only means of access to the room. There were French windows, and it was just possible that on a balmy evening like this the Duke might have left them open. Reaching the lawn after a brisk run, rosy and puffing, he discovered that he had not.

This time, Mr Pott accepted defeat. He knew men in London who would have made short work of those windows. They would have produced a bit of bent wire and opened them as if they had been a sardine tin, laughing lightly the while. But he had no skill in that direction. Rueful but resigned, with some of the feelings of Moses gazing at the Promised Land from the summit of Mount Pisgah, he put an eye to the glass and peered through. There was the dear old room, all ready and waiting, but for practical purposes it might have been a hundred miles away. And presently he saw the door open and the Duke came in.

And he was turning away with a sigh, a beaten man, when from somewhere close at hand a voice in the night began to sing the 'Bonny Bonny Banks of Loch Lomond'. And scarcely had the haunting refrain ceased to annoy the birds roosting in the trees, when the French windows flew open and the Duke of Dunstable, shooting out like a projectile, went whizzing across the lawn, crying 'Hey!' as he did so. To Mr Pott, the thing had been just a song, but to the Duke it seemed to have carried a deeper message.

And such was indeed the case. The interpretation which he had placed upon that sudden burst of melody was that it was Baxter who stood warbling without, and that this was his way of trying to attract his employer's attention. Why Baxter should sing outside his room, instead of walking straight in, was a problem which he found himself at the moment unable to solve. He presumed that the man must have some good reason for a course of conduct which at first glance seemed merely eccentric. Possibly, he reflected, complications had arisen, rendering it necessary for him to communicate with headquarters in this oblique and secret society fashion. He could vaguely recall having read in his boyhood stories in which people in such circumstances had imitated the hoot of the night-owl.

'Hey!' he called, trying to combine the conflicting tasks of shouting and speaking in a cautious undertone. 'Here! Hi! Hey! Where are you, dash it?'

For his efforts to establish contact with the vocalist were being oddly frustrated. Instead of standing still and delivering his report, the other seemed to be receding into the distance. When the 'Bonny Banks' broke out again, it was from somewhere at the farther end of the lawn. With a muffled oath, the Duke galloped in that direction like the man in the poem who followed the Gleam, and Mr Pott, always an excellent opportunist, slid in through the French windows.

He had scarcely done so, when he heard footsteps. Somebody was approaching across the grass and approaching so rapidly that there was no time to be lost if an embarrassing encounter was to be avoided. With great presence of mind he dived into the bathroom. And as he closed the door, Lord Ickenham came in.

Lord Ickenham was feeling well pleased. The artistry of his nephew's performance had enchanted him. He had not supposed that the boy had it in him to carry the thing through with such *bravura*. At the best he had hoped for a timid piping, and that full-throated baying, a cross between a blood-hound on the trail and a Scotsman celebrating New Year's Eve, had been as unexpected as it was agreeable. Technical defects there may have been in Pongo's vocalization, but he had certainly brought the Duke out of the room like a cork out of a bottle. Lord Ickenham could not remember ever having seen a duke move quicker.

And he was just settling down to a swift and intensive search for the wedding portion, when his activities were arrested. From behind the bathroom door, freezing him in his tracks, there came the sharp, piercing scream of a human being in distress. The next moment, Mr Pott staggered out, slamming the door behind him.

'Mustard!' cried Lord Ickenham, completely at a loss.

'Coo!' said Mr Pott, and in a lifetime liberally punctuated by that ejaculation he had never said it with stronger emphasis.

Normally, Claude Pott was rather a reserved man. He lived in a world in which, if you showed your feelings, you lost money. But there were some things which could break down his poise, and one of these was the discovery that he was closeted in a small bathroom with the largest pig he had ever encountered.

For an instant, after he had entered his hiding-place, the Empress had been just an aroma in the darkness. If Mr Pott had felt that it was a bit stuffy in here, that was all he had felt. Then something cold and moist pressed itself against his dangling hand, and the truth came home to him.

'Mustard, my dear fellow!'

'Cor!' said Mr Pott.

He was shaking in every limb. It is not easy for a man who

weighs nearly two hundred pounds to quiver like an aspen, but he managed to do it. His mind was in a whirl, from which emerged one coherent thought—that he wanted a drink. An imperious desire for a quick restorative swept over him, and suddenly he perceived that there was relief in sight—if only a small relief. That glass of brandy on the table would be of little real use to him. What he really needed was a brimming bucketful. But it would at least be a step in the right direction.

'Mustard! Stop!'

Lord Ickenham's warning cry came too late. The lethal draught had already passed down Mr Pott's throat, and even as he shook his head appreciatively the glass fell to the floor and he followed it. If twenty pigs had bitten Claude Pott simultaneously in twenty different places, he could not have succumbed more completely.

It was with a sympathetic eye and a tut-tut-ing tongue that Lord Ickenham bent over the remains. There was nothing, he knew, to be done. Only Time, the great healer, could make Claude Pott once more the Claude Pott of happier days. He rose, wondering how best to dispose of the body, and as he did so a voice spoke behind him.

'Hullo-ullo-ullo-ullo-ullo!' it said, and in the words there was an unmistakable note of rebuke.

Faithfully and well Lord Bosham had followed out his policy of lurking, as outlined to his Aunt Constance before dinner. He was now standing in the window, his gun comfortably poised.

'What ho, what ho, what ho, what ho, what ho, what, what?' he added, and paused for a reply.

This Lord Ickenham was not able to give. Man of iron nerve though he was, he could be taken aback. The sudden appearance of Horace Davenport earlier in the evening had done it. The equally sudden appearance of Lord Bosham did it again. He found himself at a loss for words, and it was Lord Bosham who eventually resumed the conversation.

'Well, I'm dashed!' he said, still speaking with that strong note of reproof. 'Here's a nice state of things! So you've put it across poor old Pott now, have you? It's a bit thick. We engage detectives at enormous expense, and as fast as we get them in you bowl them over with knock-out drops.'

.He paused, struggling with his feelings. It was plain that he could not trust himself to say what he really thought about it all. His eye roamed the room, and lit up as it rested on the door of the cupboard.

'You jolly well get in there,' he said, indicating it with a wave of the gun. 'Into that cupboard with you, quick, and no back chat.'

If Lord Ickenham had had any intention of essaying repartee, he abandoned it. He entered the cupboard, and the key turned in the lock behind him.

Lord Bosham pressed the bell. A stately form appeared in the doorway.

'Oh, Beach.'

'M'lord?'

'Get a flock of footmen and have Mr Pott taken up to his room, will you?'

'Very good, m'lord.'

The butler had betrayed no emotion on beholding what appeared to be a corpse on the floor of the Garden Suite. Nor did the two footmen, Charles and Henry, who subsequently carried out the removal. It was Blandings Castle's pride that its staff was well trained. Mr Pott disappeared feet foremost, like a used gladiator being cleared away from the arena, and Lord Bosham was left to his thoughts.

These might have been expected to be exultant, for he had undoubtedly acted with dash and decision in a testing situation. But they were only partly so. Mingled with a victor's triumph was the chagrin of the conscientious man who sees a task but half done. That he had properly put a stopper on Impostor A was undeniable, but he had hoped also to deal faithfully with Imposter B. He was wondering if the chap was hiding somewhere and if so, where, when there came to his sensitive ear the sound of a grunt, and he realized that it had proceeded from the bathroom.

'Yoicks!' cried Lord Bosham, and if he had not been a man of action rather than words would have added 'Tally ho!' He did not pause to ask himself why impostors should grunt. He merely dashed at the bathroom door, flung it open and leaped back, his gun at the ready. There was a moment's pause, and then the Empress sauntered out, a look of mild enquiry on her fine face.

The Empress of Blandings was a pig who took things as they came. Her motto, like Horace's, was *nil admirari*. But, cool and even aloof though she was as a general rule, she had been a little puzzled by the events of the day. In particular, she had found the bathroom odd. It was the only place she had ever been in where there appeared to be a shortage of food. The best it had to offer was a cake of shaving-soap, and she had been eating this with a thoughtful frown when Mr Pott joined her. As she emerged now, she was still foaming at the mouth a little and it was perhaps this that set the seal on Lord Bosham's astonishment and caused him not only to recoil a yard or two with his eyes popping but also to pull the trigger of his gun.

In the confined space the report sounded like the explosion of an arsenal, and it convinced the Empress, if she had needed to be convinced, that this was no place for a pig of settled habits. Not since she had been a slip of a child had she moved at anything swifter than a dignified walk, but now Jesse Owens could scarcely have got off the mark more briskly. It took her a few moments to get her bearings, but after colliding with the bed, the table and the armchair, in the order named, she succeeded in setting a course for the window and was in the act of disappearing through it when Lord Emsworth burst into the room, followed by Lady Constance.

The firing of guns in bedrooms is always a thing that tends to excite the interest of the owner of a country house, and it was in a spirit of lively curiosity that Lord Emsworth had arrived upon the scene. An 'Eh, what?' was trembling on his lips as he entered.

But the sight of those vanishing hind-quarters with their flash of curly tail took his mind instantly off such comparative trivialities as indoor artillery practice. With a cry that came straight from the heart, he adjusted his pince-nez and made for the great out-doors. Broken words of endearment could be heard coming from the darkness.

Lady Constance had propped herself against the wall, a shapely hand on her heart. She was panting a little, and her eyes showed a disposition to swivel in their sockets. Long ago she had learned the stern lesson that Blandings Castle was no place for weaklings, but this latest manifestation of what life under its roof could be had proved daunting to even her toughened spirit.

'George!' she whispered feebly.

Lord Bosham was his old buoyant self again.

'Quite all right, Aunt Connie. Just an accident. Sorry you were troubled.'

'What—what has been happening?'

'I thought you would want to know that. Well, it was like this. I came in here, to discover that Impostor A had scuppered our detective with one of those knock-out drops of his. I quelled him with my good old gun, and locked him in the cupboard. I thought I heard Impostor B grunting in the bathroom and flung wide the gates, only to discover that it was the guv'nor's pig. Starting back in natural astonishment, I inadvertently pulled the trigger. All quite simple and in order.'

'I thought the Duke had been murdered.'

'No such luck. By the way, I wonder where he's got to. Ah, here's Beach. He'll tell us. Do you know where the Duke is, Beach?'

'No, m'lord. Pardon me, m'lady.'

'Yes, Beach?'

'A Miss Twistleton has called, m'lady.'

'Miss Twistleton?'

Lord Bosham's memory was good.

'That's the girl who gave Horace the raspberry,' he reminded his aunt.

'I know that,' said Lady Constance, with some impatience. 'What I meant was, what can she be doing here at this hour?'

'I gathered, m'lady, that Miss Twistleton had arrived on the five o'clock train from London.'

'But what can she want?'

'That,' Lord Bosham pointed out, 'we can ascertain by seeing the wench. Where did you park her, Beach?'

'I showed the lady into the drawing-room, m'lord.'

'Then Ho for the drawing-room is what I would suggest. My personal bet is that she supposes Horace to be here and has come to tell him she now regrets those cruel words. Oh, Beach.'

'M'lord?'

'Can you use a gun?'

'As a young lad I was somewhat expert with an air-gun, m'lord.'

'Well, take this. It isn't an air-gun, but the principle's the same. You put it to the shoulder—so—and pull the trigger—thus. . . . Oh, sorry,' said Lord Bosham, as the echoes of the deafening report died away and his aunt and her butler, who had skipped like the high hills, came back to terra firma. 'I forgot that would happen. Silly of me. Now I'll have to reload. There's a miscreant in that cupboard, Beach, a devil of a chap who wants watching like a hawk, and I shall require you to stay here and see that he doesn't get out. At the first sign of any funny business on his part, such as trying to break down the door, whip the weapon to the shoulder and blaze away like billy-o. You follow me, Beach?'

'Yes, m'lord.'

'Then pick up the feet, Aunt Connie,' said Lord Bosham, 'and let's go.'

20

THE fruitless pursuit of Loreleis or will-o'-the-wisps through a dark garden, full of things waiting to leap out and crack him over the shins, can never be an agreeable experience to a man of impatient temperament, accustomed to his comforts. It was a puffing and exasperated Duke of Dunstable who limped back to his room a few minutes after Beach had taken up his vigil. His surprise at finding it occupied by a butler—and not merely an ordinary butler, without trimmings, but one who toted a gun—was very marked. Nor did the sight in any way allay his annoyance. There was a silent instant in which he stood brushing from his moustache the insects of the night that had got entangled there and glaring balefully at the intruder. Then he gave tongue.

'Hey? What? What's this? What the devil's all this? What do you mean, you feller, by invading my private apartment with a dashed great cannon? Of all the houses I was ever in, this is certainly the damnedest. I come down here for a nice rest, and before I can so much as relax a muscle, I find my room full of blasted butlers, armed to the teeth. Don't point that thing at me, sir. Put it down, and explain.'

In a difficult situation, Beach preserved the courteous calm which had made him for so many years the finest butler in Shropshire. He found the Duke's manner trying, but he exhibited nothing but a respectful desire to give satisfaction.

'I must apologize for my presence, your Grace,' he said smoothly, 'but I was instructed by Lord Bosham to remain here and act as his deputy during his temporary absence. I am informed by his lordship that he has deposited a miscreant in the cupboard.'

'A what?'

'A miscreant, your Grace. Something, I gather, in the nature of a nocturnal marauder. His lordship gave me to understand that he discovered the man in this room and, having overpowered him, locked him in the cupboard.'

'Hey? Which cupboard?'

The butler indicated the safe deposit in question, and the Duke uttered a stricken cry.

'My God! All in among my spring suits! Let him out at once.'

'His lordship instructed me—'

'Dash his lordship! I'm not going to have smelly miscreants ruining my clothes. What sort of a miscreant?'

'I have no information, your Grace.'

'Probably some foul tramp with the grime of years on him, and the whole outfit will have to go to the cleaner's. Let him out immediately.'

'Very good, your Grace.'

'I'll turn the key and throw the door open, and you stand ready with your gun. Now, then, when I say "Three." One. . . . Two. . . . Three. . . . Good Lord, it's the brain chap!'

Lord Ickenham had not enjoyed his sojourn in the cupboard, which he had found close and uncomfortable, but it had left him his old debonair self.

'Ah, my dear Duke,' he said genially, as he emerged, 'good evening once more. I wonder if I might use your hairbrush? The thatch has become a little disordered.'

The Duke was staring with prawnlike eyes.

'Was that you in there?' he asked. A foolish question, perhaps, but a man's brain is never at its nimblest on these occasions.

Lord Ickenham said it was.

'What on earth were you doing, going into cupboards?'

Lord Ickenham passed the brush lovingly through his grey locks.

'I went in because I was requested to by the man behind the gun. I happened to be strolling on the lawn and saw your windows open, and I thought I might enjoy another chat with you. I had scarcely entered, when Bosham appeared, weapon in hand. I don't know how you feel about these things, my dear fellow, but my view is that when an impetuous young gentleman, fingering the trigger of a gun, tells you to go into a cupboard, it is best to humour him.'

'But why did he tell you to go into the cupboard?'

'Ah, there you take me into deep waters. He gave me no opportunity of enquiring.'

'I mean, you're not a nocturnal marauder.'

'No. The whole thing is very odd.'

'I'm going to get to the bottom of this. Hey, you, go and fetch Lord Bosham.'

'Very good, your Grace.'

'The fact of the matter is,' said the Duke, as the butler left the room like a stately galleon under sail, 'the whole family's potty, as I told you before. I just met Emsworth in the garden. His manner was most peculiar. He called me a pig-stealing pest and a number of other things. I made allowances, of course, for the fact that he's as mad as a hatter, but I shall leave to-morrow and I shan't come here again. They'll miss me, but I can't help that. Did Bosham shoot at you?'

'No.'

'He shot at someone.'

'Yes, I heard a fusillade going on.'

'The feller oughtn't to be at large. Human life isn't safe. Ah, here he is. Here, you!'

Through the door a little procession was entering. It was headed by Lady Constance. Behind her came a tall, handsome girl, in whom Lord Ickenham had no difficulty in recognizing his niece Valerie. The rear was brought up by Lord Bosham. Lady Constance was looking cold and stern, Valerie Twistleton colder and sterner. Lord Bosham looked merely bewildered. He resembled his father and his brother Freddie in not being very strong in the head, and the tale to which he had been listening in the drawing-room had been of a nature not at all suited to the consumption of the weak-minded. A girl claiming to be Miss Twistleton, niece of the Earl of Ickenham, had suddenly blown in from nowhere with the extraordinary story that Impostor A was her uncle, and she had left Lord Bosham with such brain as he possessed in a whirl. He was anxious for further light on a puzzling situation.

'What the devil do you mean. . . .' The Duke broke off. He was staring at Lady Constance's companion, whom, owing to the fact that his gaze had been riveted on Lord Bosham, he had not immediately observed. 'Hey, what?' he said. 'Where did you spring from?'

'This is Miss Twistleton, Alaric.'

'Of course she's Miss Twistleton. I know that.'

'Ah!' said Lord Bosham. 'She *is* Miss Twistleton, is she? You identify her?'

'Of course I identify her.'

'My mistake,' said Lord Bosham. 'I thought she might be Impostor D.'

'George, you're an idiot!'

'Right ho, Aunt Connie.'

'Bosham, you're a damned fool!'

'Right ho, Duke.'

'Chump!'

'Right ho, Miss Twistleton. It was just that it occurred to me as a passing thought that Miss Twistleton, though she said she was Miss Twistleton, might not be Miss Twistleton but simply pretending to be Miss Twistleton in order to extricate Impostor A from a nasty spot. But, of course, if you're all solid on the fact of Miss Twistleton really being Miss Twistleton, my theory falls to the ground. Sorry, Miss Twistleton.'

'George, will you please stop drivelling.'

'Right ho, Aunt Connie. Merely mentioning what occurred to me as a passing thought.'

Now that the point of Miss Twistleton's identity—the fact that she was a genuine Miss Twistleton and not a pseudo Miss Twistleton—had been settled, the Duke returned to the grievance which he had started to ventilate a few moments earlier.

'And now perhaps you'll explain, young clothheaded Bosham, what you mean by shutting your father's guests in cupboards. Do you realize that the man might have messed up my spring suits and died of suffocation?'

Lady Constance intervened.

'We came to let Lord Ickenham out.'

'Let who out?'

'Lord Ickenham.'

'How do you mean, Lord Ickenham?'

'This is Lord Ickenham.'

'Yes,' said Lord Ickenham, 'I am Lord Ickenham. And this,' he went on, bestowing a kindly glance on the glacial Valerie, 'is my favourite niece.'

'I'm your only niece.'

'Perhaps that's the reason,' said Lord Ickenham.

The Duke had now reached an almost Bosham-like condition of mental fog.

'I don't understand all this. If you're Ickenham, why didn't you say you were Ickenham? Why did you tell us you were Glossop?'

'Precisely,' said Lady Constance. 'I am waiting for Lord Ickenham to explain—'

'Me too,' said Lord Bosham.

'—his extraordinary behaviour.'

'Extraordinary is the word,' assented Lord Bosham. 'As a matter of fact, his behaviour has been extraordinary all along. Most extraordinary. By way of a start, he played the confidence trick on me in London.'

'Just to see whether it could be done, my dear fellow,' explained Lord Ickenham. 'Merely an experiment in the interests of science. I sent your wallet to your home, by the way. You will find it waiting there for you.'

'Oh, really?' said Lord Bosham, somewhat mollified. 'I'm glad to hear that. I value that wallet.'

'A very nice wallet.'

'It is rather, isn't it? My wife gave it me for a birthday present.'

'Indeed? How is your wife?'

'Oh, fine, thanks.'

'Whoso findeth a wife findeth a good thing.'

'I'll tell her that. Rather neat. Your own?'

'Proverbs of Solomon.'

'Oh? Well, I'll pass it along, anyway. It should go well.'

Lady Constance was finding a difficulty in maintaining her patrician calm. This difficulty her nephew's conversation did nothing to diminish.

'Never mind about your wife, George. We are all very fond of Cicely, but we do not want to talk about her now.'

'No, no, of course not. Don't quite know how we got on to the subject. Still, before leaving same, I should just like to mention that she's the best little woman in the world. Right ho, Aunt Connie, carry on. You have the floor.'

There was a frigidity in Lady Constance's manner.

'You have really finished?'

'Oh, rather.'

'You are quite sure?'

'Oh, quite.'

'Then I will ask Lord Ickenham to explain why he came to Blandings Castle pretending to be Sir Roderick Glossop.'

'Yes, let's have a diagram of that.'

'Be quiet, George.'

'Right ho, Aunt Connie.'

Lord Ickenham looked thoughtful.

'Well,' he said, 'it's a long story.'

Valerie Twistleton's eye, as it met her uncle's, was hard and unfriendly.

'Your stories can never be too long,' she said, speaking with a metallic note in her voice. 'And we have the night before us.'

'And why,' asked Lord Bosham, 'did he lay out Baxter and our detective with knock-out drops?'

'Please, George!'

'Yes,' said Lord Ickenham rebukingly, 'we shall never get anywhere, if you go wandering off into side issues. It is, as I say, a long story, but if you are sure it won't bore you—'

'Not at all,' said Valerie. 'We shall all be most interested. So will Aunt Jane, when I tell her.'

Lord Ickenham looked concerned.

'My dear child, you mustn't breathe a word to your aunt about meeting me here.'

'Oh, no?'

'Emphatically not. Lady Constance will agree with me, I know, when she has heard what I have to say.'

'Then please say it.'

'Very well. The explanation of the whole thing is absurdly simple. I came here on Emsworth's behalf.'

'I do not understand you.'

'I will make myself plain.'

'I still don't see,' said Lord Bosham, who had been brooding with bent brows, 'why he should have slipped kayo drops in—'

'George!'

'Oh, all right.'

Lord Ickenham regarded the young man for a moment with a reproving eye.

'Emsworth,' he resumed, 'came to me and told me a strange and romantic story—'

'And now,' said Valerie, 'you're telling us one.'

'My dear! It seemed that he had become sentimentally attached to a certain young woman . . . or person . . . or party . . . however you may choose to describe her—'

'What!'

Lord Bosham appeared stunned.

'Why, dash it, he was a hundred last birthday!'

'Your father is a man of about my own age.'

'And mine,' said the Duke.

'I should describe him as being in the prime of life.'

'Exactly,' said the Duke.

'I often say that life begins at sixty.'

'So do I,' said the Duke. 'Frequently.'

'That, at any rate,' proceeded Lord Ickenham, 'was how Emsworth felt. The fever of spring was coursing through his veins, and he told himself that there was life in the old dog yet. I use the expression "old dog" in no derogatory sense. He conceived a deep attachment for this girl, and persuaded me to bring her here as my daughter.'

Lady Constance had now abandoned altogether any attempt at preserving a patrician calm. She uttered a cry which, if it had proceeded from a less aristocratic source, might almost have been called a squeal.

'What! You mean that my brother is infatuated with that child?'

'Where did he meet her?' asked Lord Bosham.

'It was his dearest wish,' said Lord Ickenham, 'to make her his bride.'

'Where did he meet her?' asked Lord Bosham.

'It not infrequently happens that men in the prime of life pass through what might be described as an Indian Summer of the affections, and when this occurs the object of their devotion is generally pretty juvenile.'

'What beats me,' said Lord Bosham, 'is where on earth he could have met her. I didn't know the guv'nor ever stirred from the old home.'

It seemed to Lord Ickenham that this was a line of enquiry which it would be well to check at its source.

'I wish you wouldn't interrupt,' he said, brusquely.

'Yes, dash it, you oaf,' said the Duke, 'stop interrupting.'

'Can't you see, George,' cried Lady Constance despairingly, 'that we are all almost off our heads with worry and anxiety, and you keep interrupting.'

'Very trying,' said Lord Ickenham.

Lord Bosham appeared wounded. He was not an abnormally sensitive young man, but this consensus of hostile feeling seemed to hurt him.

'Well, if a chap can't say a word,' he said, 'perhaps you would prefer that I withdrew.'

'Yes, do.'

'Right ho,' said Lord Bosham. 'Then I will. Anybody who wants me will find me having a hundred up in the billiard-room. Not that I suppose my movements are of the slightest interest.'

He strode away, plainly piqued, and his passing seemed to Lord Ickenham to cause a marked improvement in the atmosphere. He had seldom met a young man with such a gift for asking inconvenient questions. Freed of this heckler, he addressed himself to his explanation with renewed confidence.

'Well, as I say, Emsworth had conceived this infatuation for a girl who, in the prime of life though he was, might have been his granddaughter. And he asked me as an old friend to help him. He anticipated that there would be opposition to the match, and his rather ingenious scheme was that I should come to Blandings Castle posing as the Sir Roderick Glossop who was expected, and should bring the girl with me as my daughter. He was good enough to say that my impressive deportment would make an excellent background for her. His idea—shrewd, however one may deplore it—was that you, Lady Constance, would find yourself so attracted by the girl's personality that the task of revealing the truth to you would become a simple one. He relied on her—I quote his expression—to fascinate you.'

Lady Constance drew a deep, shuddering breath.

'Oh, did he?'

The Duke put a question.

'Who is this frightful girl? An absolute outsider, of course?'

'Yes, her origin is humble. She is the daughter of a retired Silver Ring bookie.'

'My God!'

'Yes. Well, Emsworth came to me and proposed this scheme, and you can picture my dismay as I listened. Argument, I could see, would have been useless. The man was obsessed.'

'You use such lovely language,' said Valerie, who had sniffed.

'Thank you, my dear.'

'Have you ever thought of writing fairy stories?'

'No, I can't say I have.'

'You should.'

The look the Duke cast at the sardonic girl could scarcely have been sourer if she had been Lord Bosham.

'Never mind all that, dash it. First Bosham, now you. Interruptions all the time. Get on, get on, get on. Yes, yes, yes, yes, yes?'

'So,' said Lord Ickenham, 'I did not attempt argument. I agreed to his proposal. The impression I tried to convey—and, I think, succeeded in conveying—was that I approved. I consented to the monstrous suggestion that I should come here under a false name and bring the girl as my daughter. And shall I tell you why?'

'Yes, do,' said Valerie.

'Because a sudden thought had struck me. Was it not possible, I asked myself, that if Emsworth were to see this girl at Blandings Castle—in the surroundings of his own home—with the portraits of his ancestors gazing down at her—'

'Dashed ugly set of mugs,' said the Duke. 'Why they ever wanted to have themselves painted . . . However, never mind that. I see what you're getting at. You thought it might cause him to take another look at the frightful little squirt and realize he was making an ass of himself?'

'Exactly. And that is just what happened. The scales fell from his eyes. His infatuation ceased as suddenly as it had begun. This evening he told her it could never be, and she has left for London.'

'Then, dash it, everything's all right.'

'Thank Heaven!' cried Lady Constance.

Lord Ickenham shook his head gravely.

'I am afraid you are both overlooking something. There are such things as breach of promise cases.'

'What!'

'I fear so. He tells me the girl took the thing badly. She went off muttering threats.'

'Then what is to be done?'

'There is only one thing to be done, Lady Constance. You must make a financial settlement with her.'

'Buy her off,' explained the Duke. 'That's the way to handle it. You can always buy these females off. I recollect, when I was at Oxford . . . However, that is neither here nor there. The point is, how much?'

Lord Ickenham considered.

'A girl of that class,' he said, at length, 'would have very limited ideas about money. Three hundred pounds would seem a fortune to her. In fact, I think I might be able to settle with her for two hundred and fifty.'

'Odd,' said the Duke, struck by the coincidence. 'That was the sum my potty nephew was asking me for this afternoon.'

'Curious,' said Lord Ickenham.

'Had some dashed silly story about wanting it so that he could get married.'

'Fancy! Well, then, Lady Constance, if you will give me three hundred pounds—to be on the safe side—I will run up to London to-morrow morning and see what I can do.'

'I will write you a cheque.'

'No, don't do that,' said the Duke. 'What you want on these occasions is to roll the money about in front of them in solid cash.

That time at Oxford . . . And I happen, strangely enough, to have that exact sum in this very room.'

'Why, so you have,' said Lord Ickenham. 'We were talking about it not long ago, weren't we?'

The Duke unlocked a drawer in the writing-table.

'Here you are,' he said. 'Take it, and see what you can do. Remember, it is imperative to roll it about.'

'And if more is required—' said Lady Constance.

'I doubt if it will be necessary to sweeten the kitty any further. This should be ample. But there is one other thing,' said Lord Ickenham. 'This unfortunate infatuation of Emsworth's must never be allowed to come out.'

'Well, dash it,' said the Duke, staring. 'Of course not. I know, and Connie knows, that Emsworth's as potty as a March hare, but naturally we don't want the world to know it.'

'If people got to hear of this,' said Lady Constance, with a shiver, 'we should be the laughing stock of the county.'

'Exactly,' said Lord Ickenham. 'But there is one danger which does not appear to have occurred to you. It is possible, Valerie, my dear, that you have been thinking of telling your aunt that you met me here.'

Valerie Twistleton smiled a short, sharp smile. Hers was at the same time a loving and a vengeful nature. She loved her Horace, and it was her intention to punish this erring uncle drastically for the alarm and despondency he had caused him. She had been looking forward with bright anticipation to the cosy talk which she would have with Jane, Countess of Ickenham, on the latter's return from the South of France.

'It is,' she said, 'just possible.'

Lord Ickenham's manner was very earnest.

'You mustn't do it, my dear. It would be fatal. You are probably unaware that your aunt expressed a strong wish that I should remain at Ickenham during her absence. If she discovered that I had disobeyed her instructions, I should be compelled, in order to put things right for myself, to tell her the whole story. And my dear wife,' said Lord Ickenham, turning to Lady Constance, 'has just one fault. She is a gossip. With no desire to harm a soul, she would repeat the story. In a week it would be all over England.'

The imperiousness of a hundred fighting ancestors descended upon Lady Constance.

'Miss Twistleton,' she said, in the voice which Lord Emsworth would have recognized as the one which got things done, 'you are not to breathe a word to Lady Ickenham of having met Lord Ickenham here.'

For an instant, it seemed as if Valerie Twistleton was about to essay the mad task of defying this woman. Then, as their eyes met, she seemed to wilt.

'Very well,' she said meekly.

Lord Ickenham's eyes beamed with fond approval. He placed a kindly hand on her shoulder and patted it.

'Thank you, my dear. My favourite niece,' he said.

And he went off to inform Pongo that, owing to having received pennies from heaven, he was in a position not only to solve the tangled affairs of Polly Pott but also to spend nearly three weeks in London with him—with money in his pocket, moreover, to disburse on any little treat that might suggest itself, such as another visit to the Dog Races.

There was a tender expression on his handsome face as he made his way up the stairs. What a pleasure it was, he was feeling, to be able to scatter sweetness and light. Especially in London in the springtime, when, as has been pointed out, he was always at his best.

EXPLORE THE WORLD OF BLANDINGS CASTLE ...

BLANDINGS CASTLE

In which an earl fights with his gardener, frees himself of a younger son . . . and learns to woo a sow.

SUMMER LIGHTNING

A missing prize-winning sow, a racy memoir that could destroy the aristocracy, and two pairs of young lovers are at the center of this hilarious romp.

HEAVY WEATHER

Galahad Threepwood's memoir is once again the object of everyone's desires. Who will get to it first: the private detective, the publisher . . . or an enormous Berkshire sow?

LEAVE IT TO PSMITH

A plot is brewing to steal an expensive necklace, and the only one who can help (or is it hinder?) the conspirators is Psmith, jack-of-all-trades.